P9-DIZ-140

PRAISE FOR
LUCHADOR
ERIN FINNEGAN

"[STARRED REVIEW] Finnegan's glorious coming-of-age story is as much a sweet and touchingly rendered love letter to lucha libre as a romance."

—Publishers Weekly

"The sweat and blood in the ring don't detract from the sweetness on display here; the setting may be outside the mainstream, but it's an old-fashioned love story at heart."

—Kirkus Reviews

PRAISE FOR
SOTTO VOCE
ERIN FINNEGAN

"[STARRED REVIEW] Finnegan's debut surprises and delights, pairing wine culture with an intoxicating contemporary romance... It's a book to be savored and enjoyed from the sweet, light beginning to the subtle middle notes, which culminate in a refreshing, delicious finish."

—Publishers Weekly

2014 IndieFab Silver Book of the Year Award Winner: LGBT Fiction
2014 IndieFab Book of the Year Finalist: Romance

—Foreword Reviews

LUCHADOR

ERIN FINNEGAN

LUCHADOR

interlude ✶✶ press • new york

3 4858 00468 2341

WESTERLY PUBLIC LIBRARY
44 Broad St.
Westerly, RI 02891
www.westerlylibrary.org
11/16

Copyright © 2016 Erin Finnegan
All Rights Reserved

ISBN 13: 978-1-941530-97-9 (trade)
ISBN 13: 978-1-941530-98-6 (ebook)
Published by Interlude Press
http://interludepress.com

This is a work of fiction. Names, characters, and places are either a product
of the author's imagination or are used fictitiously. Any resemblance
to real persons, either living or dead, is entirely coincidental.
All trademarks and registered trademarks are the property of their respective owners.

Book and Cover design by CB Messer
Source Art & Photography for Cover ©Depositphotos.com/
rawpixel/shenki/natis76/jacoblundphoto

10 9 8 7 6 5 4 3 2 1

interlude press • new york

For the exóticos, who add color and badassery to the world.

AUTHOR'S NOTE

A LOVE OF LUCHA LIBRE didn't come to me early. I grew up learning to swing a baseball bat in the backyard with my brother, not studying the intricacies of the aerial take-downs of masked wrestling. We watched college football on Saturday afternoons, not lucha libre broadcasts from Mexico City.

That all underwent a seismic shift a few years ago, when I was working with a local winemaking co-op in an abandoned Zinfandel vineyard near my home, trying to rescue fruit and valuable old vines before they were bulldozed into the earth to make room for condos. I had pulled my car up to the area where I was working, rolled down the windows, and turned on NPR while I harvested bushels of the dark fruit.

One story made me stop, climb into the car, and take a break to listen. It was about lucha libre's influence over the gay rights movement in Mexico. Specifically, it was about exótico wrestlers, and how they had developed a dedicated, passionate following in Mexico's LGBTQ community and may have influenced civil rights in their country. It also pointed out the dichotomy of these wrestlers, most of whom are gay, who typically play their characters as drag queens.

That's nothing new to lucha libre, of course, where wrestlers take on the role of defined characters in a sweaty morality play. But this was different. These wrestlers who once played the role of *rudo*—the heel or bad guy—to be booed and mocked, had come into their own in the ring. They were being credited with moving a country with deep, conservative religious traditions forward—ahead of most of the United States—on marriage equality. But they were doing it while playing one-dimensional characters that were viewed by some as aging stereotypes.

I was hooked.

I had gone to Los Angeles' famed Lucha Va Voom a few times before that and, like most of the crowd, approached the nights as bright, boozy, kitschy entertainment. But as I began to research the history and culture of lucha libre, I found it to be so much more. By the time I went to Mexico City to experience lucha libre at Arena Coliseo and Arena México, it had won me over as a mix of sport, statement, and performance art. It resembled the lights, cameras, and rock-n-roll of glitzy Lucha Va Voom—which I still enjoy—in only the narrowest of ways. At Arena México, the site of the 1968 Olympic boxing events, it is closer to the American take on this Mexican art form. There are bright lights, loud music, and ring girls. The bouts are broadcast on international networks featuring the biggest star luchadores—the super estrellas. At Arena Coliseo, an aging arena on the other side of town, you get a stripped-down, no frills lucha experience with bad lighting, worse sound, and cheap beer—with many of the same luchadores you see on TV and at Arena México.

The more I saw of these dualities, from the role of exótico luchadores to the contrast between the Mexico City lucha libre circuit and the trendy Los Angeles lucha events to the religious and cultural symbolism that pervades lucha libre, the more I wanted to set a story in this world.

A note about lucha libre terms and grammar, and what you're about to read: Much to the consternation of my talented translator, not all terms used commonly in lucha libre adhere to the rules of good Spanish grammar and spelling.

Luchador is also not a thesis on lucha libre. Liberties are taken.

My thanks to my longtime friend Pete—colleague, translator, and former Mexico City resident for his insight and support, and to RJ, Kristin, and Brew for their feedback and guidance. Thanks also to Ricardo, a lover of art and sport who made the streets of Mexico City a little less daunting and is a virtual encyclopedia of his hometown.

Thanks especially to the IP team, each of whom works so hard and sacrifices so much to create beautiful things—particularly to Annie Harper for encouraging me to get this done, to C.B. Messer for reading my mind, then going a step farther with the gorgeous cover art and design, and to Nicki and the editing team for challenging us to be better and swapping some great wrestling stories.

And finally, my thanks to Luther. You could turn dark nights into bright days and you influenced me in more ways than you ever knew. Thank you for Fanny Vice and for all those tiny moments of inspiration that will stay with me for a lifetime. I miss you, my dear friend.

PROLOGUE

1998, SOUTH TUCSON, AZ

The hand wrapped around his own, curling his small fingers in on themselves. The gesture may have been intended as reassuring, but Gabriel Romero tuned it out, shut it down, and let his senses go blank.

He forced his eyes to remain open, but allowed his mind to drift into a fog of persistent grief. His world had become a patchy blur of green grass, a hazy sky, and the drone of the priest reciting words of commitment and farewell.

He reached his other hand into the pocket of a jacket purchased hastily by his aunt and uncle, his godparents. At the bottom, he grasped the tiny figure, a worry doll his mother had made for him years before.

He gripped it tight, and didn't let go.

GABRIEL OFTEN HEARD HIS PARENTS through the thin walls of their apartment as they complained about the neighborhood. His mother worried about their safety; they needed to move. His father agreed, but answered that they couldn't afford it, not yet.

"He can handle himself," his father said. "He's tough."

"He's only ten. It won't be long—"

"Are you so sure?"

She silenced him.

"Are you *not*?"

He had always been full of focused energy that his parents channeled by signing him up for classes at the Boys and Girls Club—in karate, and baseball, and wrestling. He had taken to each sport naturally, but was drawn to wrestling thanks in no small part to his father's love of Saturday lucha libre broadcasts. They would play luchador in the family room—his father as the rudo, the bad guy, so that Gabriel, using a sheet as a cape, could play técnico—and ensure that the good guy won, each and every time.

He wrestled enmascarado, wearing a child-sized luchador mask his father purchased at a swap meet—red and white with silver trim. Climbing onto the arm of the sofa, he would leap onto his father in a perfect plancha, a swan dive that landed him prone across his father's chest. His father condoned it—so long as Gabriel's mother didn't see—allowing himself to be taken down by his son's acrobatics, pinned to the floor with Gabriel chanting, "¡Lucha! ¡Lucha! ¡Lucha!"

In that make-believe world, good always triumphed over evil. But through the walls of their apartment, he learned that the real world was not so clear-cut.

At night, he could measure his mother's worry for their safety and his father's concern for their finances. Their story spilled through the walls: the hopes and wishes, the regrets and misgivings; their steadfast belief in their family; their commitment to building a better life.

His mother wanted them out of South Tucson. His father argued that living here was manageable, practical, what they could just barely afford fresh out of school and cut off from all but the most critical of emergency help from her disapproving parents. Despite the hard-water deposits and stained carpets, even with the occasional loud parties and stray dogs scavenging through the neighborhood trash bins, 22nd Street had been relatively safe, he said, at least until the first wisps of gang graffiti appeared in the dark of night.

His parents spoke of compromise—of finding another home cheap enough to afford on their lean salaries, realizing it would never be what either had been accustomed to growing up. They needed to move on, because their modest neighborhood had become dilapidated. Its buildings were scarred with spray paint; its mall had been abandoned by businesses picking up and moving to Mesa, or Goodyear, or Phoenix.

Gabriel had seen it himself: The neighborhood toughs had taken over street corners and claimed aging apartment complexes as their headquarters. He would listen, ear to the wall, as his mother made the case that it was time to use their savings to relocate to a more secure neighborhood.

The shooting down the block sealed it.

The seemingly innocent pop-pop-pop—a sound softer than a firecracker, but followed by screams, then sirens, then the helicopter whose spotlight fired the darkness of their neighborhood with the brightness of the Arizona sun.

Tucked into a dark corner of the back bedroom, away from the street, Gabriel curled into his parents' protective arms. He kept his head low, but could see his mother catch her husband's eye, holding her stare until he acknowledged it with a silent nod.

Hours later, after the red and blue lights of the police cruisers no longer lit the room, she tucked him back into bed with a soft kiss to his forehead and a gentle touch to the tiny gold cross around his neck.

And through the walls, the persuasion began anew.

"We need to get out of here," his mother said. "You and I both know if we stay here, it's just going to get worse."

The room went silent but for the muffled sound of cushions being tossed back onto the couch, pillows that had been knocked out of place as they'd scrambled out of the room.

"A deal's a deal," she said. "We promised each other. We've been saving for better. For Gabriel. It's time. The neighborhood's gone bad."

"He's strong," his father said.

"He's small," she countered.

"He's smart."

"The world's unforgiving."

Gabriel didn't understand what she meant, but it clearly connected with his father.

"When do you want to look?" he asked.

"Saturday," she said. "After we drop him off at that birthday party."

HE KNEW SOMETHING WAS WRONG the moment he sensed eyes focused on him—hours after the water balloon fights and cannonballs into the pool had ended. The boys had demolished the sheet cake and already succumbed to the post-sugar-rush crash into the couches of the Reyes' family den to play video games.

When the doorbell rang, Gabriel expected to see his parents, running late.

Instead, it was a Tucson police officer and a woman wearing a simple gray dress and a somber face. They spoke quietly with Mrs. Reyes for several minutes before she turned, her face blanched, and stared at Gabriel.

They braved the stutter-stop congestion of Paseo de la Reforma, using it to cut through the park past the museums and onward north, hoping to beat the afternoon crowds that would later close the avenue. It was the same every Sunday. Gabriel, slumped in the backseat of his godparents' Mercedes Benz, ticked down the moments until the golden landmark triggered his weekly pre-mass sacrament. He drifted off into a silent world of his own, watching the posh glass and steel boutiques of the chic boulevard *not quite* push the city's aging mansions out of their way.

In moments, they would pass Monumento a la Independencia, the golden angel of victory most people simply called *El Ángel*. It reached high above the center of the traffic circle mere blocks from the cathedral where he worshipped with his aunt and uncle each weekend—even though there were a dozen churches between their home in Lomas de Chapultepec and the Zócalo.

The statue could be seen from kilometers away along the wide, tree-lined avenue. Each week as they drew closer, he watched for it, a golden beacon in an azure sky.

Out of habit, he pressed his fingers to his shirt seeking the outline of a small gold cross that clung to the thin chain hanging below his collarbone. Whether it was in prayer or reflection or lingering grief, he couldn't really say, but after close to eight years of making this pilgrimage, he knew that this moment belonged, each and every time, to his parents.

From the first time he had passed the landmark, he had thought of them. He had little doubt that his father would have joined the throngs of partying fútbol fans at El Ángel's base after a Team Mexico win. But it was his mother he most closely identified with the towering statue with its unfurled wings reaching skyward. Mexico City had been her childhood home, the city where she was raised, nurtured, and immersed in culture—and that she ultimately abandoned for love.

She had often told Gabriel about the city, about the museums and their storied collections. She had studied them all and was committed to making sure that her son shared her passion, or at least her respect, for their cultural legacy.

"Someday, we'll go back and we'll take you to the Museo de Arte Popular, where I met your father," she would say. She told him about the city's monuments, the colorful plazas, and the centuries-old cathedral that stood sentry over the civic core, surviving countless attacks and earthquakes.

"It's the city's soul," she had said. "But El Ángel is its heart."

He'd heard it all, dozens of times, the tour guide-like recounting of her home and the story of two recent college graduates who had stumbled into each other's arms on the museum steps. And if she were still alive he would probably be tired of it, maybe even resent it.

The details of Gabriel's Arizona childhood were becoming dust, the day-to-day little more than a blur, but some moments stuck to his memories like glue: the craft projects with his mother, the Saturday afternoon wrestling matches–on television and on the couch between father and son. His strongest memory was sensory, a feeling of freedom that he hadn't recognized as a child, but now suspected he lacked.

He had learned of his parents' deaths from a county children and family services worker and the cop at her side. Gabriel had overheard the young officer break the news of the shootout between rival gangs—bikers and drug dealers, he had said—that his parents were caught between as they exited a cafe. The woman explained that his relatives were being contacted, but he would remain a ward of the court until they arrived in Arizona.

She had been considerably more vague when she sat Gabriel down in private to break the news. At age ten, he hadn't known what a ward of the court was, but he suspected that he didn't want to be one.

He had just wanted to go home.

Instead, he'd moved into a new home more than a thousand miles and a border away.

At the graveside, his aunt had reached for his hand and found the worry doll he was clutching, a trinket his mother had made for him. She had tucked it back into his pocket and told him he was safe. He would soon have a new life, in a new country, with the predictable security he had never known as a child.

"I made a promise when you were baptized, mijo. I promised that I would care for you, protect you. You're going to come live with us now, in the city where your mamá grew up."

"I don't need to be protected," Gabriel had protested.

He still felt that way—especially once a week, as he passed by El Ángel.

As they reached the traffic circle, he shut his eyes and pressed his fingers to his heart.

SITTING ALONGSIDE HIS AUNT AND uncle in Catedral Metropolitana de México, Gabriel shifted his weight, said his Hail Marys, and knelt in prayer. It was the same every Sunday. The rigid formalities of the weekly services didn't really connect with him, but it was a reasonably fair trade. Gabriel believed in God—a god, at least—even if he occasionally questioned its motives. He probably spent as much time in the pews thinking about schoolwork or fútbol standings as he did reflecting on the merits of good versus evil, but he knew that he owed a lifelong debt to the family that had taken him in and made him one of their own, so he made their Sunday traditions his own. Of course, he didn't have much choice in the matter.

From the moment they had assumed responsibility for Gabriel's upbringing, his aunt and uncle had created a regimen designed to set him on a path to success. In their book, that included a formal education, sports, and a devotion to the church.

They had signed Gabriel up with a small legion of tutors and extracurricular activities to keep his brain and body active. His afternoons had been packed with study groups, music lessons, and fútbol practice. And as he'd prepared to graduate, they had announced that they would pay for his college education, securing his future.

"You'll be more competitive this way," his uncle had said.

By eighteen, he had taken the requisite tests and been accepted into the university, and the boredom of waiting for one academic life to end and another to begin had led to wandering, exploring his world in ways he had never before considered. It was simple enough after school, drifting through the city under the guise of an afternoon study session or team practice.

Weekends were more challenging, especially Sundays, when his ninos kept him close during their weekly ritual.

Like on every Sunday, he drifted as the congregation around him worshipped and he savored the one moment in his hectic pre-college schedule that allowed him to be bored, sitting in a five hundred-year-old cathedral, atoning for his sins. The entire routine felt almost mechanical: Worship at the cathedral, eat brunch at a hotel on the square, and race the taxis and delivery vans down the Paseo before it was shut down for cyclists and pedestrians.

This time, Gabriel lingered outside the hotel lobby. "Tía Alma, do you mind if I stay behind?"

"Meeting someone?" she asked. She smiled as if to suggest that she was in on a secret.

"Is there a girl?" his uncle asked. "¿Tienes novia?"

Gabriel grimaced, settling his eye on his Uncle Fernando with a drop-dead stare he hoped would land like a punch. This was nothing new. No, there most definitely was not a girl. And his uncle knew it.

Fernando shrugged, as if it didn't hurt to ask, yet again. Gabriel had grown numb to it. He couldn't call it exactly harmless, but there were bigger things to worry about than an uncle who hadn't quite grown into the world around him. Besides, even if his uncle was as subtle as a sledgehammer and not quite ready to accept the fact that girls were not a part of his romantic agenda, Gabriel had developed a fondness for the man who had taken him into his home and acted like a surrogate father, even if he would never truly be one.

"I'm supposed to meet some friends from school later. Our history teacher has a reputation for last-minute tests, so we thought we'd meet at the museum and maybe have a study session after," he said.

"You'll be home for supper?" Alma asked.

"There's food. Of course he'll be back," Fernando said, slapping Gabriel on the back.

"Don't hold dinner for me, but I promise not to be late."

"It's a school night," she said. She straightened his collar and tapped his cheek. "Fine, but don't be late."

"I promise," Gabriel said, kissing her cheek. "Alli nos vemos."

Pulling off his tie and shoving it into his jacket pocket, he watched them walk toward the garage, then checked to make sure they were truly gone before he doubled back across the Zócalo. He dodged in and out of the crowds in the sunny spring afternoon: the families walking after church; the tourists milling about; the street merchants hawking toys, rosaries, and Virgin Mary statuettes.

Alma would never stop him from spending an afternoon among the museum's antiquities. His gravest concern was that she'd want to tag along. And that would be a problem, because Gabriel had an entirely different plan in mind.

As willing as she was to set Gabriel loose amidst the treasures of ancient Mexico, he knew that Alma was far less enthusiastic about him spending an afternoon screaming along with a few thousand rowdy fans at the Arena México, cheering the enmascarados of the Sunday lucha libre matinee.

He had wanted to sneak out and watch the matches for a while, but his aunt didn't like the neighborhood and his uncle thought it a waste of time and money. "Why go there when you can watch it on TV?" But why couldn't it be seen as part of an extended curriculum, he reasoned. The arena was his classroom, even if his godparents didn't see it that way.

His parents would have understood. As much as his mother disapproved of him jumping off the family room couch, she valued the symbolism of the lucha match, the ritualistic battle of good versus evil that played out each week in the arenas of the Federal District, the event tents of the suburbs, and the outdoor fighting rings where dirt substituted for floor mats in the border towns. His father simply loved the showy sport and encouraged his son to do likewise.

They would have considered this moment of freedom a part of his education, of this Gabriel was certain.

"No hay mal que por bien no venga," he muttered under his breath. *There's no bad in your life that doesn't open a door to something good.*

So he told a lie—a tiny lie, really, a metirita. Harmless.

He rode the subway toward the park, where he planned to meet a friend near the museums. Tall, dark, lean—and in Gabriel's mind, at least, refined—Eduardo had been his study partner and friend in whom he found mutual skills in mathematics and similar tastes in sports, books, and music.

Gabriel wasn't sure if it was love, but it was certainly a solid crush— his first, not counting the hot history teacher from his first year at la preparatoria. Whether Eduardo shared his feelings was uncertain, but Gabriel hoped to puzzle it out during a late afternoon matinee at Arena México.

They had been in Eduardo's room studying, and had turned on the TV during a break when a raucous voiceover of a lucha libre commercial consumed the room. Eduardo rushed for the remote control but kept watching the commercial, and Gabriel saw an opening. He heard it in the announcer's blaring voice: something social, not a moment designed to get him into law school or med school, but a date that would get him a boyfriend, or possibly help to finally get him laid. He wanted the former, but he was certainly looking forward to the latter.

"Have you ever gone to the arena?" Gabriel asked. Eduardo shook his head as he watched clips of luchadores launching themselves over the ring and into the crowd. "They have Sunday matinees. We should go."

Gabriel considered everything strategically: a spring day, past the crush of college applications and exams; the clothes—a jacket, conservative enough for church but hiding slim-fit slacks and a trim dress shirt that showed off a body toned by hours of fútbol practice; the arena—a raucous safe zone of sweat, beer, and testosterone. If he had misjudged Eduardo's cues, he knew that he could at least write the day off as a shared adventure.

He took his time, catching the Metro and walking to a café outside the park, their designated meeting point. It was only a few blocks from the subway stop, but the pulse of adrenaline willed his feet to move faster than necessary through the weekend crowds. He paused at shop windows from time-to-time, feigning interest in the displays while he checked his reflection. Should he loosen another button on his shirt, maybe ruffle his hair a little? Hoping for an effortless look, he raked his fingers through his dark brown waves, then walked on until he spotted Eduardo standing on a street corner.

Eduardo wore snug jeans and a polo shirt and sat against a low wall as he thumbed at his phone. Gabriel's pulse quickened, and his thoughts spiraled. He settled his breath and reminded himself: *Even if this turns out to be nothing, at least there's lucha libre.*

But I hope it's something.

"Gabriel? How long have you been standing there?"

Gabriel snapped himself out of his reverie long enough to say hello and flag a cab to take them to the arena—a move generally considered perilous on a congested Sunday in the city. The driver veered suddenly, turning right from the left-hand lane. Gabriel hurtled across the backseat, landing against Eduardo. They lingered as the cab stabilized, and the heat of a flush crept up Gabriel's neck. He was about to speak when the taxi screeched to a halt outside the arena, and Eduardo pulled away, reaching a little too rapidly for his wallet.

They purchased tickets close enough to the ring to feel as though they were a part of the action, yet far enough back that they didn't risk having a luchador land in their laps—or getting caught in the fan cams for the television broadcast. Still, Gabriel wanted to stay close enough to the ring to feel the vibration of a takedown echo deep in his bones.

They sat in the thick of a section of fans of an estrella, a star—a former rudo, a dirty player who had seen the light and was trying to change his ways—El Diablo Azul. To their left, two suited men wore reproductions of The Blue Devil's pastel blue and silver mask, likely purchased from one of the street carts outside the arena. To their right, a group of laughing women wore blue T-shirts that read ¡SÁLVAME, DIABLO AZUL! and illuminated silver devil-horn headbands, made to resemble The Blue Devil's mask.

"I've never understood The Blue Devil," Eduardo said. "The devils, they're all rudos. They should be black or red. But baby blue? Baby blue is not a color for a devil. Besides, The Blue Demon was one of the greats—a super estrella. Why do we need a Blue Devil if we've already had The Blue Demon?"

"It's not the first time there have been luchadores with similar names," Gabriel said. "Think how many máscaras there have been: Mil Máscaras, Máscara Segrada, Máscara Magica…"

Gabriel looked around the arena, now filling with fans of The Blue Devil.

"And the Devil, he's conflicted. I think that's why people love him," he said, sipping his beer. "He used to be a rudo, but he's trying to change his ways. He's a técnico now, or at least he wants to be. Sometimes he slips. But when he's bad, it's in the service of good. I bet someday he'll change some more so that he always follows the rules, and then they'll change his name again. *Then* he'll be a técnico."

Gabriel elbowed Eduardo, directing his attention to the women next to him, who had begun to chant, "¡Diablo! ¡Diablo! ¡Diablo!"

"Considering his fan base, it may be a while."

The announcer appeared amid clouds of stage smoke, and the crowd erupted in cheers. He was well known from years of televised lucha broadcasts and his signature introductions, which extended the words so the crowd could join in. Dressed in his gray sharkskin suit and black T-shirt, he was escorted down a smoke-shrouded ramp to the ring by two bikini-clad ring girls, and as he took center stage, another one handed him a microphone.

"¡Bienvenidos a la Iglesia de la Lucha Libre!" he announced, his standard Sunday introduction. The crowd was his willing congregation and game to worship at the church of lucha.

A boisterous back-and-forth raised the collective energy of nearly five-thousand fans before the start of the first bout and fueled the decibel level as well as the arena's beer sales.

"What are we here for?" the announcer asked, pointing to the highest reaches of the packed arena.

Like a drunken assembly, the crowd bellowed back, "¡Luuuuuuuuu-chaaaaa!"

"¿Luuuuuuu-chaaaaa?" he prompted again, pointing his microphone toward the fans, encouraging their echo.

Gabriel and Eduardo laughed and shouted along with the crowd. "¡Luuuuuuuuu-chaaaa!"

Once the cheers became an organized chant, the announcer called the first bout: a trios team match between three up-and-coming rudos and a relatively unknown técnico paired with two minis, Más y Menos. The dwarf brothers, sponsored by an auto parts company, wore black-and-white costumes that resembled spark plugs. Playing the role of clowns, they were a staple of the Sunday lucha libre circuit.

Longtime fan favorites, they were now into their forties and often found themselves pitted against unknown heavyweight luchadores who played straight men to the brothers' popular routine.

"They're actually really good. Look at how fast they are, how they control the flow of the bout," Gabriel said.

Eduardo laughed. "It's staged. Of course they do."

With the three-round match tied, the minis put their skills on display. Aided by the young técnico, Más climbed up the ropes, then ran along the top line until he reached a corner turnbuckle. His partner surged at his opponent's legs, taking him down—a cue for Más to leap, hurling his tiny body into the air, catching the opponent's partner in a slam that resulted in a pileup of bodies on the mat. A quick three-count by the official, and the match was over, called, to the crowd's delight, in favor of the técnicos.

"The minis do more than buy time for people to get seated. They represent some of the great symbols of lucha libre: the little man overcoming the odds, the powerless beating the powerful. And they're really athletic. Más is a great aerialist."

Eduardo shook his head and looked at him with narrowed eyes, as if he were trying to read Gabriel's thoughts. It was a good thing he couldn't.

"You take this really seriously, don't you?"

Gabriel held Eduardo's gaze, then shrugged. "I love lucha libre."

The crowd grew rowdier as the wrestlers were announced: a match between El Grande, a thug-like rudo dressed head-to-toe in studded black Lycra and pleather, and the new técnico in blue and silver that so many in the crowd had come to watch. The women sitting alongside Gabriel began their chant anew. "¡Diablo! ¡Diablo! ¡Diablo!"

"It's his first time facing his old teammate," Gabriel said, as El Grande leapt over the ropes and into the ring. Arms folded across his thick chest, he stood near the center and glowered upstage, toward the ramp from which the técnico would emerge.

"These guys don't like each other. We may see some blood today," Gabriel said.

The spotlights focused on the Devil, led by another set of ring girls dressed to coordinate with his baby blue ensemble. He was tall and powerful, yet more sleekly built than his thick-framed opponent. Like other wrestlers, he kept his skin waxed smooth, rubbed to a sheen with oil before the match.

The Blue Devil marched to the ring, indifferent to the flash, glitz, and grinding hips. He didn't play to the crowd or dance to the beat of the music on the sound system. Focused on his former wrestling partner, he looked straight ahead, to the ring.

The announcer reignited the crowd with his introduction, raising a swell of cheers that echoed like a chorus of boos.

"¡El Diablo Azuuuuuuuuuuuul!" he called out in his resonant baritone.

"I don't think he's really a técnico yet," Eduardo said. "He's still a devil."

Gabriel shook his head, concentrating on the ring, considering the stage where this drama was about to play out.

"That's all determined by his actions," Gabriel said. "Play the devil, be the devil. He's in the middle of transforming himself. He's trying to be the hero, but he can't until the crowd accepts him as one. If he plays by the rules, then someday he will be accepted as the técnico he is trying to be."

The Blue Devil entered the ring without flare or pretense, stripping off his silver cape while staring his former partner down, biding time until the referee called him over for the ritualistic checking of his hands and feet and to meet El Grande face-to-face.

"He's fighting his own demons," Gabriel said. "He has to sacrifice… but he also has to win in order to move on."

The batalla started slowly, the two luchadores slapping at each other, sizing up their opponent. A takedown by one would be parried by a twitch or a roll, bringing the referee's three count to a halt.

The Blue Devil had always specialized in aerial moves, acrobatic flips from atop the ropes, into the ring or sometimes into the crowd. When he was paired with El Grande, the duo would use his skills as a distraction while El Grande scrambled for the takedown. On his own, the Devil recalibrated his signature moves so they ended with his legs wrapped around his opponent, flipping and spinning into a series of Patadas Voladoras, Huracán Ranas, and Tornillos. His former partner knew this pattern well, and would dart out of the Devil's grasp each time the aspiring técnico attempted a plancha into the ring.

In the third round, El Grande used the pattern to his advantage, catching the Devil by the waist on an aborted flip, heaving him over the ropes and into the cheering crowd, then diving after him, en suicida.

The rudo slammed the Devil's face into the seats, leaving him still, seemingly lifeless. The referee began a slow count as El Grande reached for The Blue Devil's mask.

"Look," Eduardo said. "His mask is loose, like he didn't tie it off. Do you think…?"

El Grande tore at the Devil's face, trying to rip the metallic fabric away, grabbing at his mouth. The Devil fought, turning his body, trying to loosen the rudo's grip, but El Grande grabbed again, and pulled The Blue Devil's head back by the crown of his mask.

Gabriel held his breath as the two struggled. They couldn't de-mask The Blue Devil right now, not in the middle of his redemption. It was too early for his identity to change, but too late to go back to his days as a rudo. Besides, it wasn't a betting match. To remove the Devil's mask meant that El Grande would forfeit the bout.

And just as the Devil looked defeated, an elbow flew into El Grande's rib cage, knocking him backward.

Gabriel leapt from his seat, cheering with the noisy women at his side. He slapped playfully at Eduardo's shoulder. "Did you see that? ¡Vamonos Diablo! ¡Dale!"

The Blue Devil slowly rose, adjusting his mask and spitting out blood. He stumbled to the far corner of the ringside seats, near the announcers, with El Grande following close behind, gripping his ribs.

Standing on uncertain legs, The Blue Devil backed up to a wall, then surged toward the stage's edge, directly at El Grande. The motion threw both luchadores into the ropes, ensnaring the rudo. The Devil grabbed his former partner by the hair and forced his face to the mat, repeatedly, until El Grande flailed his arms, finally slapping the mat, hailing the referee.

"¡Uno! ¡Dos! ¡Trés!"

The Blue Devil punched the mat inches from Grande's face and threw his arms into the air in victory.

Gabriel bounced to his feet, joining the deafening cacophony of the crowd.

For an undercard match, it had played out with brutality, stretching until the end of its third and final round. Blood was caked around the mouth of the Devil's mask, and both luchadores stumbled from one end of the ring to the other.

Eduardo pulled in close to Gabriel's ear. "He gave up? C'mon!" he said.

Gabriel's eyes didn't leave the stage, but he could feel the wisp of Eduardo's breath on his neck. He shut his eyes, just for a moment. He wasn't sure whether to savor the sensation or control it.

"That was too fast. Where did that blood come from, anyway? They have to at least make it *look* real."

"It's always real," Gabriel responded, his attention split between the action in front of him and the boy drawing close to him.

"I mean the blood. It's like it came out of nowhere. It had to be fake."

Gabriel watched the two combatants head to the locker room. He let the crowd noise simmer before he turned back to Eduardo.

"It doesn't come out of thin air," Gabriel said. "Sure, there's staging, but there's so much more to lucha than just wrestling. It's like storytelling, or performance art—but with really muscular men who could kill you."

Eduardo laughed and raised his eyebrows skeptically.

"Seriously," Gabriel said, his tone growing dark. "Luchadores have died in the ring. That's real enough for me."

"You really do love this, don't you?" Eduardo said. His tone was sweet, maybe something more, unless Gabriel was imagining things.

"My dad and I used to watch it together, and I always thought it was just fun, you know? But then I finally went to the lucha matches and saw so much more. They have to fight each other, yet work together at the same time. They're not faking those takedowns."

"I think I should give you a luchador name. What do you think? ¿El Maniaco Matemático?"

Gabriel chuckled for a moment, then looked up to the ring and gave it some thought.

"El Ángel," he said, almost under his breath.

Eduardo angled himself closer, a whisper away from Gabriel's ear. His voice was soft, flirtatious, distracting. "So you're an angel," he said. He held his gaze long enough that the breath caught in Gabriel's throat.

It was nearly a moment, nearly *the* moment, Gabriel had hoped for until it was interrupted by the voice of the announcer and the pounding beat of a narcocorrido.

The lights dimmed and the jumbotrons over the entry ramp lit up with graphics announcing the final batalla, a head-to-head bout between a rudo known for his brutality and a técnico Gabriel did not know.

Gabriel had seen this rudo wrestle before, a veteran who had long ago adopted the English name of The Henchman. A virtual wall of flesh and muscle, The Henchman approached the ring like so many others—posing and flexing as he walked a gauntlet of well-endowed models in fringed, black-and-gold bikini tops and booty shorts designed to match his signature mask.

When he approached the ring, the entourage of girls removed his cape, kissed his cheek, and left the stage to the whistles and catcalls of the fans. The Henchman grabbed the upper rope and heaved his body up and over, into the ring.

As the applause subsided, the atmosphere of the arena shifted. The lighting, bleeding red only moments before, shifted to yellows and pinks. The ear-piercing guitars of The Henchman's introduction music were replaced with a Caribo, a drum-filled sing-along dance song to a rapid-fire salsa beat.

The announcer rolled his r's to announce, "La Reina de los Luchadores! Get ready to party with La Rrrrrrrrooooooosa!"

The spotlight that lit up the ramp leading down to the ring illuminated a crowd of what looked like carnival-goers bobbing and dancing along to the infectious thrum of the music. But for the first time that afternoon, or of any time that Gabriel could recall, none of them were bikini girls.

They were bikini boys.

It looked like a mosh pit of male underwear models, swaying and dancing as if they were entering a club rather than a fight ring. Nearly a dozen young, muscular men carved their way through the crowd wearing metallic booty shorts and little else, save for floral body paint and an occasional feather boa. Some tossed roses to the fans.

They bobbed and weaved like a conga line down the ramp to a loud but mixed reaction from the crowd. Some fans cheered loudly, waving rainbow flags and singing along with the music. A few booed and taunted them as maricones. A young boy seated behind Gabriel and Eduardo had already started rolling out a series of puto taunts, over and over again.

But Gabriel was transfixed.

As they neared the stage, the entourage peeled away to reveal its leader. Ensconced in the center of the circle danced a luchador unlike any other on the afternoon fight card. With shimmering dark hair moussed high, and pink glittery eyelids lined in dark kohl stood La Rosa, the self-described *Queen of the Luchadores.*

La Rosa didn't wear traditional tights, or a wrestler's singlet, or even the trunks that The Blue Devil preferred. The wrestler wore a flesh-toned bodysuit hand-painted with roses like those worn by the dancers, leaving the impression that La Rosa was covered in nothing but flowery body paint.

The colorful luchador wore knee-high wrestling boots, though they were not black, or red, or even silver like the other luchadores—but instead a deep shade of metallic magenta with flowered inlays.

"Who is that?" Eduardo asked.

Gabriel stared at the wrestler, shaking his head. Though not tall, La Rosa had the frame of a male athlete, with muscular thighs that looked as if they could strangle a man. They betrayed years of training, but the character and the costuming were a dramatic departure from the machismo typically on display in the ring.

"He's an *exótico*," Gabriel said, hushed.

He took it all in, his eyes wide. He'd heard of exótico wrestlers before, but he had never seen one in person. He knew that in the early days of lucha libre, they performed as dandies, well-dressed wrestlers who lavished female fans with flowers and kisses. Modern exóticos were the only luchadores who performed as openly gay—and they were largely perceived as a drag act, comic relief for the fight card.

La Rosa climbed the ropes and stood on the turnbuckle. He faced out toward the crowd, arms outstretched, hips swaying with the music. As cheers echoed across the arena, La Rosa leapt heels-over-head into the ring, landing solidly on the mat, only to resume his bump-and-grind dance.

The crowd roared its approval.

"Rosa's the técnico!" Gabriel exclaimed, shouting to be heard over the crowd noise. "I thought exóticos usually played the rudo."

If that were true, the heel in the match would have had more fans than the hero, because La Rosa's fans were numerous and vocal. Along the rails of the highest balcony, a boisterous cheering section had waved rainbow flags the moment La Rosa's name was announced. Though some booed the luchador, their jeers were easily drowned out by La Rosa's rowdy fans, who joined in an organized chant: *¡Chiquitibum a la bim bom ba!¡Chiquitibum a la bim bom ba! ¡A la bio, a la bao, a la bim bom ba! ¡Rosa, Rosa, Ra Ra Ra!*

"It looks like a Pride parade up there," Gabriel said, laughing and clapping.

The announcer and entourages cleared the ring, leaving the referee free to signal the match to start. The Henchman had the quick advantage, locking La Rosa's arm behind his head, but the exótico slipped from his grasp, rushing backward into the ropes. He used them to hurl himself back toward his opponent, knocking The Henchman off balance and into the ropes.

While The Henchman struggled to free himself, La Rosa took advantage of his favorite weapon. He reached forward, grabbed The Henchman by the back of his head, and reeled him in for a brusque kiss, raising the crowd volume to ear-piercing levels. In his opponent's apparent confusion, La Rosa reached between The Henchman's legs, securing a lock on his knees that allowed the exótico to lift him off the mat and fling him toward the center of the ring.

The match seesawed back-and-forth—the rudo playing dirty, La Rosa playing to the crowd. If The Henchman threw a punch, La Rosa countered with a spin-kick. If La Rosa tackled The Henchman, he returned with a flip that landed with La Rosa sprawled across the mat. And if The Henchman stalled, La Rosa taunted him by dancing a cha-cha around the ring; his music appeared almost magically during even the slightest delay.

Gabriel watched intently, silently, as the crowd erupted around him. The sights and sounds of the arena blurred into the background. He saw only the ring, and the colorful luchador standing in the center of it.

By the third round, arena guards were standing between the crowd and the fenced-off pit surrounding the ring, as if they knew what was coming.

The Henchman circled behind Rosa while the exótico vamped for fans seated on the opposite side of the ring. In the blink of an eye, The Henchman attacked, lifting La Rosa up and over the ring to the padded floor below.

He landed in a heap against the barricade, followed closely by The Henchman, who flipped over the ropes in a perfect twisting tornillo, landing across La Rosa's back. He hoisted the exótico, hurling him into the ringside seats.

Get up. Come on.

Gabriel yelled to the flower-painted luchador sprawled on the floor. "¡Levantate!"

As the referee's count approached three, La Rosa pushed up from the floor, shaking his head, seeming disoriented. An older woman tried to help him to his feet, but the guards held her back. Shakily, La Rosa clambered to his feet as the rudo again approached him from behind, holding a folding chair high above his head.

"Here it comes!" Eduardo said.

"No, no. This is a classic ploy. Just watch—the exótico will win this one, I'll bet you."

A hand touched his forearm. Eyes locked on his, temporarily pulling Gabriel back into the moment.

"What will you bet me?" Eduardo said.

"Dinner?" Gabriel asked.

And like *that*, the moment passed as La Rosa spun around, whipping the rudo's legs out from under him and stealing Gabriel's attention back to the bout. The Henchman stumbled toward the ring, tried to climb between the ropes, but La Rosa was on him now. Showing no mercy, the exótico slapped at his face and leapt onto his back to flip the rudo over his head and flat onto the floor behind them.

Gabriel could see *himself* in the ring. He knew his strategy. He jumped to his feet, punching his fist in the air. "Come on, Rosa, make your move. ¡Dale cavron! Do it now!" he shouted, as the arena erupted in a growing chorus of "¡Rosa! ¡Rosa! ¡Rosa!"

La Rosa grabbed The Henchman's wrists and pinned him down, hailing the referee to count out the takedown, once and for all. It was over. The referee called the three-count and raised La Rosa's hand high, declaring him the victor.

Gabriel punched the air and chanted along with the crowd, "¡Rosa! ¡Rosa!"

The Caribo music started anew, blaring from the arena's sound system, and fans rose to their feet and danced along with Rosa's victory cha-cha. Gabriel, swept up in the moment, joined in without a thought of a dance partner.

Eduardo watched from his seat.

They stayed behind as the ring emptied and the crowd filtered from the arena. Eduardo took Gabriel's hand. "Let me ask you something," he said. "Was this supposed to be a date?"

"I'd hoped so," Gabriel said.

"I wasn't so sure. You were *really* into the show."

"I just really love the—"

"Yes, I know," Eduardo said. "*You just really love lucha libre.* I get it. But if this was a date, wouldn't you try to pay a little more attention to me?"

It hit him like La Rosa's diving plancha. Gabriel had been so caught up in the action that he had effectively put the brakes on the date he'd planned so carefully.

"I didn't mean to, I swear," Gabriel said. "I didn't even know if you thought of it that way."

Eduardo scratched awkwardly at his scalp and shook his head, then looked at the floor as he confessed, "I've been trying to get your attention for months," he confessed. "Probably for the best. I'll be leaving for school soon. I got in at Guadalajara."

The door was still open. It had to be.

"You still have summer, right?"

Eduardo shrugged, then nodded. He fidgeted and looked at his watch. "I promised I'd be back early. It's a school night—"

"Give me a do-over," Gabriel insisted.

"I'll see you in class."

"Please." He squeezed Eduardo's hand. "Let me make up for this."

"We can talk tomorrow."

Eduardo stood up to leave; Gabriel mirrored the action. It was no time to give up.

"Eduardo?"

The kiss—his first—was rushed and sloppy, landing off-center and ending much too fast. His lips caught the side of Eduardo's mouth. He breathed the moment in—bergamot and clove.

"Tomorrow," Eduardo said, pulling away. "We'll talk some more." He smiled, a reassuring cue, and traced his hand across Gabriel's shoulder as he left.

Somehow, Gabriel couldn't follow him out. He made excuses to linger in the arena as Eduardo departed: a visit to the men's room, a stop at a concession stand. He couldn't bring himself to leave.

What he'd seen in the ring had swept over him, given him purpose. He needed to meet La Rosa. And that needed to happen immediately.

Left behind in the near-empty arena, Gabriel headed to the foyer and turned left when he knew he should turn right. He made himself smaller than his five-foot nine-inch frame, dipping his head to blend into the throng of support teams and entourages that had collected backstage.

Dressed in church clothes he would never be mistaken for a stagehand, but if he kept his head ducked down, his sleeves rolled up, and his mouth clamped shut, he might look as if he belonged, somehow, in the sweat-drenched hallway that led to the locker rooms.

The corridor reeked of beer and baby oil and was crowded with half-dressed women and a few of La Rosa's ring boys wiping glitter off their bodies. Gabriel kept his head low and pressed on until he found a group of people in a side room, laughing and clustered around the center of their attention: La Rosa.

There was no mistaking it—the exótico was clearly the leader of this little crew. Luchadores and stagehands alike were paying their respects, congratulating La Rosa on the match. Even The Henchman, still wearing his mask, walked up and threw his arms around his opponent, encircling him in a friendly bear hug before reaching into a nearby cooler for a beer.

One by one, they greeted him, grabbed a drink, and moved on—until La Rosa was left alone, sitting before a mirror, removing glitter and makeup with a baby wipe. He had pulled his body suit down to his waist, exposing a chest already tender from the evening's match. He had run water through his hair. As it dried, flecks of gray emerged from under a layer of spray-on glitter.

Gabriel stood at the back of the room near the door. He tried to blend in, to be inconspicuous.

"Can I help you?"

Gabriel looked over his shoulder. Maybe someone was standing behind him.

Nothing.

"You, boy. Do you belong back here?" La Rosa waved his hand, indicating the backstage area.

"I was just—" Gabriel stuttered.

"You were just what? Sneaking around where you don't belong? Where's your pass?"

"I... um..."

"Well?"

"I just wanted to meet you. I am a big fan," Gabriel said.

La Rosa took another swipe at his face, scrubbing off his lipstick. "A big fan, you say? Of the exóticos?"

"Of lucha libre. I'd never seen an exótico perform in person before."

La Rosa bowed his head and smirked. "Perform? So, I'm a performer?"

"No!" Gabriel said with a start. "I've always loved lucha libre and I've only seen my first match recently and I've always been curious—"

"Curious?"

"I'd heard about exóticos, but I'd never seen one except on TV."

"Hmm." La Rosa kept his eye on the mirror, scrubbing away the makeup.

"And it was just… just… inspiring." Gabriel had yet to come down from the buzz of the bouts. His face flushed. He had to remind himself to blink.

La Rosa sighed and stood up. He turned toward Gabriel.

"Catch your breath, boy. Why don't you sit down?" He pointed Gabriel to the bench and grabbed a bottle of water from the cooler.

"Here, drink up."

La Rosa draped a towel around his neck and sat alongside him.

"So, you're gay." Gabriel nodded.

"I want to learn to wrestle."

He could feel La Rosa's eyes on him, sizing him up, judging him.

"You don't exactly look like a fighter. What are you? A college student?"

"I go to la preparatoria."

"Better yet—a prep school boy." The words escaped with a sneer.

"I've followed lucha since I was a kid."

"You *are* a kid."

Gabriel stood up, as if being on his feet somehow gave him more height, more power, more conviction.

La Rosa's expression changed. Was it a smile? A smirk? Something in between? Gabriel couldn't tell how he stood with the luchador, but he continued to press.

"I'm eighteen. I'm an adult. I want to train. I want to learn," he said. "I want to learn from someone like me."

"Someone like you, eh? We're so alike? Some rich kid wants to piss off his parents by coming out in the ring, and you say we're alike?" Rosa said, taunting.

Gabriel's voice went flat. "I'm already out."

"Good for you."

"I love lucha libre, what it means, what it represents—what *you* represent. My dad taught me to respect it. And yeah, I may live on the hill and go to a good school, but I saw what you did out there tonight. I saw what I'm supposed to do—I know it."

Rosa rubbed at his temple, then pulled another wipe from its container and concentrated on his eyebrows. "What makes you think I'd even train you?" he said.

Gabriel held up his cell phone, opening it up to a search menu. "I looked you up. You run a school."

"Miguel Reyes runs a school."

Gabriel pulled up alongside the luchador, catching his eye in the mirror. "I want to learn. I want to learn from you," he said.

"Shouldn't you be off learning to master the universe or something?"

"Teach me," Gabriel pressed.

La Rosa squinted, but said nothing.

"Please," Gabriel said. He turned so that he sat face-to-face with La Rosa. "I want be a luchador."

2

THE DEAL WAS SIMPLE: FINISH la preparatoria, then Gabriel would watch wrestlers train from an out-of-the way corner of Gimnasio de la Ciudad, a small, aging gym in north-central Mexico City where bodybuilders lifted downstairs by day and luchadores trained upstairs at night.

La Rosa made it clear that Gabriel was there to observe and to stay out of the way. "You're going to watch and learn. If you're still interested after that, we'll see," he said.

Gabriel figured that the words were nothing but talk, something to scare him off, so he showed up wearing warm-up pants and a T-shirt, ready to jump in.

La Rosa called the small group to order, and they dutifully lined up against a wall. Large, aloof luchadores stepped to the front. Clearly professionals, they carried themselves with an almost palpable disdain compared to the smaller wrestlers at the far end of the line. Two wore masks, enmascarados working out in partial costume. *Was it to disguise their identity in their off-hours? Were the wrestlers playing their characters full time? Or was it simply a matter of practicing with the constricted vision caused by the masks?* Gabriel could only guess—the luchadores weren't talking. But the sight of the masks made it all the more real for him. *I'm on the inside.*

He felt a momentary thrill, an outsider eavesdropping on a secret circle, at least until the class was called to order. As it started, Gabriel realized that there was little to be intimidated by. La Rosa looked like any other gym coach, dressed in Lycra shorts, low-profile wrestling boots, and a *Viva Lucha* T-shirt. He barked orders to a class of wrestlers in their warm-ups: stretching, cardio, and endurance exercises that any athlete might include in his training regimen. He worked up to their maromas—explaining but not demonstrating a series of drops and rolls designed to test and develop skills the wrestlers would use in the ring.

Gabriel followed along quietly, mimicking their moves from a safe distance. It was a familiar routine, not much different from warm-up exercises for fútbol practice.

From time to time, he could sense La Rosa's eye on him, as though he were being monitored, assessed.

They had been at it for close to an hour. Five professional luchadores served as the leads in every new move La Rosa taught: three in training for their competitive license exam and another two amateurs, in it for a creative workout. There were no glittery capes or flashy costumes, beyond the two masks. It was clear that La Rosa was creating a cycle of moves from simple to complex, which the professionals, serving as an example to their less-experienced classmates, integrated into a series by the end of class.

Without a partner or permission to enter the ring, Gabriel began to fidget, but he stopped in his tracks when La Rosa bellowed out at him.

"Hey, college boy, come here!"

Gabriel rushed to join the wrestlers at the center of the mat.

"It's Gabriel," he said.

The comment earned him a sideways glance, and some murmured "Oooh's" from a couple of the wrestlers.

"Boy, have you been paying attention?"

Gabriel nodded, wide-eyed.

"I'm short a wrestler, and I've got a pulled trapezius, so Raymond here will need someone to practice with."

La Rosa called over one of the trainees, an enormous wrestler the size of an NFL linebacker who dwarfed Gabriel's trim frame.

"This is Raymond. He won the bronze medal in freestyle wrestling at the 2004 Summer Games. We won't hold the fact that he wrestled for the Americans against him since he's going to be a professional luchador soon. Your job is to follow instructions, let him practice holds on you, and not die. He knows what to do. Good luck."

Gabriel looked up, his eyes bulging. Raymond had a good six inches of height on him and at least fifty pounds of muscle.

"Hello," he said, trying to mask his nerves.

"Hey, man! You speak English?" Raymond bellowed. He had a grin like sunshine. He reached out to shake Gabriel's hand, then slapped his other hand over Gabriel's, entombing it between his over-sized palms. Raymond was a two-handed shaker.

"Yes," Gabriel said.

"I knew there was a reason Miguel put us together. Nice to meet you. I'm Ray. In college, they called me The Cyclone. El Ciclón, right?"

"Yes," he replied. "I'm Gabriel."

"But now I'm The Dark Storm."

"La Tormenta Oscura," Gabriel said.

"How long have you been training, Gabe?"

"First day."

La Tormenta Oscura burst out in gales of laughter.

"This'll be fun."

He was boisterous, full of life, and Gabriel struggled to match this colossal, intimidating man with his carefree demeanor.

La Rosa paired up the other wrestlers—professionals with professionals, followed by the luchadores-in-training, followed by the amateurs. Gabriel couldn't figure out why he would match him up with Ray "The Dark Storm" Michaels.

Standing at the front of the room, La Rosa again led them through the series of maneuvers he had spent the evening mapping out. He added layers for the professionals: a flip, a roll, a pin. As far as Gabriel could tell, his own job was to duck.

"Pay attention, college boy. You need to respond to the physical cues of your partner," La Rosa barked. "Think of it like a dance. Raymond is your tango partner. If your steps aren't in line, you're going to trip him up."

On La Rosa's cue, Ray grabbed Gabriel around the waist, lifted him off the mat, and flung him to the ground in a well-choreographed flip. Then came the pin, the kill move. Gabriel took it once. He got up and brushed himself off, settled in for a second try. It happened again, with duplicated precision. And again, a third time. By La Rosa's fourth start cue, Gabriel had had enough.

He ducked and rolled briskly away from Ray's grasp, jumped to his feet and went into a wrestler's crouch.

The other students stopped and gawked. One professional—The Blue Devil himself—nodded.

Gabriel looked to the side of the gym where La Rosa stood. He was silent and grim, arms folded across his chest, watching intently.

They continued, with Ray using his size to his advantage, only to have Gabriel escape again. When Ray wasn't paying close attention, Gabriel rolled to his back, swept his leg toward the former college champ and knocked him off his feet: He scissored his legs to trap Ray around the waist, flipped and then rolled them as a unit, and finally pinned his shoulders to the floor.

The room went silent.

"Holy fuck!" Ray said, erupting in laughter. Gabriel rolled away, and Ray clambered to his feet and extended his hand. "Shit, you're fast."

"Thank you," Gabriel said, bouncing to his feet.

Ray looked to the side of the room where La Rosa stood, observing. He whispered, "I'd better shut the fuck up or I'll get us both in a lot of trouble, but nice moves, kid."

"Why?"

"You never joke around in class, and especially with a new guy. You haven't even been properly baptized yet," Ray said gravely. He gave Gabriel a wink and walked to where the rest of the class had congregated for some closing words from La Rosa. Gabriel joined them, but stood off to the perimeter of the group.

"Remember, Maria will lock you out if you don't give her your gym dues by Monday, and she asked me to say that she will personally cut off the balls of whoever pissed in the sauna. And if you know Maria, you know she's not kidding. So if it's one of you, knock it off, because I won't hesitate to turn you in. I'd rather you lose your balls than me lose my lease, got it?"

Ray slapped Gabriel on the back as he headed to the locker room. "See ya, Gabe."

As Gabriel started to leave, La Rosa grabbed him by the arm. "Hold on a moment."

He waited until the room had cleared, then pulled up a chair. He straddled it, resting his arms on the seat back.

"That was quite a display," he said. He stared Gabriel down, narrowing his eyes until wrinkles creased his temple.

"Thanks," Gabriel said, tentatively. La Rosa had him as off balance as a well-placed scissor kick.

"It wasn't a compliment," La Rosa said. "No one told you to take him down, to flip him. You don't do that without instruction."

"But he was fine with it. He was okay," Gabriel said.

"That's how people get hurt. When Raymond said it was unexpected? That's the last thing I want to hear in my class. Next time, you follow instructions, or you get your ass out of here. And wear proper gear. None of this sweatpants shit."

Gabriel let the words sink in.

"Next time?" he asked.

The instructor nodded.

"Thank you, Rosa."

"In here, it's Miguel."

"Miguel, thank you." Gabriel turned to leave.

"We're not done," he said. "You want to wrestle? Then you have to contribute. Your job is to clean this place up after practice—a thorough wipe-down, and wash the floors."

Gabriel looked at him in stunned silence. He could afford to pay, but he had a feeling this had nothing to do with money. He acknowledged the demand with a slight bob of his head.

"You can start with the sauna."

★   ★   ★

BLACK-RIMMED GLASSES PUSHED DOWN HIS nose, Miguel sat in his tiny office at the gym, scarcely bothering to look up from his bookkeeping. "You glamorize this too much," he said.

Gabriel, deep into his list of chores, stopped and leaned against his mop.

"Yes, Miguel. This is the height of glamour." He guided the mop in a graceful circle along the floor, as if leading a dance partner. "Someday I hope to step it up and become a trash collector."

Miguel glanced up, his eyebrows pinched together.

"Are you calling my gym a dump? Some of the greatest luchadores of this generation have trained here. Luchadoras, too. Professionals. People you can't hold a candle to."

"That's not what I meant."

"When you're not studying math, you'd be smart to study your craft, college boy."

College boy.

Gabriel's grades and connections had earned him an offer to La Universidad Nacional Autonoma de Mexico, where he would be expected to build the credentials that would earn him a respectable job as an attorney, or a doctor, or a businessman. He had decided to study mathematics and business, which would appease his family's wishes for his future, though he never envisioned himself in a boardroom.

His academic credentials were supposed to earn him respect, but they were a source of derision under Miguel's tutelage.

Gabriel resumed his mopping in silence. He hardly considered his work at the gym educational. He mopped and cleaned toilets. Sometimes he ran errands for Miguel or the other luchadores. But he also got to train with professionals—with El Diablo Azul and La Rosa—despite having no previous wrestling experience.

It had been six months since Gabriel first visited Gimnasio de la Ciudad, and Miguel still greeted him with the same cold contempt he'd exhibited when they first met, when La Rosa threatened to kick him out of the dressing rooms at Arena México. But he had gradually been paying more attention to Gabriel in class, even pulling him aside for brusque one-on-one instruction.

Still, the juggle of schoolwork, unpaid janitorial services, and rudimentary wrestling training sessions were a far cry from anything Gabriel considered glamorous.

"I meant no disrespect," he mumbled.

He was nearly finished cleaning the gym's floors for the third time in as many days. The last wrestler had left an hour ago. Gabriel still had a good two hours' worth of math prompts to solve before a ten a.m. class. Gradually, training and tasks around the gym were usurping his study time, and he worried that his excuses for being away from home were starting to wear thin with his aunt and uncle.

"I think it's time for you to go to school," Miguel said.

"I do that every day."

Gabriel heard laughter from the small office where Miguel was working.

"Boy, your education hasn't even started. Saturday, three p.m. We'll leave from here."

"For what?"

"Your first lesson."

★ ★ ★

No one could confuse Arena Coliseo San Ramon de Puebla with Arena México.

The center was little more than a gym, jammed with folding chairs and tables that served as impromptu concessions stands. It would host an event that was mostly a demonstration, part of a civic celebration. It was not a sanctioned bout, lacking both the venue quality and payday of matches sponsored by Liga de la Lucha Libre, the country's premier professional wrestling league that most fans simply called the Triple L. The event was off the books, so Miguel booked an assortment of lesser-known luchadores, the independents—though in a pinch, he could occasionally call in a favor and convince even a league estrella to don an unfamiliar costume and compete as a different character.

Gabriel dutifully followed Miguel around the small arena as he met with the day's slate of luchadores. It was an unfamiliar setting for everyone but Miguel—La Rosa had wrestled here before, and knew from painful experience that not all arena managers maintained equipment to his exacting standards.

"Raymond, go check el cuadrilátero, okay? I don't want anyone getting hurt in that ring. Gabriel, go help him."

It was the first time Gabriel had heard the veteran exótico call him by name and he had to let the words sink in before Ray snapped him back to attention.

"You coming?" Ray said, turning his attention to the ring.

Gabriel shadowed Ray as he ran his hands along the ropes and inspected the hardware at each corner.

"What are we looking for?" he asked quietly. He didn't want Miguel to hear him or think he didn't know what he was doing.

"Loose connections. Rust. Missing padding. Sharp edges. Torn vinyl."

"Really?"

"This isn't a palace," Ray said. "These little venues, where you don't have the league behind you? There've been problems. And our friend knows that better than anyone."

Ray nodded toward Miguel, who was meeting separately with two young luchadores, quietly discussing what Gabriel assumed would be their blocking for the match. But maybe not; he didn't know. Rosa and the professional luchadores had never shared what Gabriel assumed was an open secret: that the matches were rigged, their outcomes choreographed and predetermined in order to tell their story.

"La Rosa used to compete in these fancy leotards, bare-legged, until a line snapped and slashed his thigh a few years ago. I hear he had to be stitched up pretty good. He wears those body suits now because they cover up a couple of nasty scars."

Gabriel looked toward Miguel, then back at Ray.

"It's just a scar."

"So says the pretty boy," Ray said. "Look, that wouldn't matter much to me, but if you have a character that's supposed to be glamorous? Some Frankenstein scar isn't going to help that image much. Besides, it's not the only one. He's got a brutal surgical scar on his back, but he doesn't talk about it."

"I've seen it," Gabriel said.

"He's really careful about checking the rings now. If they look shaky, he won't wrestle."

"What about you? Are you even licensed yet? Should you be doing this?"

"I'm close enough for this little gig," Ray said. His face erupted in an ear-to-ear grin. "And I've got it on good authority that I passed my exam. It should be official any day now, and the league doesn't need to know about today."

"Congratulations!" Gabriel said. "And I can see why you wouldn't want your debut here. This place is a dump. Look at the ceiling—the paint's peeling. It looks like one of those pipes could fall at any time."

"Welcome to the minor leagues." Something creaked overhead, making them both look up. "Sometimes I wonder why I didn't just play ball instead."

"I thought you were a football player when I first met you."

Ray laughed, something Gabriel had learned was The Dark Storm's standard response to just about everything.

"Nope. That would be my kid brother Jason—defensive back, about to play safety for UCLA. He's just a freshman, and the scouts are already all over him. If things go according to plan, he'll go high in the draft in a few years."

Ray unleashed his super-sized smile. He leaned against the ropes and folded his arms across his chest.

"And when Jason signs that multi-million dollar contract, I intend to spend quality time around his infinity pool and private weight room." He bounced gently into the ropes, until he picked up a soft rhythm of drop, bounce, rebound, drop, bounce again. His face looked serenely content as he daydreamed about his brother's future largesse.

"It's good to have a plan," Gabriel said, raising his hand and getting an enormous slap of high five as Ray vaulted toward him. "You grew up in L.A.?"

"Inglewood, former city of champions."

"If you grew up in LA, how the hell did you end up a wrestler? I thought that was all in Iowa and Indiana."

"That's where I landed. I played high school ball, thought I'd play in college, too, but a friend dragged me to a wrestling team try out, and I was kind of a natural. Next thing I knew, I had a full ride as a Hoosier."

"And your brother plays football. He's big like you?"

"He's my half-brother, and he's more like you. He's *fast*—speed for days, and big enough that he can even out-jump a lot of the wideouts. You even know what that is, Gabe?"

"I grew up in a Pac 10 town," he said.

A scratchy sound system kicked in, playing musica banda. It wasn't exactly a wrestling soundtrack, but the rhythmic polka suited Ray's ring test better than the echo of folding chairs clanging against the concrete floors. Ray bobbed his head to the music. He was obviously a man happily at home in his surroundings.

"You'd like Jason," he said, raising his eyebrows in a knowing gesture. "He got the looks. I got the muscle and the smooth lucha moves." He raised his arms over his head and began to roll his hips in an awkward re-creation of a La Rosa salsa.

"No," Gabriel said. "No, no, no, no."

"*What?*" Ray laughed, and danced, and laughed some more.

"Just no, Ray. I don't need to see that. Don't quit the day job, man."

Ray dropped forcefully into the ropes and let them fully absorb his girth, then slingshot him forward. He laughed and danced over to the next line, where he repeated the move.

"What day job?"

"So this is it?"

Ray stopped, head cocked. "You mean the lucha?"

"I mean all of it. Moving to Mexico. Lucha libre. Everything."

"A means to an end," Ray said. "Someday, I'm going to use this to get into the American pro circuit. More money, a chance to be home, you know? It'd be different enough to get noticed, I think—a black luchador from south LA. And really, how is me coming here any different from what any pro athlete does? Once Jason gets drafted, there's no telling where he'll end up. It's a matter of who needs talent in the secondary and what teams have picks high in the draft."

"But he doesn't have to move to another country to do it."

"You moved to another country."

Gabriel went silent for a moment. His face fell flat.

"That wasn't by choice," he said.

Ray looked down at the floor. He knew pieces of Gabriel's history. He knew better.

"Sorry about that, Gabe. I wasn't thinking."

"Gabriel!"

Miguel had finished his talk with the other luchadores and slung a large gym bag over his shoulder. He shouted as he headed backstage.

"Yes?"

"When you see El Cadejo, tell him the locker room is down the hall and to the left."

"Who?"

Miguel simply waved his hand in the air as he walked away, a sign Gabriel had come to interpret as "just get it done." He looked to Ray for an answer and got only a shrug.

"Must be a new guy. I don't know him," he said. "But I'm guessing he should be here soon. We've got about an hour."

Gabriel excused himself and walked to the venue's foyer. As far as he knew, there was only one way into the place, so if he was supposed to meet someone, it would likely happen here—and he knew better than to disregard Miguel's instructions. The handful of times when he had, Gabriel had been saddled with more grunt work and less instruction time. But the harder Gabriel worked, the more time Miguel devoted to his training.

It seemed, at least occasionally, that he might have even secured a spot under Miguel's considerable wing, an apprenticeship of sorts earning one-on-one time with the veteran wrestler. And with it, Gabriel absorbed some of his mentor's outlook on lucha libre and its place in the world.

Once Gabriel had thought that he had a sophisticated knowledge of lucha libre. But the more he spent time with Miguel, the more he realized that his understanding of the sport and its significance in Mexican pop culture—even Mexican political movements—was on a novice level at best.

Lucha libre was no longer the simple entertainment of his childhood. Leaps, flips, and locks were trained, drilled, and earned. Masks were symbolic and served a purpose in defining characters and telling their stories. It was not just the show on television—"A circus," Miguel would complain—but a serious mélange of art, sport, and metaphor that Gabriel was only beginning to understand.

The more he learned, the more he wanted to absorb. Campus gradually took a back seat to the gym, his new source of higher learning.

So he listened to Miguel and did as he was told—usually—to ensure that his education continued. If that meant standing by a piss-soaked pillar outside a crumbling civic arena to meet someone he couldn't identify, he'd do it.

In many ways, the little venue reminded him of Arena Coliseo, the one-time boxing arena in north-central Mexico City now dedicated full-time to lucha libre. Arena Coliseo was close to fans' hearts for its history in the sport—and its cheap beer—and had seen better days. Its beach ball-colored seats were crusted with grime and acrylic paint. The sound system squawked. Its lighting bore down on the ring with little concern for staging. It didn't hold a candle to the relative glitz of Arena México, its cross-town rival that featured light shows, fog effects, booming music, and ring girls—all on display for the weekly lucha libre broadcasts aired live across Mexico and syndicated to the US.

"Excess," Miguel would say, if the topic came up, though Gabriel took it with a grain of salt. La Rosa had wrestled on some of those broadcasts, after all, and with some of the flashiest costumes and biggest entourages of all the luchadores.

Miguel clearly preferred Arena Coliseo, despite its aging surrounds. He said it brought fans closer to the authentic purpose of lucha libre— the good-versus-evil narratives played out by the técnicos and rudos each week—rather than light shows and loud music. Gabriel suspected this was why Miguel still agreed to perform in these small, unsanctioned, questionable events outside of the city.

As the ushers lifted the security gates, a small crowd of ticket holders milled about on the sidewalk: men, women, and children, many wearing reproductions of their favorite luchador's mask. Gabriel looked out on the street and saw a similar scene played out, though on a much smaller scale than he was used to in the city: the vendors hawking Lycra masks and lamé capes of champion luchadores. A few police officers stood near the doors watching the crowd develop.

A taxi rolled up right in front of him. A muscular, thick-thighed luchador hopped out of the backseat carrying a gym bag. He looked relatively young, perhaps in his mid-twenties, with defined forearms and biceps the size of birch trunks. His left arm was covered in tattoos, a half-sleeve of Mexican tribal imagery, lucha masks, and random words. He wore a tight T-shirt and jeans that told their own story of hours spent on weight machines, with a round ass that could only have been carved by squats and the gods. He already had his mask in place: a red and black Aztec-inspired design that looked like a wolf or a coyote. Gabriel didn't immediately recognize the character. He could see a wisp of black curly hair poking between the laces in the back.

He might as well have stopped time. Fans turned and stared as the luchador strode toward the arena. Gabriel followed suit.

"El Cadejo?" Gabriel asked tentatively. "I'm supposed to show you to the dressing rooms."

The luchador paused to acknowledge him and, saying nothing, followed Gabriel to the locker room—really nothing more than a large restroom with folding chairs lined up along the walls. In the far corner, Miguel stood dressed as Rosa, already applying glittery blue and silver makeup to coordinate with a shimmery cobalt bodysuit.

Miguel shook hands with the enmascarado. "Thanks for coming. I'm sorry for the last minute—"

The luchador looked at Gabriel; his gaze lingered, then he looked back at Miguel and waved his hand as if to say, "not a problem."

Gabriel took it as his cue to leave, but Miguel interrupted him. "Give me a few minutes, Gabriel. I want to talk to you. Be sure that each corner has towels and water. You're working en la esquina técnica tonight."

He set up his supplies and hung around the técnicos' corner until Miguel, wearing a hoodie over his body suit, emerged from the dressing area.

"See these first three rows? You're going to need to get them cleared out or moved back before we dive out of the ring."

"When will that happen?" Gabriel asked, wanting to eat his words as soon as they came out. He suspected a lecture was coming.

"What have I taught you? How do you read your opponent? Watch the luchadores, watch for the signs that they are preparing to clear the ropes, then get down there and move the first couple of rows back. We aren't working with our usual clearance, but these folding chairs should be easy to move. And the luchadores won't dive until they see you've made a path for them," he said, nodding toward the group of wrestlers, who were stretching, preparing for their bouts before the fans were let into the arena. "And during the breaks, give them water and towels, if they want them."

"Yes, Miguel."

"Rosa," he said. "In here, when I'm like this? It's La Rosa."

THE JOB WAS EASIER THAN Gabriel expected. The gym training, Miguel's lessons on anticipating movement, helped him prepare for the moment that wrestlers took the batalla from ring to audience, diving through the ropes and into the crowd.

The matches moved quickly: Ray and Más, the mini estrella, against his brother Menos and Gigantesco, a veteran luchador dressed in a plain green singlet who looked terribly out-of-shape in comparison to Ray's athletic frame. But Gigantesco had an established, old school following. The premise was that the tiny twin brothers had had a falling out, and were now wrestling against each other, but by the end of the match, they had turned against Ray and Gigantesco, and teamed together to take them on—and win. The crowd ate it up. The dwarf brothers were local kids, born and raised in Puebla, and their friends and family members filled an entire section of seats.

The final match pitted La Rosa against El Cadejo, a rudo named after the devil dog from Latin American folklore. Now in his costume of black Lycra wrestling tights intricately appliquéd with red eyes up the sides of each leg, the rudo was considerably younger than his opponent—older than Gabriel, no doubt, but the model of a modern luchador. He was muscular, athletic. He wasn't like the thick-torsoed El Santo or other luchadores from the early days of the sport. His muscles were intricately carved: his legs thick and powerful, his back a graceful inverted triangle of smooth skin that resculpted itself with each movement.

Normally a student of La Rosa's moves, Gabriel glued his attention to the athletic young rudo.

El Cadejo's moves were deceptive. He didn't appear to be a brawler, like so many rudos. He moved like a técnico; his moves were complex, precise, and acrobatic. Each attack, each attempted pin, was the result of a leap, a dive, or a flip. And each one was bigger, bolder, and seemingly more dangerous than La Rosa's.

He had never seen anyone quite like El Cadejo. The rudo was aggressive and threatening, yet masterful in his technique. His body looked as if it had been sculpted from marble. Gabriel couldn't take his eyes off him.

The luchadores mirrored each other for the first few minutes of the match, but El Cadejo picked up the pace, forcing one attack after another until La Rosa landed with a thunderous crash, face-first on the mat, trapped in a rana, his leg locked to his back by his opponent.

Round one to the rudo.

Round two began with La Rosa surging out of the corner, charging El Cadejo and ramming him into the ropes. The rudo paused, motionless, and La Rosa backed up, then rushed forward again, hurling his body in a patada voladora, a flying horizontal kick that landed with his legs wrapped around the rudo's neck, a helicopter move that whirled him to the ground. El Cadejo lay prone on the mat. La Rosa began his victory cha-cha, positioned to dive onto his opponent's back. But as the exótico danced, El Cadejo swept his legs out, knocking him off his feet.

It became a duel—pin, release, pin, and parry until they locked themselves into a ringside corner. El Cadejo reached between La Rosa's legs and lifted him over his head. Gabriel was transfixed, glued to the corner of the ring, watching the wrestlers' back-and-forth battle.

He didn't see it coming.

Rosa crashed into the first row of fans, spilling their beers and sending popcorn flying, landing face-first in a woman's lap.

Snapped to attention by his blunder, Gabriel rushed to the area too late and scurried to move ringside fans from their seats before El Cadejo took the match to the floor.

The rudo climbed the ropes and posed for the clamoring crowd, mocking La Rosa's signature dance, buying Gabriel time. As the last of the front row fans shifted back and La Rosa pulled himself up on his forearms, El Cadejo turned his back to the crowd, faced the ring, threw himself into a back flip off the turnbuckle, and landed with his feet hitting La Rosa squarely in the upper chest.

Though he lurched backward, La Rosa was prepared for the move. He flipped their bodies so that the rudo landed back-first in the aisle with his body pinned at the feet of the ringside crowd.

The referee made sure it ended quickly, calling his three-count and raising La Rosa's hand high from his spot in the aisle.

Round two to the técnico.

La Rosa rose slowly and stumbled dramatically toward the ring as the crowd clamored for more. Several of his ring boys rushed to his aid, but La Rosa waved them off. He pulled himself up into his corner and heaved himself into the ring for round three.

Though he had won the second round, the odds didn't look good for fans of the técnico. The rudo was younger, stronger, and, by definition, played dirty.

El Cadejo rushed La Rosa's corner to begin round three. He gripped the técnico's body suit. In turn, La Rosa tore at his mask, revealing his dark eyes. El Cadejo slapped at him, and grabbed at his own mask, trying to ensure it stayed in place—giving La Rosa time to attack.

As if energized by the move, La Rosa sprung at the ropes, rebounding and accelerating toward the rudo. He used his momentum to leap into a scissor kick, twirling their bodies until El Cadejo had been flung to the mat. Before the rudo could recover, La Rosa rose, and rushed to the ropes.

He leapt to the upper corner, turned toward the center of the ring. Before El Cadejo knew what had hit him, a blur of flying sequins spun at him, hitting hard, and landing flat across his body with a thunderous bang.

La Rosa rolled El Cadejo so that he lay prone on the mat, and pulled his arm securely against his back until the referee's hand slapped the mat once, twice, three times.

Round three and the match to La Rosa.

Gabriel stood by the ringside seats at the corner of the ring, in awe of the display, a true parejas increibles. And as the wrestlers stumbled from the ring, he sensed two sets of eyes squarely focused on him. He knew that one of them belonged to the man who would surely lecture him about the difference between watching the bout as a fan and participating as support staff.

He deserved that.

It was the other set that left him off balance.

★　★　★

THE MATCHES IN THE CITY were easy. Late nights studying were the norm in college, and the time went largely unnoticed at home. He had settled into studying economics at school, and the comparative styles, strengths, and weaknesses of professional wrestlers in the ring.

The shows outside the city—in tents, community centers, and even cockfighting rings—required lies. After a few months, he needed quite a few of them, because Gabriel had become the go-to support for Miguel's troupe of traveling luchadores.

As often as his academic schedule and family allowed, Gabriel was running errands, acting as support, and no longer forgetting his cues to clear the front rows if the arena didn't have enough room for the wrestlers to leap from the ring safely. He would pack a change of clothes under the books in his backpack and tell his aunt and uncle that he planned to stay on campus with friends from a study group.

In return, Miguel stepped up his training, coaching him one-on-one on days without classes, and pairing him to train with professional luchadores on days with them.

He could feel the eyes on him during training. It sometimes drove Gabriel to distraction, until he began to make an effort to eavesdrop, to catch snippets of conversation that could confirm whether he had begun to make inroads with his gruff mentor.

He had been sparring with a classmate when he saw Ray lean up against a wall in the training room alongside Miguel. Gabriel waved off his opponent, calling for a break, leaning over the ropes in apparent exhaustion. He rolled his head down, closed his eyes, and focused on the mumbled conversation occurring nearby. He could only make out fractions of words, but it was enough to get his attention.

"He's special, huh?" Ray asked, bumping Miguel's shoulder.

Miguel's response was rapid-fire.

"What makes you say that?"

"Nothing. I've just never seen you spend as much time with anyone as you spend with the kid."

"Maybe he needs that much work."

"Or maybe," Ray said with a wink, "maybe he's *the chosen one.*"

Miguel chuckled and shook his head as he walked away. "Oh, and Raymond?"

"Yeah?"

"I wouldn't let him hear you call him a kid if I were you."

His head still bowed, Gabriel couldn't help but grin.

Miguel had been the sole trainer at Gimnasio de la Ciudad since he started the business, years before. He'd always had enough willing talent in the room to help him demonstrate concepts and moves, but he had never been compelled to hire an assistant.

That lasted right up until the moment that Arturo Guerra walked through the door.

He marched into the gym with an authoritative attitude and a chiseled body, interrupting a conversation without apology to speak to Miguel. They spoke for a few minutes, looking at Gabriel. Miguel clapped his hands to get the class's attention.

"I want to introduce you all to Arturo. He's going to be helping out coaching, working on your acrobatics. This is a chance for you all to up your game. So listen to him like you'd listen to me—and no jokes, Raymond."

Ray laughed. "Since when do I listen to you, Miguel?"

Whether it was his body or the way he carried it, something about Arturo seemed familiar. His thick arms bulged under a gray long-sleeved compression shirt. His black hair was a kaleidoscope of curls, only slightly softening the sharp angles of his face.

Gabriel couldn't take his eyes off him.

Arturo pulled off the warm-up pants that covered muscular thighs and black Lycra shorts and moved to the front of the line along the wall for the group's first set of maromas. Every move that Miguel called out to the class, Arturo demonstrated, leading a conga line of students through choreographed rolls, lunges, dips, and falls. His movements were fluid, flawless, and powerful.

As the warm-ups concluded, Miguel hailed Arturo. He leapt over the upper rope with ease and landed in a somersault that left him standing in the center of the ring.

At Miguel's command, he hurtled himself to the upper rope, stood in the corner, and straddled the turnbuckle. He prowled the ring like a tightrope artist, pausing mid-way between corners to perform a backward swan dive back into the ring, landing as solidly as an Olympic gymnast.

Arturo was nimble and acrobatic in ways Gabriel had seen only occasionally, from La Rosa, El Diablo Azul, and the super estrellas of the televised league broadcasts.

When it came time to pair up and wrestle, Arturo worked with The Blue Devil, occasionally rotating to spar with Ray, who would never be a proper lucha aerialist due to his size. But with Arturo, the former wrestler champion exhibited a surprising talent for diving out of the ring. The move would be important in the pros, especially in team bouts, when luchadores would coordinate their plunges into ringside crowds.

Gabriel had moved up the ranks of the class rapidly, but still could not be considered a true luchador, so he sparred with other experienced amateurs, braving occasional glances at Arturo, but neither wrestling nor speaking with him.

Something about the new luchador left Gabriel feeling edgy and awkward in a way he had never experienced in the gym, and he wasn't going to risk making a fool of himself. Miguel took care of that for him.

As the class dispersed, Miguel called them both to his office.

"Gabriel, I've asked Arturo to work with you. He's an acrobat, and you still need to develop those skills. I think he could be a big help to you," Miguel said.

"But you're my trainer," Gabriel said.

"There's a lot you can learn from him. He's been doing acrobatics since…"

"Since I was a kid," Arturo interrupted. He looked at Gabriel, seemingly unimpressed. "Circus family."

"I'll still be working with you and running your training. You two coordinate your schedules. I'd like you training outside of class time at least twice a week."

Gabriel nodded, and extended his hand to Arturo. "It's good to meet you."

"Oh, we've met before," Arturo said, shaking his hand, and holding it firmly while he finished his introduction. "I wrestle as El Cadejo."

Arturo had just moved to Mexico City from Jalisco, where he had begun to carve out a career on the independent lucha libre circuit. There had been talk of his joining one of the big lucha leagues—there was no question of his talent—but rumors of erratic behavior had dogged his climb.

Miguel was the first promoter to show faith in El Cadejo, perhaps because he had the skills that Miguel hoped to instill in Gabriel. Perhaps because Gabriel and Arturo had similar strengths, bodies, and ambitions. Perhaps because his own body was beginning to betray him after years of abuse. Whatever his motivation, Miguel welcomed Arturo as an assistant, his right hand at Gimnasio de la Ciudad.

They were evenly matched in size. Though Arturo had the advantage of a mature frame, Gabriel was rapidly growing into his body. He was no longer the scrawny boy who had sneaked into an old exótico's dressing room and demanded wrestling lessons. The workouts and training had broadened his shoulders and defined his torso. His arms were developing the taut form of a professional athlete. Gabriel didn't see it in himself, not right away, not until his aunt asked him if he had found a weight room on campus.

With wits and with speed, Gabriel could handle himself against almost anyone, but there were similarities in their comparative strengths that made training with the new rudo valuable.

They both presented the picture of the modern luchador: as much athletes as performers; toned where older wrestlers had been thick; leanly muscled rather than pumped up like over-inflated gym rats.

The instruction, though withheld from Gabriel, had been made clear to Arturo: Show him the ropes; ready him for the acrobatics that would eventually be demanded of a técnico. They started on the mat, progressed to the ropes, and eventually had him mastering dizzying aerial attacks from atop the ring—flying helicopter takedowns designed to dazzle the fans.

Though he entrusted the development of Gabriel's technical skills to Arturo, Miguel insisted that Gabriel continue his own, unfathomable tutoring. It was classroom work, of sorts, a training of Gabriel's mind that only Miguel could explain—but steadfastly refused to do so.

His unconventional training included handing Gabriel a list of research assignments. *Study the rise of the PRI and the role of Superbarrio in the emergence of opposition politics. Watch and compare the El Santo movies of the 1960s to the El Santo movies of the 1970s. Contrast and compare American professional wrestling performance to lucha libre.*

"I know who El Santo is. My dad used to watch his movies with me when I was little. But how is watching *Santo vs. las Mujeres Vampiro* relevant to my getting a pro license?" Gabriel asked. He spat out his words in a rapid-fire complaint.

Miguel smirked and tossed a magazine across the room. "Read this," he said.

"*Lucha Semanal?*"

Miguel nodded, as if acknowledging a secret he hadn't shared.

"A thirty-year-old magazine? I wasn't even born yet."

"That's the point, college boy," Miguel said, going back to work, smiling to himself.

Gabriel trudged into the gym with a backpack full of books—only some of them textbooks—dropped them in a corner, and slumped against a wall. Ray watched him walk past and burst into laughter.

"Homework?"

Gabriel shot him a fiery look.

"You don't get it, Gabe. You think Miguel does that for everybody?"

"You mean the special torture that is C-grade movies and history lessons from wrestling magazines?"

"What's up with you? I thought you loved this shit. You came in here talking history and symbolism, now suddenly you don't like it?"

Gabriel rolled his head back until it rested against the wall. He sighed, oozing drama.

"How many people walked into this gym on their first day knowing the history of lucha libre, huh? I already knew this stuff."

"We all know who El Santo and Mil Mascaras are, Gabe," Ray said. His stern tone dropped away into a laugh. "Okay, I didn't—but I do now."

"You know what I mean. I just don't see how this makes me a luchador. How are movies and magazines supposed to help me in the ring? I don't see anyone else leaving class with homework or being told to mop up every night, and I just take it. I do everything he tells me, because I keep thinking that someday I'm going to learn some big secret about lucha libre. But every day, it's 'Gabriel, stack the mats' or 'Gabriel, clean the toilets,' or 'Gabriel, study the imagery of political movements in lucha libre circa 1968.' Who cares? I'm not getting tested on political movements. I'm going to be tested on whether I can do a competent quebrador con grio. And Arturo's teaching me that."

Ray slid down alongside Gabriel and settled on the floor. He scratched at his freshly-shaved head, as if deep in thought.

"You know why I train with Miguel?"

Gabriel shook his head.

"When I first came down here, the leagues were all over me. I could have signed with them, trained with them, I could have already been on the Sunday broadcasts. I mean, they knew who I was, and they were ready to put me in the ring based on that bronze medal."

"Why didn't you?"

Ray laughed again.

"Because I might have an Olympic medal and an NCAA title, but I didn't know shit about lucha libre, other than it looked cool and I knew some luchadores were making it into the American pro circuit."

"But Miguel just has you working those little weekend gigs. You would have already been on your way."

"And I still wouldn't know fuck-all about lucha. But I heard about Miguel, and I asked around and found out that people really respect him. He's old school. He makes sure his students understand what they're doing and why they're doing it. When he's done with you, you're a pro. No one's going to question your credentials, man."

"He doesn't make *you* clean toilets."

"Nope."

Gabriel stared into his lap.

"He doesn't like me," he mumbled.

Ray bumped his shoulder. He grinned.

"Hey, I thought you were smarter than that," he said. "Don't you get it? Wax on, wax off, man."

Gabriel shrugged. Ray made no sense.

"Dude, you're being Miyagi'd."

★ ★ ★

STAND ON THE ROPE. CENTER *your weight. Balance. Tune out everything outside the ring. Focus on nothing but the leap, the next move, and how you land it.*

Again!

Gabriel, a natural athlete, had little experience in acrobatics, other than those moments as a child when he would leap from the arm of the couch, pretending to be a wrestler launching himself from the ring. Now, the only thing holding him back from becoming a professional luchador was his lack of aerial skills.

Round off! Back flip! Dive! Roll!

Again!

Slap the mat as you land! Harder! Make it loud!

Again!

He stole spare moments—at home, on campus, in the park—to practice using improvised props: a handrail that doubled as a balance beam, a dining room chair that served as a spotter for handstands. He soon felt that he had earned a shot at the license Miguel absolutely demanded he secure before competing even in the smallest of unsanctioned events.

"I don't understand why he won't let me wrestle in one of these little weekend bouts," he complained. "I'm good enough."

"Probably because of that attitude," Arturo said. "Back to the ropes—plancha."

It was after hours. The class had dispersed more than an hour before, and Miguel left with a silent nod to Arturo and a reminder to Gabriel to stack the mats before he left for the night.

Arturo had tested him all evening, forcing him to push, then push more, and push even harder through move after repeated move. He pursued Gabriel relentlessly through the evening's routine, pinning him again and again—by his wrists, or his ankles, or face-first into the mat.

He was already sore from the beating, and Arturo simply demanded, "Again"—again, and again, and again.

Between Miguel's flat refusal to put Gabriel into a professional bout and Arturo's antagonism, Gabriel had had enough.

"That's it!" he barked, stripping off his sweat-soaked shirt and retreating to a corner. "No more drills. Best of three falls. I win, we're done. You win, then do what you will."

Arturo nodded and backed into the opposing corner. "Go ahead," he said, waving his hands in invitation. "Your move."

Gabriel took a breath and moved slowly toward the center of the ring. Arturo mirrored his movement.

"Show me what you got, Gabriel. Show me how you deserve to be a pro."

Gabriel lunged, grabbing at Arturo's waist, trying to draw his left arm to his back. The lock lasted only a moment—Arturo slipped free and turned his body so that he had leverage on Gabriel, hurling him to the mat. He straddled Gabriel's back and pulled his leg forward until Gabriel's foot reached his lower back, and counted to three.

"That's one," Arturo whispered in his ear. He released his hold and walked slowly back to his corner.

Gabriel scampered to his feet and ran toward the ropes, using the force to propel him into a back flip toward Arturo. He twisted his body, raising his feet, striking Arturo in the upper chest. He fell face-first onto the mat, but spun away as Gabriel dove toward his body.

"Got to be faster than that," Arturo taunted. He rolled back toward Gabriel, attempting the takedown, but Gabriel was prepared. He leapt to his feet and jumped atop the ropes, launching himself toward his instructor. He landed prone across Arturo's chest and pinned him flat against the mat.

"That's one," Gabriel said, his tone mocking. He didn't move immediately, but locked eyes with his teacher before he jumped to his feet.

They stared each other down from across the ring before either moved again. Arturo was slick with sweat. Gabriel's heart pounded. He gasped for air, trying to regain control of his body.

He charged.

They hit the mat as one. Gabriel moved fast, but Arturo's every move was infused with aggression and experience. Gabriel used every hold, every trick he had learned, to wrest control from Arturo, but just as he secured a hold, Arturo would slip out and turn the move against him.

He pulled behind Arturo and tried to lock his arm, but Arturo spun out of the move and turned the tables. He slid in tight behind Gabriel, grabbed his arms, and flipped him head-over-heels, flinging him to the mat.

Arturo followed him down, aligning and locking their bodies so Gabriel had no hope of escape. His pulse echoed through his ears. He drew a sharp breath, and looked up to eyes dark with intent.

"Show me how you break the hold," Arturo commanded.

Gabriel twitched. He couldn't control the rush flooding his body. He couldn't focus. He certainly couldn't break free.

"Should I count it out?" The words slipped through Arturo's lips like a hiss.

Gabriel squirmed and grunted. "No," he said firmly.

Arturo's breath brushed against Gabriel's ear. It left his mind unfocused, his body shaky.

"Wrap your legs around me," Arturo said.

Arturo reached down and grabbed Gabriel's thigh, pulled it until Gabriel dug his heel into the small of his back.

"And the other one."

Gabriel lifted his other leg from the mat and let it mirror the earlier motion. He took a deep breath and relaxed into it. He let his back dip into the mat.

"Now, rock your way out," Arturo said.

He tried. He shifted his feet to the mat for leverage. When that failed, he tried to roll Arturo off him.

Gabriel closed his eyes, trying in vain to focus, but it was no use. A hum, a buzz, raced through his head, charging his senses and draining his will.

He was finished. Panting, he dropped his head to the mat.

Arturo lifted himself up and reached for Gabriel's hand, drew it over his head, and pressed it flat against the mat. His face was close enough that Gabriel could feel Arturo's breath on his cheek.

Without a word, he angled his face to Gabriel's and pressed their mouths together. After the rush of the bout, the graze of Arturo's lips lingering on his was surprisingly, shockingly, gentle.

Stunned, Gabriel didn't respond. His lips quivered; his eyes refused to shut. As Arturo pulled away, Gabriel snapped back to life, lifting his head from the mat and chasing Arturo's mouth. He grabbed for Arturo's hair, reached behind his head, and pulled him back.

Arturo released his grip on Gabriel's wrist and drew his hand to Gabriel's cheek, enveloping it in his palm, pulling him closer, deeper. His other hand traced Gabriel's body until it landed firmly on his hip.

Their bodies connected, Arturo slid his knees between Gabriel's thighs, slotted between them, pressed their pelvises close.

Having fought all evening—first against Arturo, and now against his own body's traitorous excitement—Gabriel accepted defeat and gave in to the pleasure flooding through him. He buried his face in Arturo's neck and rolled his hips upward as Arturo ground down again and again.

He lost control of his breathing as his body built to a climax and he could scarcely huff out the words through his groan: "No pares. Por favor, no pares."

He shut his eyes against the rush and collapsed into the mat. Spent, Arturo rolled off and stretched out alongside him.

"That's two," he whispered. "I win."

ARTURO HAD MADE IT PAINFULLY clear from the outset that if this were to be a thing, if this were to be *anything*, it had to be conducted discreetly, quietly.

Secretly.

Even the scant two months that Gabriel had spent casually dating his study partner Eduardo after his graduation from la preparatoria had felt more like a relationship than this.

It wasn't that Arturo hadn't made his intentions clear. He had spelled out his conditions from the outset, from the moment that first night when Gabriel had gathered his courage and stepped behind him, wrapping his arms around Arturo's waist, and tentatively nuzzled the base of his neck.

He could feel how Arturo's shoulders had squared, how his frame had stiffened at the touch. It wouldn't be the only time it happened.

Over time, Arturo's response had become a refrain: "If you're looking for someone to hold your hand, I'm not your man."

Gabriel didn't challenge it at first. He had simply let Arturo slip from his grasp.

He didn't want to rock the boat. Arturo would come around, in time. But Gabriel couldn't help but wince every time Arturo got up to leave without sentiment, without the moment to linger that Gabriel had always assumed went hand-in-hand with sex.

"It's got nothing to do with you," Arturo said, sounding nonchalant. "Don't you realize that the reason I'm able to wrestle as El Cadejo is because no one knows? I bet you didn't even know at first. I have no choice in this."

"Of course you do," Gabriel said. "I do."

"Why? Because you're out?"

"Yes."

"And it's the reason why you'll end up like the old man," Arturo said. He nodded toward Miguel's office. "You're out—but you'll end up wrestling exótico because of it."

His words landed like a roundhouse. And Gabriel, on the ropes, put up his defenses.

He had been inspired by that first moment when he saw La Rosa wrestle at Arena México, but he had never once considered following in Miguel's heeled footsteps. Gabriel had never considered his sexuality relevant to his own wrestling. They were separate things. Yes, he admired Miguel for being an out luchador. Yes, he appreciated the history of exótico wrestlers—Miguel had seen to it. But Gabriel Romero had always assumed he would, simply, wrestle.

No feather boas, no lipstick, no problem.

And though he didn't intend to join the exóticos, his instincts told him to defend them.

"What's wrong with that?" Gabriel charged.

"Nothing. You want to wrestle exótico? Good for you. You want to play dress up? Then you're all set. You've had the perfect trainer."

"Every luchador wears a costume," Gabriel countered.

Arturo huffed out a dramatic sigh. If it was intended to make Gabriel feel small, young, and inexperienced, it succeeded. "You know what I mean. You want to become a super estrella? You want to be on TV every week? You want people wearing your mask to the arena? Then don't wear a dress."

"Miguel doesn't wear a dress."

"You've got the skills and the looks to make it, but everyone already knows about you—and that's going to hold you back."

"You don't know that," Gabriel said.

"Really? You just wait and see. When the league offers you a contract—and it will—it's going to be as an exótico."

"It doesn't have to be that way. Things are changing—"

Arturo shook his head. "Really? What are you going to do? Take over the leagues? Change the pinche management? Exóticos are *tolerated* because they bring in cash."

"Fans love the exóticos," Gabriel said.

"And the league still treats them like fools. Sure, they have their own fans now. The leagues figured out they could build a new audience, so now they're gaybait. The exóticos may not get jeered at the way they used to, but they're still nothing more than the leagues' drag queens. I don't care how much they mean to the fans. If you're in a league and you're out, you're going to be told to wear glitter and kiss the ref."

"You act like being exótico is second class."

"So do you," he said. "You defend them, but tell me, Gabriel—do you want to be one?"

Gabriel went silent.

"There it is," Arturo said. His voice was softer now, less combative. He had won this round. "You'll still go far. I'm not saying you won't. It's just that I've had these plans for a long time, and getting what I want means keeping up El Cadejo's image."

He reached out to trace Gabriel's lips with his fingertips, then ran them down his chin and along his throat until he struck the tiny gold cross. Arturo twisted it his hand, rolling it from finger to finger.

"Do you ever plan on coming out?" Gabriel asked.

The slow shake of Arturo's head was almost indiscernible. "While I'm wrestling? Why would I? I have tradition to fall back on. Enmascarados have always been secretive. There's nothing unusual about keeping my private life private. Masked luchadores have always done that."

"But you'd be leading a double life."

"What luchador doesn't? It's an act, and El Cadejo's just a character."

Gabriel turned away, but Arturo reached for his arm, drew him back. He pulled Gabriel close so their foreheads touched, and lowered his voice.

"You think I wouldn't like what you have? I just want this more. I've wanted it as long as I can remember. But you don't get top billing if you're gay. It's as simple as that. And I want to be a super estrella. If you're not comfortable with that, I get it."

He kissed Gabriel again, a caress more tender and inviting than the urgency they had shared just moments before. He dragged his lips along Gabriel's jaw, lingering in front of his ear.

"But I hope it's not," he added.

It was a fleeting gesture—just enough to turn the heat of anger to the spinal chill of excitement. Just long enough to convince Gabriel to take a chance on the man who frustrated, intimidated, and thrilled him. He let himself be enfolded in Arturo's embrace and slowly wrapped his arms around Arturo's neck, then reached up to draw him in and not let him go.

Gabriel surrendered to the kiss, to its implications, its complications, and to the inevitable marks it would leave on his life. His hand dropped down Arturo's spine, palm flat against the warm skin.

Arturo could leave him feeling furious and worked up. He could also leave him breathless. Gabriel wasn't sure which was better, or worse.

Arturo pulled away and looked down at the cross hanging from Gabriel's neck. He toyed with it, twisting it in his fingers for long moments.

"You shouldn't wrestle with this thing," he said.

★ ★ ★

A MAN ON A MISSION, Miguel marched into Gimnasio de la Ciudad. He hadn't yet changed into his workout gear. He was still in the jeans and a Club América jersey he'd worn while running errands: the Pemex, the athletic supply house, the post office. He clutched an envelope in his right hand and rapped it against the wall as he scanned the gym.

"Where's Gabriel?" he barked. "¡Oye, pendejo escolar!"

Mop in hand, Gabriel poked his head out from the office. Someday, this *college boy* nonsense would stop.

"There you are!"

"Where else would I be?" Gabriel said. He had been cleaning the gym for close to an hour while other wrestlers mingled. He was in no mood.

Miguel taunted him, waved the envelope in front of Gabriel's face, and then fanned himself like a flamenco dancer. "Well, if you don't want to see this, I can wait all day," he said.

Gabriel dropped the mop. "My results?"

Miguel nodded and handed him the letter. "Congratulations. Have you decided on your nombre de batalla?"

Gabriel tore at the envelope. He had fantasized about his wrestling name since childhood, but now that the decision was, maybe, imminent, his mind was blank. "You don't even know if I passed," he said.

"Oh, yes I do. Now, what are we going to do about your character?"

Gabriel pulled the paper from the envelope, took a moment to absorb its contents. He shut his eyes, feigned stoicism, and tried to bite back the grin that ultimately won out. It had taken more than eighteen months before Miguel cleared him to test for his license to compete professionally, to finally earn the right to be called a luchador.

It had seemed like a decade.

Ray had reminded him—many times—that eighteen months from first lesson to professional status was nearly unheard of, but eighteen months can seem like eighteen years when you want what you know you have the skills to do.

Gabriel just didn't have his mentor's permission.

Even as he cleared Gabriel for his license, Miguel admonished him that his education was far from over: Balancing the demands of the audience, the business, and the demands of promoters were all virgin territory for his apprentice.

"There are things you can only learn in the ring, with an audience. And there are people who'll want to run you, and people who'll want to ride your coattails when you succeed."

Gabriel nodded, and Miguel reached under his chin to make eye contact. "And you will, Gabriel. I have every confidence. So we're not going to worry about those other things today, okay?"

He turned and whistled loudly to attract the other wrestlers' attention. "We have a new luchador in the house!" Miguel called out, slapping Gabriel on the back. "We're closed for the night. Drinks are on me."

It had become a tradition in Miguel's gym. When a wrestler passed league-sponsored exams to become a certified professional, when they truly earned the title of luchador, he would take the newly minted professional wrestler, and whomever else was in the gym, out for a round of drinks. But this was the first time he had stopped everything and cancelled classes.

They met at a bar a few blocks away, near Arena Coliseo; the bar had long been a watering hole for luchadores, trainers, and promoters. It was dark and loud, with floors sticky from beer and walls littered with collections of treasured clutter: championship posters, autographed photos, and framed masks of some of the sport's greatest stars. It was a shrine to lucha libre.

Over Victoria beer and tequila shots, the group toasted Gabriel's future and made sport of planning it. The naming of the newly minted luchador was a beer-fueled rite, a confirmation ritual of the small, tight-knit community of independent professional wrestling.

Suggestions were shouted out from across the bar, by wrestlers and patrons, from traditional and time-honored to laughable.

He's small and fast. Call him El Conejo!

Gabriel grimaced. He would *not* be a rabbit.

How about El Gringo?

"I'm as much a Mexican as I am American. And Ray's an American. Why don't you call *him* that?"

Because he's bigger than us!

"I wanted to be El Rayo. Lightning. Perfect, right? Like the superhero I was meant to be. But they gave me the thumbs down," Ray said, to a friendly chorus of boos and raised glasses.

"It also means sunbeam," Gabriel said.

"Like a *Ray* of sunshine? Like I said, perfect."

Call him Pretty Boy!

He has to shave that peach fuzz off his chin first—and wax!

Gabriel whirled around to see where the comments came from.

"Maybe we should use Miguel's name for you—College Boy," Ray said.

He glared at Ray. *College Boy* had taken on many teasing forms since Gabriel first joined the gym, and there was no way he was going to let it follow him into the ring.

"I had a boyfriend once who said I should have a lucha name after my studies, like El Maniaco Matemático," Gabriel said.

As his colleagues gave the idea a boisterous thumbs down, Arturo sat grim-faced near the end of the bar. Gabriel had told him about Eduardo, how his high school crush had briefly become his first boyfriend, his first everything. It never failed to sour Arturo's disposition.

"You never have time to date, Gabe. Maybe we should call you Lonely Boy," Ray said, laughing at his own joke, even as the entire bar again groaned and booed.

"Whatever you do, don't be a devil," said El Diablo Azul, still wearing his mask as he stood at the bar, occasionally posing for selfies with the patrons. "It will take you years to live it down."

It would be the last time that Gabriel talked to the Devil.

Days later, the veteran luchador would be de-masked in the ring, led away by a fellow técnico. Minutes later, he would re-emerge: new mask, new identity, and new allegiance in place. He would be La Nube de Plata—The Silver Cloud—a full-fledged técnico at last. It was anticipated, of course, but the wrestler and the league, and, more than likely, Miguel, had kept the event a well-guarded secret as crowds continued to build with each of El Diablo Azul's final bouts. They knew the moment was coming, the day the Devil would be exorcised from the ring, once and for all. With each match the crowds grew larger, and the league delayed the inevitable, stretching out opportunities for box office gains.

"I used to think about being some sort of angel," Gabriel said.

"But you're going to be a rudo," Arturo chimed in, finally speaking up. He shot a glance at Gabriel. He was cocky, self-assured, and apparently trying to make a point.

"I could be a Dark Angel, an Avenging Angel," Gabriel snapped back.

"He will be neutral for now, so no names that scream rudo or técnico. He has to play both sides of the fence," Miguel said, and then turned to Gabriel. "You're a rookie, so you need to be ready to float for a while, be whatever's needed until you get established."

"No Dark Angel?" Gabriel asked.

Miguel shook his head.

"No Avenging Angel?"

"Afraid not."

Gabriel made a face as if the bar smelled even worse than its native aroma of stale, spilled beer.

"Phoenix," Ray said, interrupting.

"What was that?" Miguel asked. He had tuned Ray out at Lonely Boy.

"Phoenix. Rising from the ashes?" He looked at Gabriel. "And, you know, Arizona."

Miguel looked around the group, scratching his chin, until he glanced at Gabriel with a "What do you think?" expression.

"It's better than Lonely Boy," Gabriel said. "But it sounds more técnico than rudo."

"Dark Phoenix, Light Phoenix. We can make it work either way," Miguel said.

"You sure it shouldn't sound stronger?"

"All in good time," Miguel said. He turned toward Gabriel, seeking a moment of privacy in the crowded bar.

"A word?"

He picked up their beers and led Gabriel to a corner table, away from the increasingly raucous group. Only Arturo was mute, silently watching Gabriel and Miguel walk away.

"I'm happy for you," Miguel said. "You've worked hard for this."

"You made me."

"Do you regret it?"

"No," Gabriel said. "I know how long it can take to get licensed."

"Three, four, even five years for some wrestlers, the ones who stick with it," Miguel said.

Gabriel allowed himself a smile. "I'm just hoping this means I don't have to wipe down the sauna anymore."

Miguel laughed and slapped his back. "Yes, you've graduated. No more mops and piss."

He sipped at his beer and looked over to the bar. Ray was dancing, sort of, with two women who had been lingering around the perimeter of the group of luchadores.

"You're going to wrestle with us?"

"I'd like to," Gabriel said.

Gabriel turned his beer bottle clockwise, picked at the moist label, and then spun it counter-clockwise.

"Something's on your mind," Miguel said. Gabriel's focus stayed fixed on the bottle.

Turn, pick, spin. Repeat.

"Look at me," Miguel said. "Spit it out."

Gabriel stopped, tapped his fingers on the table, and finally looked up, meeting Miguel's eye. "Are you going to make me an exótico?"

"What?"

"Are you going to make me be an exótico?" he repeated with more force.

"I can't make you anything," Miguel said.

"I heard I would be an exótico, that I don't have a choice."

"Who told you that?" Miguel asked. Gabriel glanced to the end of the bar, and Miguel's gaze followed. "Gabriel, look at me. You're a rookie. You're just starting out. And I don't represent the leagues. As far as I'm concerned, you can be whatever you want. But the future? I can't predict that. You become a league wrestler, and they'll have a say in the character they want you to play."

Gabriel looked down, grim and silent, poking at his cuticles. Miguel wasn't telling him anything he didn't already know.

"You have choices, you know," Miguel added. He narrowed the gap between them to be heard over the din of the bar, as if sharing a secret. "You don't have to join a league."

"But then, I'll never get to the top," Gabriel said, not bothering to look up.

"Does that really matter?"

Miguel dipped his head, forcing Gabriel to make eye contact. He didn't move until Gabriel acknowledged him, albeit with a grunt.

"I told you, you have choices to make. You're a good wrestler. You could become a great luchador. But success? Only you can decide what that means to you. Is it money? Television? Fame? Then you become a league luchador and you play by their rules."

"And an exótico?"

"Maybe," Miguel said. "Or is success something else, Gabriel? Is it being the luchador that you want to be? Not letting an empresa decide that for you? Then maybe you stay independent."

Gabriel measured the words, sometimes acknowledging with the slightest of unconscious head bobs, occasionally glancing over to where Arturo stood at the bar.

That didn't go unnoticed.

"No one can make these choices for you. Not me, not anyone else."

Somehow, Miguel knew, and acknowledged it without the judgment Gabriel expected. "Whatever you decide, understand that at some point, you're going to have to sacrifice for it."

"I don't understand."

Miguel leaned back in his chair and looked at the ceiling, as if the dim bulbs and acoustic tiles held the answer to life's great mysteries. "You will."

Gabriel wasn't sure what Miguel meant, but knew he wouldn't get an answer even if he asked. So he responded with a simple "yes," and nodded, and carried on—just as he'd done dozens of times before.

"You know, Ray likes to say that when you get all cryptic you're just Miyagi'ing me."

Miguel finished off his beer and rested his chin on his hands. "I have no idea what that means."

"It means you're playing head games with me."

Miguel laughed. "Raymond—our savant. Maybe I do. But this isn't a head game. You haven't wrestled in front of a crowd yet, and once you do, you're going to start getting fans. You need to learn to play to them, to cultivate them. And then you'll need to deal with the empresas who'll want you for their own matches, and know whether they're looking out for your best interests or just trying to ride your coattails."

"Does that include you?"

Miguel's face suggested that he had to at least consider this a possibility, even if it was just for his own amusement. But when he spoke, he grew serious.

"You know I look out for you. Not everyone will. Promise me that when someone tries to get you to sign on for *extrema*, you'll say no, whatever they offer."

"I've never even seen an extrema match," Gabriel said.

He had heard stories, of course, but as a protégé of Miguel's, he was unlikely to see one of the controversial bouts. Miguel would have nothing to do with them and didn't want his stable of wrestlers to pander to them, either. Too great a risk, he told them. Fight extrema and don't expect to be let back into his gym, he warned.

Gabriel had talked with wrestlers who had tried lucha extrema. He'd heard their stories of big paychecks and bigger risks, of surviving, bloodied and injured, and vowing never to do it again.

Playing on the fringe of lucha libre, outside of its traditions but drawing big promotions and bigger crowds, extrema matches added elements of danger to the ring. There were no rules, no staging, no ethics. They were often fought in a cage, and the ring would be littered with broken beer bottles, nails, even razor blades. Several luchadores would fight simultaneously, without teams, or rudos and técnicos, or even storylines. The last man standing won.

More often than not, extrema wrestlers got injured, sometimes seriously. Sometimes permanently.

But they were paid well.

"Like I said, you define your success, so be choosy. Stay true to your principles. And if you have to do something extreme, stick to the hair matches, okay?" Miguel said. He placed his hand on Gabriel's scalp and mussed his mop of dark brown waves. "You have plenty to spare."

"I just have one question," Gabriel said. He drained the last of his beer and set the glass down on the table.

"When do I start?"

★ ★ ★

A LICENSE TO WRESTLE WAS not an invitation to jump into the ring.

Gabriel spent weeks working with Miguel fine-tuning his character, his look, his costumes. He shadowed Miguel. He accompanied him to the wrestling suppliers, to the designer's studio, to the fabric shop.

In the car, they would talk of strategy and of show, of the masters of lucha libra, and why they were so beloved decades after their careers had ended. El Santo's path may have led him from the ring to B-grade movies, but he was still beloved by fans as lucha libre's greatest técnico long after the day when he was buried wearing his silver mask.

It takes something special, Miguel would remind him: a character story that resonates with fans, a style unlike other luchadores. People needed something, or someone, to cheer for.

"And I can do that as a rudo?" Gabriel asked.

"You can do that as anyone. You just need to be compelling."

They started with the costumes. As a rudo, the look was simple: black wrestling boots and Lycra tights with gold and burnt orange lamé flames appliquéd up his legs. But the Phoenix would also have to play the técnico in some matches. For those, Miguel ordered the same costume with a base of white instead of black.

"And what about a mask?" Miguel asked. The look on his face said he already knew the answer.

"Yes, always," Gabriel said. "If I'm keeping the same identity for both rudo and técnico, I should wrestle enmascarado."

Miguel had already asked his designer to create samples with a continuation of the appliqué works from his tights, so flames framed the front of his two masks—one black, one iridescent white.

"You want to try these on?" he asked, pulling them from a bag. "We can have these made without the laces or the mouth, but I don't suggest it. You can tighten them this way, or loosen them up if you need to. That will help if you have to be de-masked."

He stepped behind Gabriel, helped him adjust the white mask until it settled neatly across his face, and then tightened the laces. It had a deep cutaway around the mouth, with room to show off his pouty lips. The last time he had worn a mask was as a child, wrestling on the family room couch with his father.

"Why would I ever want to be de-masked?" Gabriel said. He touched the mask, tracing the flames up his cheeks and around his eyes. "I'm never letting anyone claim my mask."

Miguel didn't argue. Being de-masked was rarely the luchador's choice. But should Gabriel's professional identity change—as it inevitably would—he would have to surrender his mask, his identity.

"It's a good fit," Miguel said.

When it was time to schedule Gabriel's debut, he arranged for a trios parejas, a tag team match with familiar faces, with opponents who could be trusted to work with the rookie luchador.

Gabriel would be paired with Arturo and The Henchman as rudos against Ray, The Silver Cloud, and himself as técnicos at Arena Coliseo. It was a high-profile matchup for a debut, but Miguel had looked out for his protégé, as promised.

"You're going to be my padrino?"

Miguel nodded.

"You okay with that? I thought I'd be there to help coach you through it, to make sure everything goes right."

They scheduled practice time with all six luchadores so Gabriel would be comfortable with the ebb and flow of the multi-wrestler format. As a rudo, he'd have room for error. If he broke from protocol, he would simply be playing the rule-breaker. Still, he needed to know when to step out and when to stay in the ring.

Miguel sketched out the pairings carefully, based on skills and body types. The Dark Phoenix would face La Rosa, El Cadejo would square off against The Silver Cloud, and the La Tormenta Oscura would pair up against The Henchman. He coached Gabriel and Arturo to coordinate their acrobatics with flying takedowns and side-by-side tornillos to trap their opponents outside the ring. Ray and The Henchman, both heftier than the other combatants and skilled in traditional wrestling, would use their time to feature locks, holds, and power moves in the ring.

"You're as ready as you're going to be," Miguel said as they finished their final workout. He wrapped his arm around Gabriel's shoulder. "Now your family finally gets to see you wrestle. How many tickets should we pull?"

"They're in Cuernavaca this weekend," he said. Gabriel spoke rapidly and looked the other way, avoiding Miguel.

"On the weekend of your debut?" he asked.

Gabriel hedged, biting at his lip. He kept mum, hoping for a change in subject.

That didn't work.

Miguel's eyes narrowed. He was onto Gabriel's game.

"They do know, don't they? Have you lied to them?"

"I haven't lied," Gabriel said.

Miguel tilted his head and pursed his lips.

"Not exactly."

The squint became a grimace.

"Have you told them anything?" he asked.

"There didn't seem to be much reason. I'm still in school."

"And how long is that going to last?"

Miguel had that look on his face. Gabriel had seen it dozens of times before and knew it wouldn't do him any good to draw out his deception.

"I cut back on my units."

Miguel said nothing.

"It was too much: the classes, and all the extra training sessions. I didn't want my grades to suffer."

Miguel folded his arms across his chest. Gabriel stammered.

"I just don't think it would have done any good. They wouldn't have let me—"

"Are they still paying your tuition?" Miguel asked.

Gabriel nodded.

"And where is that money going?"

"I haven't dropped out," Gabriel said.

Miguel leaned back against the ropes, bounced a little, and dropped until he was sitting along the edge of the ring, resting his back against the ropes. "Take a seat," he said, patting the space alongside him.

Gabriel did as he was told and settled on the edge of the platform.

"You're out to your family, right?"

"Yes," Gabriel said. He thought he heard a muffled grunt.

"But you can't tell them you're a luchador?"

Gabriel couldn't voice his response, not right away. He answered with the slightest shake of his head and then searched for his words. "They wouldn't approve."

"Do you know that for certain? Have you tried?" Miguel spoke cautiously. "Do they accept you?"

Gabriel nodded. "In their way. They try. They're not flying rainbow flags or anything, but they've never exactly objected, either."

"Then why do you think they won't accept the lucha libre? A lot of parents would be proud to have a luchador in the family."

"I think they'd rather have a doctor or maybe a politician." Gabriel's voice was low, resigned.

"That's why you still go to school? To make them happy? Or is it to fool them?"

"I like school. I want to finish. But right now, I want this *more*. This is what I'm meant to do."

Miguel patted Gabriel's knee. "I think you need to tell them and I think someday you'll regret that your family wasn't here for your first bout, but that's your call. You have your familia luchistica, and they'll all be in that arena with you tomorrow."

He stood up gingerly, gripping his thigh as he rose. "Now, quit sniffling. I want you to get some rest. No fooling around with cute boys tonight, you understand me?"

He looked to off to the far side of the gym, where Arturo lingered near the staircase.

"I understand," Gabriel said.

GABRIEL ARRIVED EARLY TO ARENA Coliseo in jeans and a T-shirt with the Dark Phoenix costume stashed in his backpack. It was a good hour before the arena was to open to staff and wrestling crews, but he had a friend at the box office who let him in, let him walk the space and get a feel for the venue that he had sat in so many times before as a fan.

He climbed into the ring between the ropes, a pedestrian move that would be replaced by a luchador's vaulted flip in a few hours. Alone in the center of the ring, he looked up and absorbed the stark confines of Mexico City's aging wrestling palace: the netting that protected drunken fans from falling off the upper decks; the thick coats of robin's egg blue paint that stretched from floor to ceiling, four levels up; the empty beer stations standing sentinel at each corner of the room.

Arena Coliseo had little outward charm and had been overshadowed in recent years by the flash of laser light shows, jumbotrons, and booming sound systems at Arena México. But it owned the sport's history, its glory, and many of its ghosts. Miguel's history lessons flooded over Gabriel as he looked into the empty seats. During World War II, the archbishop had blessed the arena before it opened for its first bout. Over the years, two luchadores had died wrestling in its ring when planned maneuvers went awry.

Fans of the spectacle watched lucha libre at Arena México.

Fans of lucha libre watched it at Arena Coliseo.

Miguel's choice of venues for Gabriel's debut had not been accidental.

Gabriel looked at the ceiling, at nothing in particular, and mindlessly touched the base of his neck, feeling the gold chain and the cross that hung from it. His fingers traced it while he shut his eyes and exhaled.

"You ready?"

Gabriel looked up to see the silhouette of a man standing near the top row of the floor seats. Arturo had arrived long before the evening's card demanded.

"How long were you standing there? And why aren't you wearing your mask? You always wear your mask to the arena."

"Long enough. And I don't wear it when I'm this early. I was looking for you."

Even after months together, Arturo could unravel Gabriel with just a look. Simply by entering the room, he could lay claim to Gabriel's unwavering attention. His power, his intensity, and his authority combined in a siren call, leaving Gabriel self-conscious and on-edge.

Part of it, admittedly, was simple attraction. Even hidden behind his mask, El Cadejo had lured Gabriel in from the first time they met. And months after their first night together, simply knowing what that body could do to him threw him off balance and filled him with want. That Arturo was also his senior, his instructor, left him feeling stripped of power, which he had willingly surrendered.

"I've been trying to reach you," Arturo said. He picked up Gabriel's bag from the floor and handed it to him.

"I thought I'd spend some time alone with the room before tonight."

Arturo nodded. "I was hoping to go over the match last night, but you didn't answer my texts."

"Miguel told me to rest up."

"Miguel." Arturo grunted.

"I needed rest."

Arturo walked him backstage, toward the locker room. He tilted his head toward Gabriel's ear and lowered his voice. "Is it true that your family's away this weekend?"

Gabriel tried to hide the smile creeping onto his lips.

"For a couple of days."

"Why didn't you say anything?" Arturo said, hushed. "I could have come over. We could have had a night together. Don't you want that?"

Gabriel dipped his head and lowered his voice to match Arturo's. "Of course I do, but Miguel was right—I needed rest."

"Does he have so little confidence in you?"

Gabriel bumped Arturo with his shoulder, teasing him, trying to lighten the mood, then pulled away quickly in case anyone entered the room.

"El Cadejo, always so surly. It was just one night—and they don't come back until tomorrow afternoon."

He glanced up and down the hall and pulled Arturo by the wrist into the locker room. He let the door snap shut behind them, and spun Arturo until his back was pressed against it.

"Come over tonight," he said, his face inches from Arturo's. "We'll celebrate."

Arturo's eyes scanned the room, darting from side to side before settling on Gabriel's face. He raised an eyebrow.

"I promise," Gabriel shivered against his lips. "Come over."

THEIR BOUT WAS SCHEDULED LATE in the program, just before the headliner, and bodies jammed the locker room as they readied for the match: wrestlers, trainers, and nearly a dozen gold lamé-wearing bikini boys—La Rosa's fight day entourage, and Miguel's answer to the posing, ubiquitous ring girls of Arena México, known for their big hair, bigger breasts, and miniscule costumes. His group, mostly young go-go boys culled from Zona Rosa dance clubs, took up the scarce mirror space in the locker room as a makeup artist went down the line, dusting their hair in gold glitter and applying shimmery neon eye makeup in golds, blues, pinks, and greens.

Miguel pulled out all the stops for the tag team match: the weeks of preparation, the dancers, his new rainbow-colored bodysuit and matching cape.

Despite his planned theatrics, he kept a low profile in the locker room, alone in a dank corner, away from the hubbub of the crowd. He sat on a folding chair with his bodysuit pulled to his waist and slowly rolled his head to the right, then the left, as he started his pre-bout stretches.

Though his precisely painted lips and glitter-tossed hair spoke to his character's glamour, his exposed torso told its own story with bruises and scars, including a long line stretching from shoulder blade to armpit, the remnant of a long-ago surgery normally hidden beneath workout gear.

He breathed slowly, his eyes closed, as if in a meditation that locked out the activity around him.

"You ready for this, boy?"

His eyes opened with laser focus on Gabriel, dressed for the first time in rudo black.

"You need help with that?" Miguel pointed toward the mask Gabriel gripped tightly. Miguel waved his fingers in a "come here" gesture. "You don't want to get de-masked in your first bout."

Gabriel knelt on the floor in front of him while Miguel adjusted the black-and-orange mask so that it rested like a second skin across his face and gave him a clear sightline.

"How's that feel?"

Gabriel nodded. "Good."

"Turn around. Let me lace it up for you."

Miguel's hands worked quickly, pulling the mask snug at the back of Gabriel's head, then securing it with a double knot that he tucked under the bottom of the mask.

"Let's see."

Gabriel rose to his feet and turned. Before Miguel stood a luchador, head carried high, torso cut with muscle, the muscles in his thighs clearly visible through the black Lycra tights.

"We should line your eyes," Miguel said. Even with much of his face now covered by his mask, Gabriel could squint, and sneer, and make it clear he was not on board with the suggestion. Miguel simply rolled his eyes, changed the subject, and reached toward Gabriel's boots. "These on tight enough?"

"I know how to lace my boots, Padrino."

Miguel stood and looked Gabriel up and down. He reached into a bag in his locker and pulled out a small makeup tube. "Put this on," he said, handing it to Gabriel.

"Lipstick?"

"Just to plump them up a little. The mask is a cutaway. It'll help. Trust me. Hurry up or I'll make you do the eyeliner, too."

Gabriel rolled the makeup in his hand.

"Don't worry," Miguel said with a wink. "It's not pink."

Gabriel applied the gloss, and Miguel stood back, hand to chin, assessing his appearance.

"Remember to watch me for your one-on-one cues," he said.

Gabriel nodded.

"And watch Arturo for group cues, when you leap into the crowd."

"Yes, Miguel."

"And remember, you're a rudo. Don't be humble. You need to strut."

"Yes, Miguel."

"When you take me down, you own it, you hear me? Pose. Be arrogant."

Gabriel bit his lip. "Yes, Miguel. I understand."

"And when I take you down, protest! Play it up! *Overplay* it."

A chuckle bubbled up from Gabriel's chest.

"And don't you go easy on me. Those spinning scissors you've been practicing? Use them. Lock onto my neck and I'll follow you down to the mat—and don't forget to distribute your body weight as you land so you don't get hurt. And land with a slap! Make it loud, Gabriel."

"Miguel?"

"—you understand?"

"*Miguel.*"

"What?"

Gabriel stepped alongside Miguel and placed his hand on his shoulder. "I know."

The door to the locker room opened, and an arena attendant called the parajas de luchadores to line up—rudos first, técnicos second.

They would enter the arena by status, with the captains for each team appearing last. Gabriel stood by the door, waiting for Arturo, who leaned against the lockers, and The Henchman, who was attending to Ray's face.

Maybe he needs lip gloss.

The Henchman dotted Ray's forehead with what looked like a styptic pencil, as if applying pre-emptive first-aid.

"You ready for this?" Arturo asked, stepping in line behind him.

"Everyone keeps asking me that,' Gabriel said. "I think I should be asking you. Are you going to take those off?"

Arturo still wore his warm-up pants and a skin-tight compression shirt that showed off every detail of his chest. He also wore a new mask: the same black and red design as before, but a full-coverage variety made of Lycra without the traditional laces or cut away for his mouth. It amplified his already aggressive costume.

"Thought I'd mix it up a bit today," he said. "Hey, Henchman, you good to go?"

The Henchman waved, raised a finger—just another minute.

"What are they doing?" Gabriel asked, eyeing the spectacle as The Henchman stood up and muscled his way to the front of the line, towering over the assemblage of bikini boys. He tapped the shoulder of the attendant, who radioed to the booth to announce the match.

"Just stepping up the drama," Arturo said. "Don't you worry."

As Gabriel approached the door, he felt a hand at his elbow. Miguel, now in full La Rosa regalia, took one last moment to coach.

"Remember to strut. Preen. Own the moment. Hit hard; land loud. Okay?"

The door opened, and the Dark Phoenix acknowledged the coaching with a silent bob of the head. He crossed himself and let his fingers drift to the chain hanging from his neck, then turned to enter the arena.

THE ANNOUNCER DIDN'T HAVE MUCH to say about him. "For the rudos, rising from the flames, *El Fénix Oscuro!*"

It was enough. There would be no announcing that this was his debut. The game was to look like a master, not a rookie. The crowd would play along, even if they knew better. The arena rang out with his entrance music, a popular reggaeton piece fueled by guitars and rap.

Gabriel took a settling breath and seated his shoulders, straightened his posture, lifted his chest. He shut his mind to the thumping of his heart and the growl in his stomach. He looked forward, toward the ring, and took his first step as a luchador.

And tripped.

Laughter rang in his ears. Popcorn pelted his face. A hand slapped his ass. He turned. A group of middle-aged women cheered and high-fived each other.

Breathe.

He focused again on the ring, nothing but the ring, ignoring the outstretched hands of fans wanting to high five the luchador on his march.

Hold your head high.

He reached the ropes and placed his hands along the upper line.

Own the moment.

He stepped back, giving himself room to build momentum, and then ran at the ring. He hurled himself up and over with a flip, sticking the landing.

Be arrogant.

He raised a fist as a salute to the crowd. As the noise settled, he turned and bounced against the ropes, waiting for the rest of the team.

The arena's sound techs ensured that he wouldn't wait long. A scream of heavy metal guitars scorched the room. The volume rose through the vibrations in the ring.

El Cadejo stepped into the room, accompanied by a booming bassline, holding his palms outstretched for fans to slap. He still wore the skin-tight shirt and warm-up pants over his black knee-high boots.

As he approached the stage, he launched into a handspring to vault over the ring, and landed in a summersault on the mat. The crowd went wild—men raised their beer cups, children waved luchador masks over their heads. Arturo approached the center of the ring, and placed both his hands at the front of his waistband. He ripped at the tear-away pants, revealing a new costume: His traditional wrestler's tights had been replaced with black trunks appliquéd at the hip with the familiar red eyes.

He shot a look at Gabriel as he paced the ring, his arms outstretched to the crowd. Women and more than a few men screamed. Gabriel nearly joined in. He hadn't felt a pull this strong since the first day he had seen Arturo in the ring—and had missed his cues.

The lights dimmed, and the rudos' captain emerged from the locker room to the now-familiar strain of narcocorrido music. He had donned a flowing black cape with the hood pulled deep over his mask.

The Henchman could not be bothered with dramatic leaps into the ring. He separated the ropes and climbed in, tossed his robe to a ringside assistant. He replaced a theatrical entrance with a dramatic costume: His tights, sleeveless T-shirt, and mask were painted to resemble a ghoulish apparition.

He approached the corner, faced forward to the ringside seats, and jumped so that he stood on the middle rope, mugging for the fans. When he had one side of the arena riled up, he moved to the next corner and started all over again.

The announcer turned to the técnicos, and the energy in the room shifted; the music was brighter, the luchadores were more accessible.

Ray emerged first, slapping hands as he bounced down the ramp in a fighter's bob and weave from fan to fan. As La Tormenta Oscura, he had adopted a costume of rich blue Lycra tights trimmed with pewter. When he had booked his first professional bout, he'd told Miguel that he had decided The Dark Storm would wrestle without a mask. He said that the American pro circuit would welcome his unconventional brand: an Olympic medalist for Team USA, a black wrestler from South Los Angeles joining the US pro circuit by way of Mexico City's lucha libre leagues.

"Besides," he had reasoned, "why would I hide this pretty face?"

Yes, Ray Michaels had a game plan.

Though it was unusual for someone of his seniority, Miguel had decided that La Rosa should be introduced second, along with his entourage. To the strains of the exótico's signature dancehall party music, the bikini boys burst from the dressing room, tossing roses to fans. They parted as they approached the ring, revealing La Rosa in a shimmering multi-colored unitard and his rose-colored knee-high wrestling boots. On his head, he'd added a crown of deep red roses. He raised his arms over his head and swung his hips from side to side in a ringside salsa, encouraging the crowd to follow suit.

A man sitting ringside shouted "¡Viva La Rosa!" and tossed him a rainbow flag. La Rosa caught it in mid-air, and continued to wave it as he danced around the ring, until he tossed it to one of his dancers and vaulted over the ropes to the cheers of his fans.

Though he was La Rosa's junior, The Silver Cloud served as the team's captain. He had become an enormous celebrity in the lucha world since his transformation from El Diablo Azul to La Nube de Plata, and crowds clamored to see the recently "baptized" técnico.

The bout began with El Cadejo and the Cloud confronting each other, both crouched and ready to charge. The Cloud pounced first, running at El Cadejo with arms outstretched, aiming for a tackle. But El Cadejo ducked, diving at his knees, aiming for an off-balance takedown. They both landed ass-first on the mat, and El Cadejo used his speed to roll out of the fall, up and over the larger wrestler, scrape at his face, pull at his mask, tear at the fabric. He wrapped his forearm around the Cloud's elbow, pulling it behind his back and locking it down.

The cue is coming. Deep breath. Focus.

The Cloud reached his arm toward the tecnicos' corner, just shy of his partner's fingertips, trying to evade the referees' count. With seconds to spare, La Rosa slapped at the Cloud's outstretched hand, granting him a break from the ring. La Rosa ran toward El Cadejo but the Phoenix, on cue, countered his move, entering the ring without a proper tag, as a rule-breaking rudo would do.

The two luchadores lunged at each other and missed, aiming instead for a rebound off the ropes, propelling themselves back toward each other with renewed momentum.

La Rosa struck first, hitting the Phoenix with a last-second flying dropkick that set the young rudo off balance, falling into the ropes. The Phoenix recovered, turning and hurling himself toward Rosa, his high kick landing with his ankles wrapped around the técnico's neck, twisting his body to take his mentor down headfirst onto the mat. Both luchadores somersaulted together out of their falls, but the Phoenix grabbed a handful of La Rosa's glittered hair, pulled the exótico on top of him, and locked his legs around La Rosa's waist.

Miguel reached for his back as if in pain and whispered to Gabriel, "Good. Now, flip me."

Lock your leg. Roll. Stay focused.

The Phoenix rolled La Rosa onto his back, using his foot to lock down the exótico's leg while the referee began his count. Writhing in apparent pain, La Rosa rocked back and forth, dislodging the Phoenix as the referee counted down. The Phoenix was slow to rise, but La Rosa bounced to his feet and swayed to his salsa victory dance.

As if incensed by the action, The Henchman and The Dark Storm both rocketed into the ring and began grabbing at each other's faces, fighting for leverage. The Henchman slapped at the Storm's exposed face, striking with a vicious smack. The Storm reached for his forehead, burying his face in his hands. When he pulled his hands away, his face and hands were covered with blood.

The crowd gasped as one.

Ray.

Gabriel fought his instinct to rush to Ray's aid, stopped by a hand on his forearm and a quick glance from Arturo. It was planned, staged between the two combatants, who had cut and patched Ray's forehead in the dressing room before the bout so that it would bleed on impact in the ring.

The Storm stared at his blood-stained hands, then countered by slamming The Henchman face-first into the mat; the collision ripping through the arena like thunder. When The Henchman rose, he also seemed injured: Blood dripped from the corner of his mouth.

What the hell?

The Dark Phoenix lingered at a far side of the ring as the fray continued. After a confirming glance indiscernible to the crowd, he charged and lifted La Rosa off his feet, heaved him over the ropes toward the ringside seats. He strutted and posed for the crowd amidst cheers and boos. The move drew a heated response from the Cloud, who lunged toward the young rudo, with El Cadejo fast on his heels. The Phoenix darted away, circling to El Cadejo's side. They ran at the Cloud and pushed him out of the ring, toward La Rosa, and then both backed up to rush the ropes. They vaulted into spinning tornillos over and onto the mats below, at the feet of ringside ticket holders, and landed on their prey.

Miguel, rolling from side to side as if injured, winked at Gabriel. He broke Gabriel's hold and threw him to the floor. The match had followed its script to the letter.

Until it didn't.

Arturo's attention shifted abruptly, directed at the exótico and his protégé as they wrestled into the crowd. He separated himself from the Cloud and threw himself on top of La Rosa, then kneed him in the groin. A shriek rose from the dogpile, and the wrestlers fell apart to reveal La Rosa, curled into fetal position at the base of the ring. But the referee didn't flag the foul and El Cadejo didn't give up. He attacked again, attempting to cast La Rosa toward the front row seats.

Uncertain what to do, Gabriel clung to the ropes. Rudos were by definition rule-breakers, but Arturo's movements were unscripted, unexpected, and threw the match into disarray. He looked to Miguel, but, knowing he shouldn't defend the técnico, ultimately choose to dive to the floor alongside Arturo, as if in a planned rudo attack.

On the floor, pretending to slap at La Rosa, he appealed to Arturo in hushed tones. "What are you doing?" he whispered.

"On the offensive," Arturo responded.

Looking for help, Gabriel glanced around the ring. The other wrestlers had slowed the action and retreated to their corners as the battle between La Rosa and El Cadejo spun out of control. Only Gabriel was close enough to do something about it. He remembered an early lesson from Miguel:

Rudos are consistent only in their inconsistency. They break the rules. They turn on each other if there is a gain in it. It's the rudo way.

Gabriel improvised, redirecting his attention to his partner. Feigning anger that his opponent had been stolen by the other rudo, he sprang at El Cadejo, violently knocking him off La Rosa. The move slowed the action just long enough for the exótico to regain his footing.

La Rosa stumbled to his feet and jumped El Cadejo, wrapped his leg around his back and muscled himself on top of the rudo. He turned to Gabriel.

"You're on the Cloud now," he said. "Break his hold once or twice and then let him pin you. This one's mine."

La Rosa held on for dear life as El Cadejo rocked and grabbed for leverage beneath him. As the Phoenix sacrificed himself to The Silver Cloud, La Rosa angled for the kill move, and locked El Cadejo's shoulders to the floor as the referee counted the pin out and done. The técnicos were declared victors—one round earlier than planned.

The referee grabbed La Rosa's hand to raise it in victory, but Miguel held off, kept Arturo locked in the hold long enough to make a point. He stared the rudo down and let go, then rose to his feet.

Usually, La Rosa would dance following a victory, encircled by his entourage, encouraging fans to join in. He would celebrate a win with a cha-cha to each corner, playing to the crowd at each side of the ring. But Miguel stayed only long enough to be declared the winner. He stormed from the ring and to the locker room. Gabriel and the other luchadores followed close behind, leaving Arturo alone.

Drinks had already been set on ice in anticipation of a post-match party, but they went untouched as the luchadores milled silently around the room. The Henchman cleaned the cut on Ray's face. The Cloud grabbed a towel to wipe baby oil off his chest. Miguel stood with his back to the group and peeled off his false eyelashes in front of a mirror hung from the inside of his open locker.

Across the room, the door creaked open. Arturo, looking solemn, slipped into the room.

The remaining bikini boys grabbed their street clothes and left. The Silver Cloud and The Henchman stood together in a far corner. Gabriel sat quietly in front of a locker with Ray standing by his side.

Metal crashed against metal to break the silence. Miguel slammed his locker shut and spun around to confront Arturo.

"What was *that*?" Miguel demanded. "Where in any of our preparations did it say it was okay to leave your man?" He stalked the room, stopping in front of Arturo.

"It was better my way," Arturo said. "Did you hear the crowd?"

"You got a problem with the plan? You talk it out ahead of time. But you don't rewrite the story in the ring. Someone could have gotten hurt."

"It's lucha libre. Wrestlers get hurt. What do you think people are paying to see? Shakespeare?" Arturo fired back.

"It was Gabriel's first bout. You don't go off script like that. We have to be able to anticipate what's happening."

"That's exactly why I did it! Your stories are stale, old man. Gabriel got noticed *because* we were unpredictable. We kept the crowd in the match. You should thank me."

Gabriel turned to Arturo, putting his body between his mentor and his lover. "Arturo, don't—"

Miguel moved to one side, sidestepping Gabriel to confront Arturo again. "*Thank* you? Who's going to *thank* you when someone ends up in the hospital?"

"Miguel, please—"

The two men were face-to-face now, ready to square off, ignoring Gabriel's pleas to stop. He stepped between them again, hoping to prevent the fray.

"Miguel, it's my fault!"

"I have no reason to believe that. Get out of the way," Miguel said, his eyes never leaving Arturo. He waited for a heartbeat, then pushed Gabriel aside and lunged.

"And this is when the big man steps in." Ray wedged himself between the combatants just as they were about to come to blows. He held them back, one hand on either man's chest. The Henchman and The Silver Cloud joined him from across the room, each grabbing a man from behind.

"I should kick you out," Miguel said, spitting out the words.

"Miguel, please. I was nervous and freezing up, and he was just trying to help," Gabriel said, shooting a glance at Arturo, "No matter how misguided it was, he was trying to make it better."

Miguel glared silently at his assistant, sized him up, and then glanced briefly at Gabriel.

"Please, give him another chance," Gabriel said.

"Right now, I want him out of this locker room," Miguel said. He shifted to his left, just enough to catch Arturo's eye. "Get your shit and get out of here. And if between now and Tuesday you can figure out what you did wrong here, we'll talk about whether or not you still have a job."

Without a word, Arturo stepped to his locker, grabbed his gym bag, pulled on his warmup pants, and stormed from the room, still wearing his mask.

Miguel didn't flinch until Arturo had cleared the room. When Ray and the other luchadores finally gave him room to move, he turned to Gabriel.

"And you," Miguel said. "You don't take a fall for someone unless it's planned."

GABRIEL DIDN'T WASTE TIME AT the arena. He didn't shower. He didn't socialize with the other luchadores. He didn't celebrate his debut.

He made a beeline for home, rinsed out his Dark Phoenix costume, and filled a tub with hot water. He lingered there, beer in hand, for thirty minutes or more, occasionally submerging, drifting into an underwater cocoon. Being underwater, feeling that pressure against his ears, gave his head a welcome sensation of peace.

He climbed out only when the beer ran dry and the water ran cold, and slipped into an old pair of soft, worn sweatpants and a plain T-shirt: the perfect uniform for an empty evening of nothingness.

No studies. No workouts. No conflict.

He opened another beer and sank into the couch, only to be disrupted by a rap at the front door. Gabriel peeked out a window to see Arturo standing on the front porch, cleaned up and changed into street clothes. He opened the door only wide enough to talk. "What are you doing here?" he asked.

"You invited me. Do I get to come in?" Arturo took a step forward and stopped. "Please?"

Gabriel hesitated, then stepped aside and opened the door. As Arturo passed, his hand drifted across Gabriel's abdomen. Before the door could close behind him, he turned and reached around Gabriel's waist.

"Don't."

"What?" Arturo said. His lips had already found their way to Gabriel's neck.

"Stop it," Gabriel said, forcefully this time. He shut the door and slipped from Arturo's grasp. He stepped back and folded his arms across his chest.

"Don't you even care what you did tonight?"

"I gave you a better match. You got to show off your skills, and we woke up the crowd."

"The crowd was awake. The bout was already good. I can fend for myself. Now you could lose your job, and Miguel's pissed at me for defending you."

"I won't lose my job—not unless I want to," Arturo said. He followed Gabriel across the room and reached for his hand. "He needs me."

"Miguel doesn't seem to think so. He nearly fired you on the spot."

"He needs me because *you* need me," Arturo said.

"I don't need you," Gabriel whispered.

Arturo took Gabriel's hand in his and kissed his fingers, one by one.

"You do. You can have all the history lessons you want, but you got into this for the thrill." He kissed Gabriel, letting his lips linger. "And that's me."

"You have to apologize," Gabriel said.

Arturo kissed him again. His lips drifted down. He murmured against Gabriel's neck, "The old man can take it."

Gabriel set his palms flat on Arturo's chest and gently pushed him away. "Not to him," he said.

"What?"

"You attacked my coach. You ruined my debut. If we're going to be together, I have to trust you. And right now, I don't."

The rebuke landed. Arturo furrowed his brow, buried his head in Gabriel's shoulder. "Sorry," he mumbled. "I was trying to make it better."

Gabriel lifted Arturo's chin until they were eye-to-eye. "It can't happen again."

Arturo shut his eyes, nodding his assent. "Forgive me," he said. "Don't leave me."

★ ★ ★

THE RING HAD BEEN SET up outdoors, on a plaza, improvised in a dusty courtyard that would serve as the center of the little town's bicentennial celebration. It was a far cry from the arenas of the Federal District. But it was the norm for a rookie luchador, even one who had debuted at the historic center of his sport, high on the match card, alongside some of lucha libre's most popular wrestlers.

To his credit, the work had been steady. It had also been largely anonymous, scheduled outside Mexico City, in small towns and outlying areas seeking to book luchadores for entertainment and promotion, and not high-profile arena matches.

Gabriel knew he should see it as paying his dues, the price one paid for being the new kid, a rookie. He suspected it was something more: payback for his defense of Arturo after his debut and punishment for trying to keep Arturo on staff at Gimnasio de la Ciudad. Even that had failed. Arturo had walked out a week later, moving to a competitor's gym across town.

Miguel never said it explicitly, but a chill crept over their relationship in the months following Gabriel's debut.

He thought it was working out. He had, after all, kept the pieces of his life relatively in place. He was a working professional luchador. He had told his family of his pastime, and they grudgingly accepted it, as long as he finished school. He still trained with his mentor and found moments to spend with Arturo. His life had become an ever-more-complicated juggling act, but he had managed to keep the balls in the air.

And though it took frustrating months to get there, he sensed a gradual shift in his career. He was being booked on the undercard of regularly scheduled lucha libra batallas. The bouts were more frequent; the civic celebrations and demonstrations dwindled. A small following developed—women and more than a few men that he started to recognize as regulars inside and outside the arena.

He walked past the street vendors outside Arena México, past the ladies and their daughters selling knock-off masks, capes, and flags representing the sport's great and most popular luchadores: El Santo, Mil Mascaras, Rey Mysterio, La Parka.

He looked up and, tucked in the back corner, he saw it for the first time: a black Lycra mask, its mouth cut away, the face framed by burnt orange and gold appliqué flames.

El Fénix Oscuro.

The vendor didn't recognize him and, when he purchased the mask, she told him it was a good choice. "I just got that one in yesterday," she said. "I've already sold three."

When he returned to wrestle the Tuesday night undercard a week later, he saw two ringside fans wearing his mask. One was a woman with bleached blond hair and a low-cut T-shirt, a regular at the arena. Gabriel recognized her from his very first bout and had seen her frequently since he started to be booked for repeat matches at the arena. The other was a child no more than ten years old, cheering the rudos. The child was enthusiastic and loud and reminded Gabriel of the boy he had once been.

But it was odd that the man next to him, whom he assumed to be the child's father, seemed so disengaged, spending the entire match scribbling in a small notebook.

4

THE COVER OF *LUCHA SEMANAL* magazine screamed in neon letters about Luchadores de Nueva Generación, but the accompanying photograph featured just one: El Fénix Oscuro, airborne, his black boots wrapped around his opponent's neck, spinning him into what was quickly becoming his signature takedown.

And like the cover, the story inside was largely devoted to the rudo character's rise in the Mexico City lucha libra circuit. The magazine profiled four other young luchadores and one luchadora, or at least featured their stories about how they joined the lucha libre scene.

Luchadores, especially enmascarados, were notoriously elusive and sometimes downright dishonest about their backgrounds. They kept their identities and their histories as tightly masked as their faces. Few shared their real names publicly. Fewer still were honest about them.

Gabriel, on the other hand, shared the moment that inspired him to become a luchador.

> **Lucha Semanal: What is your first memory of attending lucha libre?**
> **El Fénix Oscuro:** Oh, I've loved lucha libre for years, but I didn't see it in the arena until I was a teenager. The time that stands out was the night I took a date to Arena México

and saw La Rosa for the first time. I knew right then that I was destined to be a luchador.

Lucha Semanal: What about the match made you decide to study lucha libre?
El Fénix Oscuro: La Rosa brought so much energy to the room, and the arena got up and danced along with him. To see so many rainbow flags, and for gay fans to have someone to rally around, was so inspiring.

Lucha Semanal: And what happened to your date? Does she like lucha libre?
El Fénix Oscuro: I think I enjoyed it more than he did.

Arturo threw the magazine in the trash. He spun around, shaking his head. "If you had any chance of joining a league without becoming an exótico before, it's gone now," he said. "You outed yourself."

"There was nothing to out," Gabriel said. "I'm already out."

"...to your friends..."

"And to anyone else who bothers to ask."

They were shutting down Gimnasio de Campeones across town, where Arturo had quickly been snapped up as an assistant trainer after leaving Gimnasio de la Ciudad. The gym was well known in wrestling circles as home to numerous luchadores from la Liga de Campeones—known to fans as the LC, an upstart lucha libra league high on style and low on tradition.

The LC didn't sweat the details of lucha libra like the Triple L did. Owned by a social media entrepreneur, its style was flashier, louder—more like American professional wrestling. It booked Arena México each week and its matches there were recorded for later broadcast on both Mexican and Spanish-language American television.

Miguel detested la Liga de Campeones. But in it, Arturo had found a fit, a home of sorts, among ambitious, like-minded luchadores.

The change suited him and his goals. He got a contract and his own apartment and tried to convince Gabriel to follow suit.

The ink had hardly been dry on his deal when he'd persuaded Gabriel to at least make Gimnasio de Campeones his second home, to continue his training with Miguel while secretly working with Arturo and the luchadores of the LC.

"Don't worry about the old man. He doesn't have to know," Arturo had said. "Work out with us, and you'll get an education you'll never get from Miguel; you'll have the best of both worlds. Miguel can have his traditional mumbo jumbo over at Ciudad, but over here, you'll learn about showmanship."

Gabriel had found it hard to argue with the logic, even if he'd felt a twinge of betrayal.

El Gimnasio de Campeones was everything Gimnasio de la Ciudad was not: new, stylish, well-equipped, located just outside the premier arena of lucha libre. It had an excess of new equipment, an abundance of experienced luchadores, and well-established contacts within the league's power structure.

Arturo gained status at the gym for bringing in an up-and-coming luchador from Miguel's gym, and Gabriel began to be booked for more and more prestigious bouts after following Arturo over for weekly workouts.

At Gimnasio de la Ciudad, the changes didn't go unnoticed. Gabriel had picked up strength and aggression, adding them like building blocks to the foundation of fundamentals Miguel had instilled.

In the audience, the number of Phoenix masks grew, as did the number of rainbow flags waved during his bouts, along with a smattering of trash talk from ringside fans. For every fan screaming "¡El Fénix Oscuro!" he was just as likely to get catcalls or hear someone call for his opponent to "take out the puto!"

His small fan base began to grow: men, women—some who would linger after his matches, hoping to get an autograph or a glimpse of the face behind the mask, or maybe something more.

But one stood out. He had been in the same corner, wearing the same gray suit, keeping his arms folded across his chest, for three, four, maybe even five, of Gabriel's bouts in a row. Gabriel had lost count.

The man didn't linger. He disappeared as soon as the Dark Phoenix finished each night. So when Gabriel showed up at the arena as a fan—sitting ringside to watch El Cadejo—he was surprised when the man in the gray suit took a seat beside him.

"I know you can't confirm this right here, but I'm a fan of your work," the man said, extending his hand. "Oscar. I've been looking forward to meeting you."

It was late, and Gabriel knew that Miguel was probably asleep. But each unanswered text heightened his need for an answer, resulting in a string of increasingly agitated messages.

I need to talk.

Are you up?

I have news.

Where are you?

THIS BETTER BE GOOD GABRIEL.

Gabriel sighed with relief. Miguel would get over it.

He texted his response: *Need to talk.*

The response was slow to arrive. Gabriel wondered if Miguel had drifted back to sleep, until his phone buzzed to life: Breakfast. El Cardenal. 9 a.m.

Gabriel walked into the cafe with his hair more unruly than usual and his clothes wrinkled. He slung a backpack over his shoulder, the one that usually held his laptop, some schoolbooks, and his wrestling boots. He sat down across from Miguel and placed the bag in his lap.

"Those texts made a racket last night. Nearly got me in trouble," Miguel said.

Gabriel reached into the backpack and pulled out an oversized envelope.

"They made an offer," he responded.

Miguel sipped an expresso and held out his hand, beckoning for the paperwork. "The league?" he asked.

Gabriel nodded.

"Which one?"

Gabriel hesitated. Miguel sipped again at his coffee.

"I know about Gimnasio de Campeones, Gabriel. Which league?"

"The Triple L," Gabriel responded.

"Good. When did this happen?"

"Last night."

"You weren't on the card last night," Miguel said. He pulled a pair of glasses from his breast pocket and started reading the documents.

"I went to watch—"

"Never mind," Miguel said, waving him off. "You sure you don't want an expresso? You look like you could use it."

Gabriel shook his head. "I don't know how you drink that shit."

Miguel waved the waiter over and ordered without looking at the menu—aporreado con huevos. The waiter turned to Gabriel, who just shook his head.

"You should at least try the chilaquiles," Miguel said. He kissed his fingertips. "Magical."

"Fine. Chilaquiles, y tambien un jugo de naranja."

Miguel laughed, and kept his nose in the paperwork. "Give it time."

They sat quietly, sipping their drinks, while Miguel read on, occasionally mumbling to himself. He finally set the papers down and took off his glasses.

"So they just pulled you aside and said, 'Join the league'?"

"There was this man, he's been hanging around a lot lately," Gabriel said.

"I bet."

"He asked me to meet with him last night."

"And he offered you a contract?"

"Yes."

"Most people would be celebrating, Gabriel."

"There are strings attached," he responded.

"Aren't there always?"

Gabriel took a long gulp of his orange juice, set the glass down, and leaned across the table toward Miguel.

"They want me to be an exótico," Gabriel said, hushed.

"Are you surprised?"

Gabriel shook his head. There had been enough discussions of the subject for him to know what the Triple L would want from him.

"And what does your man have to say about this?"

Miguel's casual reference to Arturo, and to a relationship that had been kept secret, silenced Gabriel. Clearly, Miguel knew they were together, but it was something they never discussed, especially after Arturo's departure from the gym.

Gabriel bit his lip and nodded. "Mainly he just said, 'I told you so.'"

"Do you want to wrestle for the league?"

"I love wrestling for you. It's not that. You know I've always wanted..."

"More. Yes, I know Gabriel. You want to become a super estrella. You want it all."

"But I'm not... I don't do..."

"Drag? Is that it? You don't want to do drag? Are we back to that?" Miguel cocked his head. He looked exasperated, tired.

Gabriel hunched his shoulders, curling in on himself.

"You know? I was proud of you, saying what you did in that magazine," Miguel said. He leaned forward, folding his hands on the table. "You didn't sound much like a rudo, but you did sound like a man who knows who he is."

Gabriel rocked slowly in his chair with his eyes settled on the tablecloth.

"Arturo said I never should have said that, that I should have made something up."

"I'm not surprised," Miguel said. "But what are your thoughts? You tell me what Arturo thinks, and you ask me what I think, but I don't hear much about what you think."

Gabriel looked up and glanced across the room. The restaurant was already filling with families and a smattering of tourists. It wasn't the place for a discreet conversation, but it was neutral turf—free from luchadores, and empresas, and boyfriends.

"You're right. Technically, I already have everything I want by wrestling as an independent," he said.

"Technically?"

"I don't want it to sound like I'm putting it down. You've done so much for me, but the league has more to offer."

"But at a price, or at least what you see as a price?"

"You don't think that being told I have to be something I'm not *isn't* a price?"

"We all play characters, Gabriel."

It reminded him of a time, months before, when he had said nearly the same words to Arturo. Yet when they were directed back at him, they sounded hollow.

"Why is it that if I want to be out in the league, I can only be one type of character?"

"That's the trade-off, isn't it? Are you really that uncomfortable being an exótico? What happened to the boy who was so inspired by us?"

"I was—I *am*. But it's just not me."

"What is it?" Miguel asked. "The drag? The act? Tell me how that's any different than being enmascarado, Gabriel. What's the difference? If you go out there and play straight, you're playing a character that isn't you. Whether you're a técnico or a rudo, you're still playing a character. So why not play one that honors others like you?"

"Honors?" Gabriel scoffed. "By wearing lipstick, and grabbing ass, and kissing referees?"

"We give people hope. Let me tell you something. Think about our history, the role we've played in this country. We're not just entertainment. We give people something to rally for, and against. Lucha's been a part of politics and our social order, always has been. Why do you think I made you study it? And exóticos? Do you know how many men have come up to me after a match and thanked me? How many kids have said we've given them courage to come out? We may not be your picture of the perfect postmodern gay or whatever your generation calls it, but we paved the road for you with our glitter and makeup."

Gabriel looked down; his voice was muted and low. "I respect that, I do."

"You may admire us, and train with us, but you don't want to be one of us. You want to be out and you want to be one of them. Well, let me tell you, mijo, you play straight like Arturo? That's no different than playing camp with us, because that's an act, too. Besides, he's right about one thing—it's too late for that."

He hated to admit that Miguel might be right—or Arturo, for that matter. Practically speaking, he had two choices: to wrestle as an independent and control his character, but give up a chance at commercial success, or to sign with the Triple L, where he would pay for increased exposure by agreeing to terms he didn't entirely agree with.

"You talk about hope, but imagine how much hope a successful out-luchador would give them, someone who didn't compromise, someone who didn't play by their rules?" Gabriel said.

Miguel stabbed at his half-eaten eggs. "You play with the league, you play by league rules."

"Is that why you are La Rosa? So you can wrestle league matches?"

"I wrestle league matches because they know me, and trust me, and know I can sell tickets," he said. "I'm La Rosa for a lot of reasons."

He set his silverware on his plate and pushed it aside, effectively ending the conversation.

"Did I offend you?" Gabriel asked.

"I've heard worse." Miguel tapped the papers against the table, then lined them up to slide them back into the envelope. "Did they give you a new character?"

Gabriel looked up, grim-faced.

"That bad?"

Gabriel rolled his eyes. "I wish I could just stay El Fénix Oscuro."

"You can if you stay independent."

"I just want to wrestle," Gabriel said. The words escaped his mouth as a breathy exhale.

"But not in a dress." Miguel said, smirking.

"Preferably not."

Miguel scratched his chin and looked around the room. He waved his hand at a waiter, asking for the check.

"Maybe," he said. "Maybe we can work with this. Maybe we can find a way to… adapt? I've known Oscar since I was first starting out. Maybe we can create something a bit more subtle. What did you say they wanted your character to be?"

Gabriel rubbed his temple and groaned out the name. "La Muñeca."

"Oh."

Miguel looked at the floor, shaking his head. His expression slowly changed. Gabriel could see him trying to hold back the grin and then lose the battle, breaking out in laughter.

"All right, *Baby Doll*, I'll see what I can do."

★ ★ ★

THEY CALLED HIM EL REY, the king of lucha libre empresarios. His real name was Oscar Chavez, and he'd joined the Triple L as a low-level promoter at the birth of the league nearly forty years ago. At the beginning, that meant copying promotional fight cards on mimeograph machines and handing them out at busy street corners around the Federal District.

He'd climbed from street corner to corner office by clinging to the traditions of the ring while modernizing the marketing machine that kept lucha libre relevant in Mexico.

He didn't tinker with success, at least not in the ring. Fans liked traditional lucha libre—storylines of good versus evil, of rudos versus técnicos. But they also clamored for something new, so he delivered laser light shows, rock music, and the ever-popular ring girls.

And the formula worked, thanks to television revenue from Mexican networks and from syndication rights sold abroad, as well as the vice-like contracts that locked wrestlers into characters developed, owned, and controlled by the Triple L.

Triple L luchadores stood a decent chance of becoming stars, even super estrellas. But they had no control over their characters and could even have their personas stripped from them if the league found a new luchador to slip into the spot.

Few wrestlers signed their first league contract with representation, and fewer still found ways to wriggle out of the Triple L's strict contract terms.

But played right, the terms were negotiable, Miguel said. He'd warned Gabriel that he was unlikely to get everything he wanted. "Some of these things have to be earned," he said. "So let's figure out what you can live with and live without."

With a strategy in place and an appointment made, they met outside a fashionable glass-and-steel office building along the Paseo de la Reforma.

Gabriel had never seen Miguel dressed quite like this: not in the campiness of the ring, nor in the simple workout gear of the gym. He looked more underwriter than wrestler, dressed in a conservative blue suit tailored neatly to fit his athletic physique.

"You look like my uncle," Gabriel said.

"Handsome?" Miguel asked.

"Like a banker."

He also looked as if he belonged. The building, home to the Triple L, had a posh foyer that appeared as much gallery as office. Art lined its walls, from pre-Hispanic artifacts to modern Mexican masters. Gabriel strolled in a slow circle, taking them in, as Miguel spoke to a building security guard. His mother's voice was clear in a crisp memory of lessons detailing the connectedness of the eras of Mexican history, culture, and art.

"Fourteenth floor, second bank of elevators," the guard said, handing Miguel their security passes.

"That's quite a collection," Gabriel whispered as they entered the elevator.

"You like art?"

"My mom," he said. "She loved it."

The elevator doors opened to a brightly colored office, which was a museum unto itself, documenting the history of lucha libre with memorabilia and framed posters of historic championship matches. A glass case enshrined the original masks of some of the league's first and most famous luchadores. In another, a floor-to-ceiling enclosure, sleek mannequins wore costumes from the 1960s, 70s, and 80s. It was as if Miguel's favorite bar near the Coliseo had gone upscale.

"Miguel! So good to see you!" Oscar Chavez, a well-dressed fireplug of a man, emerged from a back office. He wore a gray suit, a pinky ring, and a slick smile.

He patted Gabriel on the shoulder as he shook his hand. "I think I owe you a thank you drink, letting us have your star pupil. How are you, Gabriel? Ready for all this?" He waved his hands at the showcases. "Ready to become a part of history?"

"I'm well, thank you." Gabriel said, shutting up the moment he felt Miguel's eyes on him.

"Oscar, can we maybe meet in one of your conference rooms? We have some questions about the contract."

"Certainly! Anything for my old friend."

He led them back to his office, a spacious corner suite overlooking the Paseo and the central city. Maybe two blocks down the avenue Gabriel could see Monumento a la Independencia glistening against the sky.

Chavez showed them to a seating area in his office, away from his desk, with leather chairs, a sofa, and a wet bar.

"More comfortable than a conference room," he said. "So what's up, my friend? The last time I saw you, you were wearing sequins and body paint."

"I still do, but I'm here for Gabriel today."

"A very talented young man," Chavez said.

"Yes, but we're concerned about how you plan to market him."

Gabriel kept his mouth shut and let Miguel control the conversation. He presented his case like a litigator, spelling out Gabriel's background, training, and potential before finally making his request.

"You're a traditionalist, Miguel, and this is a traditional contract. Gabriel's open about who he is," Chavez turned to Gabriel, "and we like that about him. It also means he'll be an exótico. You know better than anyone how that works."

It was clear that this was the opening Miguel was waiting for. It was a part of his strategy to let Chavez introduce the issue, and for Miguel to offer the solution.

"I think you're missing an opportunity here," Miguel said.

"How so?"

"First of all, have you seen him wrestle? He may not be the biggest luchador out there, but he's one of the most athletic. He's the fastest, and he flies like El Ángel herself. And he's got a body like a statue—a perfect welterweight."

"The boys are going to love him, yes," Oscar said.

"But that's my point," Miguel countered, closing in, about to ensnare Oscar Chavez in his favorite trap—commerce. "You're cutting off half your audience."

"What do you mean? He's exótico. He's there to pull in the gay crowd and the old ladies who'll want to mother him."

"But what about the young women who want to fuck him?"

Miguel had never mentioned this part of his strategy. Gabriel fought to keep his expression neutral, not to betray the stream of panic entering his mind. He nearly interrupted, but Miguel was on a roll and not about to let Gabriel jump in with anything other than his designed patter. He got up from the couch where he had been seated and gestured toward Gabriel.

"Look at him. Ladies love him. Trust me. I took him out to dinner the other night, and we nearly had to beat them off—and the men, too. You put him in drag, you're going to miss an opportunity."

"But he's an exótico," Chavez said.

"Oh, I understand, but what if we played with that idea a bit? Pushed the envelope? Just a little, just enough to maximize his audience potential? What if we make Gabriel the luchador wanted by men *and* by women? A character that's hot, but ambiguous. He could be both masculine in a way that appeals to the women in the crowd, and beautiful to appeal to the fans of the exóticos. We don't have to be so campy with him. Look at him. He's strong, but he has fine features. Women think he's handsome. Fans of the exóticos will think he's beautiful. And men? They're about to meet one tough luchador. Think about it, Oscar. I know what I'm talking about, and you know it. You could have an opportunity to have a luchador unlike any other. And you know what that means."

Chavez leaned forward, occasionally glancing at Gabriel, as if sizing him up, but focused on Miguel's pitch. "What are you thinking? Give me specifics."

Miguel had him. He ticked off a laundry list of ideas. Anything that deviated too far from the norm was there by design, to create negotiating space for his real ideas, the look and identity he was truly angling for: a costume based on wrestler's tights, or maybe trunks, but not a leotard or minidress like most exóticos wore. Fine, Chavez said, so long as they were designed in a style that made it clear Gabriel belonged to La Rosa's team.

He should be beautiful, but strong and heroic. He should be a wrestler that women and children would cheer for, a técnico to take advantage of both the audience and Gabriel's advanced skills. His brand of wrestling was about athleticism and grace, not brute force, Miguel argued.

"And I think," Miguel said. "I think he needs to keep his mask."

"*What?*" Chavez's voice boomed across the room. "Exóticos don't wrestle enmascarado, and his face is one of his best assets."

"There haven't been many masked exóticos, but there's precedent," Miguel said. "And it will add to his mystery. We've been using a modified cutaway mask on him already. Maybe we take that a little deeper, to show off that jaw and those lips of his. We give them a little color, maybe a little glitter, and people will understand."

Gabriel sat still, praying this didn't go further than his comfort level.

"And of course, to attract the women, he will need a different name. Women want to cuddle a Baby Doll, not fuck it. Gabriel's brand of exótico will be about being *exotic* and mysterious. We need something strong but romantic, something that still hints at an exotic character."

He saved the dealmaker for last.

"Oscar, if any of this makes you uncomfortable, make it a trial contract. Sign Gabriel for a year. If you don't like how it turns out, you can just walk away."

Chavez didn't say a word. He got up and walked across the room to his desk. He picked up a notepad and started writing. "And this character you're talking about—did you have any suggestions?" he said.

"I have an idea," Gabriel said.

The give-and-take lasted for nearly two hours. When they agreed on the finer details—a concept, a character, a name, and an abbreviated duration that gave Chavez a sense of security and Gabriel options beyond it—Gabriel agreed to terms, shook Chavez's hand, and followed Miguel out to the street.

"So, you still want this?" Miguel said as they left the office. "You know, there are others. It's risky. You need something to help you stand out, maybe something more to the name. And we have to work on this character, your look. You got lucky today. Right, Baby Doll?"

"Please don't call me that."

"It could have been worse," Miguel said. "He told me on the way out he was going to call you Pretty Baby."

Gabriel threw his head back in disgust.

"See what a little help and experience can do for you?"

"Yes, thank you, Miguel," he mumbled.

"What was that? I'm not sure I heard you."

"Muchos gracias, Señor Reyes."

"For what, Gabriel? What did I do?"

"For saving my ass."

"That's right. Now what are you going to do for me?" Miguel had a wicked smile on his face. He was enjoying himself.

"I'm assuming I'm mopping the floor, maybe washing the windows? Perhaps there are some toilets in my future."

"No."

"No?" Gabriel was genuinely surprised.

"Tonight, you are coming to my house and enjoying a home-cooked meal, and we'll talk about your character some more, figure this thing out."

Gabriel had never been invited to his mentor's home and didn't know anyone who had been. Miguel was famously private among the luchadores and did not discuss his life outside the ring.

"Rosa's cooking something special tonight. You're in for a treat."

He looked at Miguel to see if he was pulling his leg, but Miguel kept walking without the slightest hint that he was kidding.

They arrived at the modest home in Roma Norte, a once-fashionable neighborhood made less so by time and trends. Miguel had scored a deal on the house when a friend had to sell fast. The former homeowner, a one-time lucha libre announcer, apparently got out of town one step ahead of a loan shark he had been evading for years.

Miguel fished for a key to the oversized wooden door that shielded a modest, tiled courtyard from the street. To one side was a small staircase and another door that led into the home.

He opened it, and the smell of roasting poblano peppers filled the air.

Miguel breathed in deep, shutting his eyes and smiling. "Aah. Heaven," he said. "Rosa? I'm home. And we have a guest for dinner."

A middle-aged woman with long, braided salt-and-pepper hair and laughing eyes entered the room, wiping her hands on a towel. She kissed Miguel on the cheek.

"Always full of surprises."

She walked over to Gabriel, shook his hand. "You must be Gabriel. I'm Rosalinda. Miguel talks so much about you. He said you were a handsome boy, but he didn't do you justice."

"Umm... thank you, hello. It's nice to meet you."

Gabriel looked at Miguel, his brow wrinkled.

"Gabriel, would you like something to drink? Iced tea? Or some wine or a beer?"

"Nothing just yet, thank you," he said.

"It looks like you two have things to discuss, so if you need me I'll be in the kitchen. I'm making Chiles en Nogada tonight. I hope you like them. They're Miguel's favorite. They should be ready in about an hour."

As she left the room, Gabriel turned to Miguel, his eyes narrowed. "I don't understand," he said.

"What?"

"Who is that? Is she your roommate?"

Miguel waited a beat before answering.

"You could say that," he said. "She's my wife."

"But—"

"But what?" Miguel said. He smiled.

Nothing that Gabriel could say would be a surprise, it seemed.

"But how?"

"How can I be an exótico and be married?"

"... to a woman?"

"To a woman, yes. You know there have been straight exóticos, right?"

Gabriel thought back to all the times that he had seen Miguel wrestle as La Rosa, escorted by an entourage of bikini boys, his body and unitard painted in bright roses, dancing to salsa, kissing referees, and grabbing opponents' asses to throw them off balance—being an inspiration to Gabriel because he appeared to be out and successful in the macho world of lucha libre.

"There's no way you're straight," he said.

Miguel laughed.

"So you *are* gay."

"Oh, Gabriel. I think you could use that drink now."

He poured two glasses of wine, then decided to take the entire bottle, and led Gabriel out to the little tree-lined courtyard, where they settled in at a patio table.

"Have you never considered that there are other options that aren't black and white? Sometimes, things don't end up as cleanly defined as you expect."

He took a long sip of the tempranillo and stared into the glass.

"This is one of the first times I've let my worlds meet," he said. "But it's time, and I thought maybe this would be good for you."

Miguel leaned back in his chair and sipped his drink. The blare of traffic, muted behind the thick walls of the tiny courtyard, played as a soundtrack to his story.

He and Rosalinda had been friends since childhood, as close as two people could be, when a drunken night after a school dance led to a pregnancy and a forced wedding. They had a son, at least for a while.

It all had happened just as Miguel began to notice men, began to question his sexuality, and he'd started running off at night for a series of short relationships and one-night stands, leaving Rosalinda home with an infant.

"I was a terrible husband," he said. "I'd go out to clubs and not come home. I slept around. And the bouts, there were always fans afterward who were... willing."

"Why'd you stay?" Gabriel asked. "Why did *she* stay?"

"Because of our son and our partnership. Our friendship has always been strong. I always cared about her. My attention was just... elsewhere, at least until our boy died."

Miguel's face looked like ash. His eyes were red, lacking the focus that was his usual signature.

"She kept it together all that time. She put up with me and my engaños, my indiscretions. And I realized how much I loved her. So I made a vow to be a better man. You wanted to know if La Rosa is me. The answer is yes, every day. Playing Rosa gives me an outlet for another side of me. But the real Rosa? She's right up there. I wrestle as La Rosa for me, but I also do it for my Rosalinda."

"But you like men."

"Yes. And women. But I *love* my Rosa."

Gabriel looked toward the kitchen. He lowered his voice. "And she's okay with that?"

"Mijo, when you finally realize you only want to be with one person, you tune out the rest of the noise. She understands me, and that takes more strength than you see in any gym."

The door to the house opened, and Rosalinda stepped outside. "Do you two think you can take a break for some dinner or would you like to eat it out here?" Her voice was warm and inviting.

Miguel grasped Gabriel's hand and gave it a squeeze.

"No, we're done here. We'll be up in a moment."

Much of the work got done around the kitchen table that night: the discussion of character, the give-and-take about appearance and costume, and how they should reflect the balancing act that Gabriel would undertake with his new name.

For this, Rosalinda joined in, contributing a rapid-fire succession of ideas to combine concept, character, and a sense of tradition with standards that reflected and redefined exótico.

Miguel pulled out a sketchpad and tried to pencil out the ideas to share with his designer, whom he had already contacted about the job. But while his imagination embraced the colorful, his art skills hovered somewhere between stick figures and paint-by-numbers.

"Give it to me," Rosalinda said, holding out her palm. "Pencils, too."

Dutifully, he turned them over, and Rosa sketched the soft outline of a male form, then filled in the finer details they had discussed: the mask, white with gold accents, the mouth and jaw deeply sheared off; the gold bands to be worn along his biceps; the white wrestling trunks trimmed in gold lamé that replaced tights after a heated debate; and the boots—the true crowning touch, which through a simple design shift, took the costume to another level.

She traced the outline with her index finger, as if reading braille, and turned the blotter around for the others to see.

"Your costume should help tell your story, don't you think?"

Gabriel inspected the sketch with bright eyes. He took an audible breath, and exhaled through an emerging smile.

"I like it," Miguel said. "But it's still missing something."

"A little more drama?" Rosa said. "How about if we add something for your grand entrance?"

She pulled more pencils from the case and began a second drawing, making additions and adjustments to color and detail.

"When you first described your character, it reminded me of something very particular. Do you know Jorge Marín's work?"

She turned the pad toward Gabriel, showing him a dramatically revised costume.

Miguel grinned.

Gabriel felt as though he'd had an epiphany.

"I told you," Miguel said. He leaned over and kissed Rosalinda on the cheek. "She gets me."

"What do you think?"

Gabriel rolled over, pulling the sheet with him, reaching for his copy of the sketch from the nightstand. He reeled it in and curled back into Arturo, holding the paper above them.

"Do you like it?"

Arturo grunted and reached for the drawing.

"What does that mean?" Gabriel punched at his stomach playfully. "If you don't like it, give it back."

He grabbed for the paper, but Arturo pulled away, holding it away from Gabriel. "Very dramatic," he said. "Considering your options, good."

"Considering my options? Give it back."

Arturo laughed, and waved the drawing above Gabriel's outstretched hand. "I'm just saying that it could have been a lot worse. Now, let me look at it."

Gabriel snuggled into his shoulder as Arturo held the sketch above them.

"It'll get noticed."

"It's meant to," Gabriel grabbed the paper and set it aside. "You don't like it, do you?"

"It does its job. It's flashy. It's sexy. And you better model it for me before you wear it in the ring."

Arturo rolled until they were face-to-face. He dragged his fingertips along Gabriel's hairline, across his jaw, down his neck.

"I just hope you're paying as much attention to your wrestling as you are to your costume. You're in a whole new league now."

"You know I work out. I work out with *you*."

"Sometimes," Arturo said. "You work out with me sometimes. I'm just saying that when you start wrestling for the league, at the big arena, with the cameras and the lights and the sound—you need to up your game."

"How?"

Arturo's hand drifted farther down, along Gabriel's arm, to his hip.

"What if you give the crowd some shock factor? What if the exótico isn't just a niño bonito? That it isn't just about the besos? What if he's the toughest guy in the ring—or one of them? Now *that* would get you noticed."

"I thought I was tough," Gabriel said.

"You're good. You're fast. But you can be more."

"And do you have an idea who should coach me?"

He pulled Gabriel closer.

"I might just," Arturo said, rolling him onto his back.

★   ★   ★

DAYS FROM HIS LEAGUE DEBUT, Gabriel's schedule consumed him—costume design meetings with Miguel and the league, classes at the university, training with Arturo, church with his family, more training with Miguel, an occasional night across town at Arturo's apartment.

He finished his workout at Gimnasio de la Ciudad drenched in sweat, rested his back against the wall and slid down, down until his butt slapped the floor.

"You need this more than me, man," Ray dropped down, handing him a bottled sports drink. "Get those electrolytes back up."

Gabriel exhaled, shut his eyes, and gulped down half the bottle in one swig.

"You keeping it together?" Ray asked.

Gabriel nodded and raised the plastic bottle like a chalice. "Thanks," he said. "You're a lifesaver."

Ray laughed, his answer to everything. "You slowing down yet?"

Gabriel rolled the chilled bottle against the back of his neck. "Yeah. That was it. No more training before Saturday. No more meetings. No more classes. Done."

"Good, 'cause the drink's a bribe," Ray said. "I was wondering if you had anything happening tomorrow."

He grinned, eliciting a raised eyebrow from Gabriel.

"My brother's coming for a visit before he has to start back up with football practice. He flies in tomorrow—"

"You need a ride?"

"It's that or a taxi," Ray said.

"You don't want to do that," Gabriel said, waving his hand. He knew too well the erratic bob-and-weave style of Mexico City taxi drivers, not to mention their loose, evolving interpretation of "fair" rates. "So I get to meet Jason, huh?"

He'd certainly heard enough about Ray's half-brother to feel as though he already knew him. He was the family celebrity, at least as far as Ray described it—a defensive back carrying the weight of the UCLA secondary and catching the eyes of NFL scouts. The university had already started a Heisman campaign featuring Jason Michaels on television commercials and freeway billboards across the Los Angeles basin.

Ray followed his brother's college career intently, and knew all of the hotels with the fastest free Wi-Fi where he could settle in with his laptop on Saturday afternoons to watch Jason's games on the web. Gabriel had lost count of how many times he had walked in on Ray talking, texting, or video conferencing with his brother.

"He's coming along to your bout on Saturday," Ray said. "He's going to get himself a quick education in lucha libre."

★ ★ ★

Mexico City traffic had a reputation rivaling some of the world's worst: the volume of Los Angeles, the aggression of midtown Manhattan, the erratic lane changing of Boston and, if the lanes were open, the no-holds-barred speed of the autobahn. Gabriel preferred taking the subway where he could, but his aunt and uncle had bought him a small Volkswagen when he turned eighteen, a graduation gift he made use of for occasional travel outside the city. A cab ride required a certain level of bravery, and the trip to Mexico City International Airport required wheels.

Volkswagen Polos were not designed with a passenger the size of Ray Michaels in mind, but he hardly seemed to care. He opened the window and extended his arm like a wing, raising and lowering it when Gabriel built up speed along occasional open stretches of road.

"By the time we've got Jason and his luggage in here, this is going to look like a damned clown car," he said. He grinned. "Thanks, man."

Ray was even more animated than usual—playing with the car's radio and air conditioning and chatting a blue streak all the way to the airport. He pointed out old churches, pink taxis, and storefronts that he found amusing. Gabriel nodded and smiled with each new discovery.

By the time they stood outside the frosted glass partition at the international terminal, waiting as the assortment of vacationing families and business travelers from the Aeromexico flight from Los Angeles cleared customs, he had become downright fidgety, shifting his weight from foot to foot and craning his neck to catch a glimpse of his brother.

"Whoo! There he is!" he hollered, his voice booming across the room. "J! Over here!"

There was no mistaking Jason Michaels.

Though he only vaguely resembled his half-brother, he looked every bit the football player. He walked with the casual swagger of a top athlete. A silky long-sleeved T-shirt clung to his torso; a duffel bag was slung over his shoulder. Jason was taller and leaner than Ray, and meticulously chiseled to someday take on a cadre of NFL running backs and receivers. While Ray's eyes were warm and dark, Jason's were piercing green. A casual observer wouldn't have recognized them as brothers, at least not until Jason saw Ray across the room, and they flashed the same thousand-watt smile.

Jason dropped his bag, and they fell into a bear hug of back slaps and laughter, the accumulation of years of brotherly love and a lengthy separation. When the greeting concluded, the laughter carried on.

"What? Not gonna flash me that Heisman pose? Don't tell me you're not practicing it," Ray teased.

"C'mon. Knock it off. That's a long shot. And how are you doing, Ray? Still into masks and stretchy pants?" Jason shot back, chuckling.

"Says the football player—"

"Nothing but NCAA-sanctioned unies, baby."

Gabriel stood off to the side, giving the brothers a moment to reacquaint.

"Hey, Jay! This is Gabriel, my friend I told you about."

Jason slipped into the automated motion of a handshake while turning to greet Gabriel.

And stopped.

It was fleeting, but his grin slipped as if it needed a momentary gut check. His face went blank and recovered. He held out his hand.

"Gabriel. I've heard a lot about you," he said. His rich baritone settled over Gabriel like comfort food: delicious, impossible to say no to, and undoubtedly unhealthy.

Gabriel wanted to say something clever, something striking, but the best he could muster was, "It's good to meet you."

They shook hands, maybe a little longer than necessary.

"I don't know whether to thank you or congratulate you," Jason said.

"For what?"

Jason reached over and slapped Ray on the back. "For keeping this chucklehead out of trouble."

The smile was back, along with a distracting set of dimples.

"How about I go get the car? I'll circle around and meet you by the curb," he said, seeking an escape. "I won't be long."

He left Ray and Jason curbside in a sheltered corner away from the smokers congregated outside the terminal doors. As he rounded the corner to the garage, he glanced back to see Jason still watching his departing figure.

When Gabriel pulled up to the curb, he found the brothers deep in conversation, so much so that they didn't immediately see him. He popped the trunk and climbed out of the car, catching the end of a conversation.

"I had a feeling this would happen," Ray said.

"What? I was just saying that he's—"

"You're just saying nothing. I have eyes. I saw what was going on. The entire arrival area saw... Hey, Gabe!" Ray laughed and picked up his brother's bag. Jason looked away and folded his arms across his chest, looking thoroughly uncomfortable.

Ray threw the bag into the trunk and then heaved his body into the back seat of the tiny city car, a favor to himself and to his brother. He stretched across the seat, improvising legroom.

He chattered his way across the city from the back seat, quizzing Jason about home, about NFL scouts, about their father, about the friends and the girls he'd left behind.

"Ray, we've got all week to catch up. How about we take Gabriel out to lunch, say thanks?"

"My day's free. I could give you the tour, if you like," Gabriel said. He glanced in the rearview mirror, catching Ray's eye. "Unless you have plans?"

Jason turned around in his seat, looked at Ray, and raised his eyebrows.

"Fine," Ray said. "I don't need my legs."

Gabriel drove a circuitous route around the city, pointing out murals, monuments, and churches dating back centuries. Jason looked as though he absorbed each word, splitting his attention between the sites and his tour guide.

Ray stretched out across the backseat, scrolling Twitter.

"I think we should stop for lunch," Gabriel said in an exaggerated whisper. "I'm not sure I've ever seen Ray grumpy before."

"Then you've never seen him hungry before," Jason said.

"Don't mind me," Ray said, not bothering to raise his eyes from his phone. "You two carry on."

They stopped at a café, and Gabriel made a point of engaging Ray in the conversation. It had been so easy—too easy—for him to drop out of it in the car. So they talked football. They talked wrestling. They talked about Ray's plans to join the American pro wrestling circuit some day and about Jason's prospects in the NFL.

Through it all, Gabriel sensed that he was being watched. He would look up to green eyes, keenly focused on him.

"You're coming to the arena Saturday?" Gabriel asked while Ray settled the check.

"Wouldn't miss it," Jason said. "Your first?"

"First with the league," Gabriel said. He took a breath and exhaled slowly, a calming exercise he had learned to combat pre-bout jitters. "First with a new character."

"So I'm guessing you're busy between now and then?"

Gabriel shrugged. Realistically, he knew he should say yes, he was busy. No, he could not carve out time for sightseeing. No, he shouldn't, because there was someone in his life and he knew what he was feeling.

"Well—"

They rushed through the questions, stepping on each other's answers, racing to the natural conclusion.

"Because I'd love to see the museums, but they're not really Ray's thing."

"They're my favorite thing," Gabriel said. "Want a tour guide?"

Jason rested his cheek on his hand; his eyes didn't leave Gabriel's face.

"I'd like that."

Jason could dedicate the next day to Ray, to a soccer match and a sports bar and a club to follow. And Friday? Friday would be a great day to explore.

"This looks cozy." Ray slapped Gabriel on the back and laughed. "What did I miss? Or do I want to know?"

"We're just planning a museum tour," Gabriel said.

"Count me out," Ray said.

"That's why we were planning it," Jason said. "Friday, then?"

"It's ..." Gabriel caught himself. "It's a plan."

★ ★ ★

HE'D MAPPED IT OUT TO the minute, a course that would take them through or at least past some of the city's landmark halls of history, culture, and art. They wouldn't see half of what was on the route, but he included what he thought of as the gems of the city, with options for more.

He drove first to Coyoacán, to Casa Azul, the electric-blue home of Frida Kahlo, hoping to beat the line of visitors that would stretch down the street as the day wore on. Despite the cobalt paint, Casa Azul felt as if it had invited nature in; its parklike garden wrapped the home-turned-museum in a warm embrace.

Gabriel led Jason through its rooms like a docent, pointing out details in Kahlo's self-portraits, the relevance of the letters and photographs. They stepped outside, to the cafe in the courtyard, and sipped coffees under the canopy of trees.

"Where did you learn all this?" Jason asked.

"This was one of my mother's favorites. She said Casa Azul was full of life, that you could feel Frida's energy in the home, how she channeled herself into her art. It's so vivid, but peaceful."

"So your mom's the art lover."

"My mother was an artist. She loved folk art." Gabriel said.

Jason's expression shifted to one of recognition, of respect for the dead.

"Ray didn't tell you?"

Jason shook his head.

"It's why I'm here. I grew up in Arizona. My aunt and uncle took me in when my parents died."

"I'm sorry," Jason said.

"She was from here. Even when I was little, she'd tell me about the art. She said we'd come back some day, see it all together. So once I moved here, it kind of became a thing for me."

"A pilgrimage," Jason said.

"I never really thought of it that way, but maybe, yes."

Jason leaned back in his chair. The shade of the sky rivaled the blue on the walls of the home. "I could sit here like this all day."

"No, you really can't, not if you're serious about seeing museums. We've got to move."

"Where to?"

"The other side of the coin," Gabriel said.

He inched them away from the city center, to the Diego Rivera Museum—Anahuacalli—five kilometers and a half-hour's worth of traffic away.

"You want to see them back-to-back. It's like seeing two sides of the relationship," Gabriel said. "Besides, the Anahuacalli is free since we went to Casa Azul first."

"Free's good."

Stark and dramatic, the Diego Rivera Museum was built of volcanic rock; its lower levels were illuminated through small, slat windows. Dark and somber, navigated through narrow halls and stone staircases, it was the antithesis of Casa Azul. Not until they reached the top—a bright expanse of a room housing pre-Hispanic artifacts and the sketches for Rivera's famed Rockefeller Center murals—did the building open itself up to a wall of glass that welcomed in the late morning sun.

"I love going to these two back-to-back. It's not just about getting a feel for the artist, but I feel like I walk away with a glimpse into their lives, how they were so different, but still connected. You can see it here," Gabriel said.

"You know what I feel here?" Jason said, looking around the room. "Ego. It's amazing, but it feels like a castle, like it's meant to keep people out."

"And Casa Azul?"

Jason smiled. "Passion. It was like you said, full of life, full of love."

"I wanted to make sure you saw those two," Gabriel said. "From here, we have choices. The Palacio if you want to see the murals, or Bosque de Chapultepec."

"The what?"

"Sort of our version of Central Park," Gabriel said. "Lots of museums, and the castle, sort of a forest in the middle of the city."

He had spent countless hours in the massive, central city park. It was home to some of the city's largest museums, as well as lakes, a zoo, and what seemed like endless hiking trails. When he was old enough for his aunt and uncle to trust him alone in the city, he'd found refuge as much in the busy halls of the Museo Nacional de Antropología as in the quiet of the park's forested sprawl.

He led them along paths that had served as his jogging routes, committed to muscle memory, until they reached the northern edge of the park.

"So, exactly how many museums are we talking about?" Jason asked.

"This is Mexico City. There are always more museums," Gabriel said. "Modern art? History? Anthropology?"

"That's the big one, right?" Jason asked.

"Yeah, once you get past the old dioramas, it's pretty impressive, lots of pre-Hispanic stuff. When you get to the main hall with the Aztec exhibit and the giant calendar, it's really something. It puts a lot of things in context."

The calendar dominated the room, attracting a line of tourists and students waiting for their turns to take selfies in front of the enormous artifact. Gabriel and Jason found a stone bench off to one side and sat down as Gabriel recited the details with a familiar ease.

"These images? They're all over lucha libre. In the characters and especially in the masks. I mean, it's all part of the show, but a lot of the characters have ties to these gods."

Jason soaked it in, quietly absorbing every word.

"So tell me—the lucha libre? I understand why Ray loves it—he likes to tackle people. But you? What's a guy who can tell me about the relationship between Aztec gods and pop culture doing wrestling for a living?"

Gabriel rested his forearms on his thighs. He clasped his hands together, twiddling his thumbs.

"My dad never missed it. I used to watch it with him."

"And that made you want to wrestle?"

"The ah-ha moment was when I saw my coach in the ring the first time," he said.

"Miguel?"

"Everything just fell into place. There was the lucha libre, and this badass luchador who was gay and out and surrounded by hot boys. What wasn't there to love? I dare you to find that in any other sport. So I talked my way into a class, and that was it. Hooked." He shrugged.

Jason bobbed his head. "And what would your mom think?"

Gabriel took his hand and pulled him up. "Dad was sure she hated it," he said.

Of course, his father was wrong. The mask Dad had purchased at the swap meet had not been Gabriel's first. That honor went to a multicolored work of construction paper and crayon that his mother had helped him piece together and attach using a string of elastic.

"She was the one who taught me all about the imagery and the narrative of lucha libre—that it's performance art as much as sport. She knew who all the luchadores were and their backstories. But she let dad think that she hated it."

THEY DARTED IN AND OUT of the souvenir and snack stands toward the street. It was well into the afternoon, and they hadn't eaten since morning.

"Will Ray call out a search party if we stop for a late lunch?"

"I told Ray I wouldn't be back till late," Jason said. He smiled. Again, that smile. "I didn't define 'late.'"

He led Gabriel across the intersection, but stopped in the median at an art installation encircled by tourists snapping pictures. They lined up to pose in front of the statue, a pair of outstretched golden angel's wings.

"Well, well," Jason said.

Gabriel read the plaque along its side; his memory was jarred by the information: *Alas de México by Jorge Marín*.

"I've got to get a picture of you with this," Jason said.

Had he been in the ring, Gabriel would have folded his arms across his chest and glared at the camera. But in this moment of freedom, he stretched his arms up over his head so they were aligned along the upper edges of the wings, rolled his head to one side, and closed his eyes as Jason snapped away.

"Now, you," Gabriel said. He began to step down from the platform, but Jason took his wrist, stood beside him, and held his phone aloft. He looked at Gabriel and grinned. "Ready?"

They shot frame after frame, a series of selfies they sorted through and shared over lunch.

"This one goes to Ray," Jason said. He pulled up a picture that a tourist had shot for them, both laughing, each with one arm around the other's waist, and their other arm outstretched in symmetry with the wings.

"C what U missed?" Jason texted. "Late lunch—hungry?"

Mmmhmm, was the sole response.

"Ray's never been much of a day person," Jason said.

"I've noticed."

With plenty of time to waste, they lingered over lunch until it could be considered dinner. They compared notes: on families, on attitudes, on sports, and on their futures.

And on the big question—how an out football player could make it in the NFL. It had been tried. It had never succeeded.

"It probably helps to be a Heisman candidate," Gabriel said.

"It doesn't hurt—but I'm not a Heisman candidate until the *end* of the season."

"But what about when it's time for the draft?"

"I think it all depends on my stats," Jason said. "There've been some great out-players who tried to go pro, but somehow didn't go high in the draft. A couple even made it to the NFL—and ended up on the practice squads. They deserved better."

Gabriel had already had this conversation, or bits of it at least, with Ray. Brimming with confidence, but with a trace of concern, Ray considered his brother to be the best of the best of the class of 2010.

Of course he did.

But Gabriel had done some research of his own. He was, after all, a football fan—a Pac 10 follower. It made sense to look up senior UCLA standout Jason Michaels.

And if Jason Michael's senior season was anything like his junior, sophomore, and even freshman years—when he was called upon to fill in for an injured senior, and ended up with the job—he would be a top five draft pick. An argument could even be made that he was the most attractive candidate in next year's pro draft.

Gabriel wouldn't argue with that.

"What do you think your chances are?" he asked.

"For the Heisman? Realistically, not great. It doesn't matter how good you are, Heismans go to QBs and running backs. Wide receivers hardly even have a chance. But a safety? I might get nominated, but I think that's as far as it goes. No respect for defense."

"And the draft?"

"There's the million dollar question," Jason said.

"Or more," Gabriel added.

"It's different for you, isn't it? I mean, Ray says there's a whole culture of gay wrestlers down here."

"Yes, and some of them are big stars," Gabriel said.

"I sense a *but* coming."

"But you don't have a lot of choices about who you are in the ring. You're expected to be outrageous, campy."

"It's a show, right?"

Gabriel grinned.

"I can neither confirm nor deny…"

"Yeah, yeah. Ray gives me the same line," Jason said. "So then, your character—"

"—is an exótico. I choose to be out in the ring."

"So there are luchadores that aren't."

Gabriel nodded.

"So they don't have to be a—what was it?"

"*Exótico.* Yes."

Jason pushed his plate aside and rested his elbows on the table. He laced his fingers together.

"Tell me if I'm out of bounds, okay?"

Gabriel nodded.

"Ray says you're seeing someone, but it's some kind of secret. Is that true?"

Gabriel rolled his eyes and offered up a sweet, noncommittal smile. "Oh, Ray."

"Is that a yes?"

"There are some things I can't talk about," Gabriel said.

"It's okay. Just asking. Selfish interest. I shouldn't have asked."

Gabriel raised a brow and cocked his head.

"You know," Jason said. He ducked his head, and lowered his voice. "Because I want to know what would happen if I kissed you."

Gabriel took a deep breath and exhaled in a soft shudder. If this had been a date, that would be the perfect end to it.

But it wasn't.

"I'm with someone," he said.

It had only been a day of sightseeing, but it was everything that he missed with Arturo—time together, in public, unafraid of the consequences of being seen as a couple. There were times—too many of them, he realized—when he questioned whether he could consider what he had with Arturo to be a relationship at all.

There was attraction, there was sex—outstanding sex, as far as he was concerned—and private companionship. But it came attached with a price tag: the secrecy, the occasional outbursts, the absolute refusal to go out in public together. Whatever he had with Arturo had never seemed like how he'd imagined a real relationship to be. It wasn't the loving partnership he had seen with his parents, or even his godparents.

Even his short time dating Eduardo, when they had explored the city and enjoyed a series of firsts for a few short weeks, had seemed more like a relationship than the captured moments in an empty gym and short nights with Arturo.

He wanted something more, but for the time being was unwilling to compromise what he had.

"I'm sorry," he said.

"Naw, my bad. Sometimes, I just dive into things without thinking. Ray warned me. I figured it wouldn't hurt to ask." Jason shrugged. "So who is he?"

Gabriel shook his head. He couldn't.

"Another wrestler?"

"Yes."

"An exótico?"

"No."

The "ah" signaled Jason's moment of recognition. "I see," he said.

"It's complicated."

"Should it be?" he asked. "I mean, don't get me wrong, but doesn't that drag you into the closet with him?"

"It's a professional issue."

"Does that make it a professional issue for you, too?"

"Honestly?" Gabriel said. "I don't know."

ARENA MÉXICO WAS MAYBE TWO-THIRDS full—not bad for an early undercard match. It would fill as the evening wore on, but Gabriel wasn't concerned about that.

He peeked around the corner of the stage entrance to the arena to the ramp leading down to the ring through a gauntlet of rowdy fans and bikini models, through plumes of stage smoke and laser lights.

Gabriel adjusted the final details of his costume with Miguel, who positioned his cape and tightened the drawstring on Gabriel's mask before leaving for the arena floor.

His opponent stood at his side, a veteran rudo with a consistent following among the most dedicated fans of the league, but never a major star. It was an open secret that he planned to retire soon, and it was pre-ordained that Gabriel's introduction to the league would be Titus' goodbye.

"It feels like the wrong way to start," Gabriel said.

Titus snapped the straps on his singlet.

"This is how it works. There's no victory lap. You give up your mask and you move on. I'm good with it," he said. "You know how long I've been thinking about hanging this ugly thing up?" He slapped Gabriel on the back. "Time to get nasty. See you on the other side."

Gabriel shut his eyes. He drew a deep breath through his mouth, exhaled slowly through his nose, and then did it again to settle his nerves. He bounced on his toes, stretched his arms upward, and fell forward, folding his body, pulling his chest to his thighs. And the final, unconscious habit—he crossed himself, then kissed his fingertips and reached down to touch the tiny gold cross he'd worn since childhood.

He looked at the stage assistant and gave a thumbs-up.

He stepped into the darkened arena, marching, seemingly aloof to the scene surrounding him. He turned toward the audience and stopped.

"… here to save us! In his Triple L debut, El Ángel Exótico!"

Pyrotechnics erupted around him, surrounding him in explosive white light. He raised his arms, with the stiffened edges of the cape in hand, and put his costume and his character on full display.

The cape unfurled into gossamer wings. Extended, they revealed the drama of his white-and-gold costume: the trunks with metallic accents feathered along his hips, and the shimmering pearl-toned mask with wings set around the eyes and a golden cross laced down its back. It was enough to hide his identity, but not his lush, painted lips. At first blush, the costume could have belonged to any técnico.

The boots told his story, signaling Gabriel's identity as an exótico, even if he wasn't costumed in traditional drag. Working from Rosalinda's sketch, Miguel had collaborated with his costume maker and wrestling supply house to fashion a custom boot for El Ángel Exótico. He had told Gabriel to "think Chanel" as he first unwrapped them: white patent leather with gold trim and laces and an extended shaft that stretched the normally calf-high boots into thigh-high fashion statements. The kick pads, designed to blend into the boot shaft, were trimmed with golden wings.

Gabriel strutted down the ramp like a runway model, just as Miguel had taught him in his final training sessions. His stride was strong, yet vampish. He held his chin high, avoiding eye contact with the crowd, seemingly above the fray.

As he approached the ring, he stretched his arms upward, rolled his head back, and shut his eyes.

Women screamed. Men shouted—some with the derisive rhetoric that had long followed exóticos into the ring. *¡Maricón! … ¡Chupa mi pito! … ¡Puto!*

Some made exaggerated sounds of kissing.

Some purred propositions. *Déjame ser tu papi.*

Gabriel ignored it all, tuned it out, remained aloof and untouchable, an exotic character designed to be worshipped by his fans. By wrestling exótico, Gabriel had willingly placed himself in front of the words, but that didn't make the slurs any less jarring. He would use them as fuel, as motivation for aggression in the ring, but more often than not, he would simply let them slip into the white noise of the arena.

Releasing his pose, Gabriel unlatched the cape, let it drop, and looked at the fans along the ramp, at a boy no older than twelve who held out his hand. Gabriel winked and stretched out his hand for a low five.

He ran for the ring, launching himself over the ropes in an elegant swan dive. He landed in a somersault and bounced to his feet to an explosion of cheers. He quickly climbed the corner turnbuckle and raised his hands, outstretched, to the audience. The crowd, a willing congregation, roared its acceptance.

Gabriel glanced across the ring to his corner, where Miguel, in street clothes, stacked towels for the match. He would be in Gabriel's corner for the fight, no longer La Rosa, but an assistant who would double as coach.

He looked to the ringside seats, where Arturo sat near the wrestlers from Gimnasio de la Ciudad, just a row in front of Ray and Jason.

He couldn't help but see it: Jason cupping his hands to his mouth to yell; Ray grabbing his arm, stopping him; Arturo wheeling around. Whatever happened between them was uncertain, but it ended in what looked like an introduction, a handshake, and a stern look as Arturo turned back toward the ring.

IT WAS PROMOTED AS *CARRERA contra carrera*—career versus career. The loser would be forced into retirement.

Of course, only one career was truly on the line. The other was just starting, and on an undeniable upward trajectory. The wrestlers knew it. The officials knew it. The fans that showed up to see Titus one last time knew it.

There wasn't much reason to be jittery. It wasn't his first time in the ring. It wasn't even a featured bout. But so much rested on El Ángel Exótico's wing-tipped shoulders: the launch of one career; the conclusion of another; the introduction of a character that adhered to some rules, while breaking others; the opportunity for Gabriel to carve his name into the lexicon of beloved luchadores. And though crowds of fans rarely fazed him, there were three people that he couldn't ignore: two that he wanted to impress, and a third that he didn't want to let down.

Gabriel held his breath as the umpire checked his boots, a ritual before the start of each bout. He shut his eyes and pictured what he was supposed to do, replaying the script in his mind before launching himself toward Titus in the center of the ring.

He would put on a show like never before, careful to counter his moments of success with failure, with action designed to make Titus look good in his retirement match. El Ángel Exótico would appear defeated, repeatedly, hung up on the ropes while Titus hurled his body at the young técnico.

Eventually, Titus would miss, miscalculating a diving attack and leaving room for El Ángel Exótico to roll away and regain his balance. He eventually arose, renewed, and reclaimed his acrobatic finesse. He cornered the rudo, and the crowd began its chant, "¡Beso! ¡Beso! ¡Beso!"

He had settled into the pace of the bout by then, calmed his nerves to the point that wrestling was second nature. But the rhythmic cheer caused his breath to stutter once more. Gabriel braced himself for the moment no amount of training could prepare him for.

With Titus trapped in a corner, El Ángel Exótico grabbed him by both cheeks, as though he was about to level him with a head butt. Instead, he crashed their mouths together.

The crowd went wild. It was not a simple kiss, a little smack like so many exóticos incorporated into their act. Ángel dove in forcefully, opened his mouth, and put on a show rarely seen in Arena México.

As Titus pushed him away, Gabriel chanced a glance around the arena. In a corner off to the side of the ring, Miguel grinned. A couple of rows back, Jason whooped. And one row in front of him, Arturo stood, indifferent, his arms folded across his chest.

Titus played it up, looked shocked, protested to the referee and the crowd. El Ángel Exótico took advantage of the distraction, tripped him up, and rolled him into a decisive pin. After the referee held his hand up in victory, he knelt as if in prayer, crossed himself, and bowed to kiss the mat. Only after the bout had been called in his favor did El Ángel Exótico reach behind Titus' head and loosen his mask. He grabbed at it and ripped it away.

Titus' career was over.

El Ángel Exótico's had just begun.

5

CHIN HIGH, SHOULDERS BACK, GABRIEL stayed in character until the moment he crossed the threshold into the locker room.

Only then did his body relax, his shoulders sink, his eyes drift across a sea of familiar faces. He soaked it in, letting the space envelop him.

He was home.

The roar of Ray's voice finally broke Gabriel's concentration.

"Yeeaaahhh!! That's what I'm talkin' about!"

The room erupted in cheers, and the luchadores of Gimnasio de la Ciudad and the Triple L circled him, slapping his back, reaching out to shake his hand. Off to one side, Miguel hung up El Ángel Exótico's cape, exchanging it for a bathrobe. He tossed it across the room.

Gabriel caught it with one hand, mouthing "Gracias" as he slipped it on.

The wrestlers who weren't needed in the ring were ready to party—a fête that had been postponed after Gabriel's original debut as El Fénix Oscuro. In a corner, they'd filled a tub with ice and drinks.

Titus reached into the tub and pulled out two bottles. He waved each at Gabriel. *Water? Beer?* Gabriel nodded toward the water.

Titus slapped him on the back and wrapped his arm around Gabriel's shoulder.

"Well done," he said. "You're an estrella, chico."

He tapped the neck of his beer bottle against Gabriel's and offered a smile, then turned toward his locker.

"Wait," Gabriel said. "Your mask—"

Titus shook his head. "It's yours now," he said. "Ángel's first."

"It's from your final match. I can't take it."

Titus laughed and gulped down most of a bottle of Bohemia.

"I've got a case of them at home—and I'm never putting that lousy thing on again. Keep it."

Gabriel stretched the Lycra mask across his hand and then shoved it into the pocket of his robe.

"You did Rosa proud."

Miguel stood beside him, quietly smiling to himself.

"Which one?" Gabriel laughed.

"Both. She's out in the seats for the rest of the card, but she wanted you to know that she thought you really sold the walk and that she'll give you a proper hug later. Oh, and she's sitting with your aunt and uncle. Don't worry. They seem proud, but they think maybe you should go to confession tomorrow."

He winked.

"How did you ever convince me to tell them?"

"If I'm not mistaken, I believe I Miyagi'd you."

Ray barreled across the room, pushing Jason through the crowd like an earthmover plowing dirt in Gabriel's direction.

"Gabe! Look who just got his lucha cherry popped!"

Jason hit the brakes, turned around to face his laughing brother, and shook his head.

"Gross, Ray. That was disgusting. Show some class."

He turned to Gabriel and lit up his smile, holding out his arms to welcome Gabriel in an embrace.

"Congratulations! That was something else. We could use some moves like that on the field. And the wings—"

He slapped Gabriel's back as they hugged, but didn't release his hold. Gabriel could feel both the repetitive workouts of football training

130

and the soft comfort of his greeting. He would happily hit the pause button.

"And I like the boots," Jason whispered in his ear.

A rush of heat flared across Gabriel's cheeks.

"That was your first lucha libre match?" Gabriel asked, circling the conversation back to safe terrain.

Jason pulled back. He was wide-eyed and, even as he released his embrace, he reached for Gabriel's forearm. "I'd only seen it on TV, looking for the big man over here. That was crazy. I loved it."

"Ahem."

Ray was still standing behind his brother, dramatically clearing his throat to get their attention.

"So when all this…" Ray waved his finger between the two of them, "When you're all done here, we were talking about taking this party to a club. Someone suggested Zona Rosa." He raised his eyebrows in a manner only he could think was salacious.

Gabriel cast him a sideways look.

"*You* want to go to a gay bar?"

Ray howled.

"It's your night, man. I'm here for you. We all are. So we decided it's time to take one for the team. I'd just change out of that costume first—unless…" He tilted his head and cocked an eyebrow.

"I'll be changing," Gabriel laughed.

He looked up to see Miguel glaring at the entrance to the room, where Arturo lingered in the doorway.

"I'll be back," Gabriel said, excusing himself.

Arturo stood apart from the fray. He ducked his head as Gabriel approached.

"You got your first mask," he said.

Gabriel shoved his hands in the pockets of his robe, trying to look casual.

"What did you think?"

Arturo spoke without looking at him, focusing here and there around the room.

"You looked hot," he said. He was stoic, but it was clear to Gabriel that he was fighting the urge to smile.

"The match, Arturo. What did you think of the match?"

"I told you." He finally turned. "You were good. You looked great. You had your character down. I'll give the old man that."

His eyes narrowed as he looked over toward Miguel.

"We can talk later. Are you coming over?"

"The guys made plans to go out. They've even convinced Ray to go to Zona Rosa. Come on. Come with us. It'll just be guys hanging out. It'll be fun. No one needs to know that it's El Cadejo."

"At a gay club? I don't think so."

"Don't you want to celebrate with me?"

"That's why I was asking if you were coming over."

Gabriel turned his back to the room so he could speak with some level of privacy.

"Let's have a night out," he said. "We never go out. We can drink, we can dance. No one cares."

Arturo shook his head. "You know I can't." He turned to leave.

"Text me if you change your mind."

"MEXICO CITY SEEMS LIKE A long way to go for sushi."

Jason eyed the seafood salad in the center of the table.

"Ceviche, Jason. Not sushi. You're from LA and I know you speak a little Spanish, so I'm betting you know the difference."

"Same difference. Raw fish." He took a sliver of jalapeno-topped albacore from the dish and popped it in his mouth. He bobbed his head in approval. "You didn't need to do this."

"I wanted to," Gabriel said. "It's been a good week. I just hope Ray doesn't mind me stealing you for a couple of hours on your last day here."

Jason would board a flight to Los Angeles in the morning, back to summer workouts and training for his final college season, as well as the planned maelstrom of athletic department promotions that accompanied a Heisman campaign.

He had spent plenty of time with his brother over the week, but he had also shared a sizeable amount of time with Gabriel.

And whether it was a thank you, or a goodbye, or a chance to linger for another hour or two, Gabriel had asked him out for lunch. The lively bustle of Contramar could hardly be considered a date, just a last chance to enjoy a good meal with a new friend before Jason left for home.

That's what he told himself.

Repeatedly.

"I should be taking *you* out, after the whole scene with Ray on Saturday night," Jason said. He buried his eyes in his palm in embarrassment.

"He was just having fun," Gabriel said.

Since Gabriel first met Ray at Gimnasio de la Cuidad, he'd come to think of him as the older brother he'd never had: someone who watched over him, whether he liked it or not; someone who had his back. Ray Michaels was an oversized teddy bear, but he was also a protective, trusted friend.

He was family.

As they grew close, Gabriel found that little about Ray surprised him. He may have had the body of a bouncer, but he exuded an overwhelming sense of joyous adventure in nearly everything he did. He'd go anywhere, try anything. So it hadn't been a complete shock when Ray had suggested that they celebrate Gabriel's first league bout at a gay club.

It *had* surprised him when Ray joined the club's house dancers on a small side stage.

"He was dancing with half a dozen go-go boys when he wasn't trying to fix us up," Jason said. He shook his head. "Say what you will, the man's always looking out for me."

"Me too," Gabriel said.

Jason turned his beer bottle aimlessly, shaking off the condensation, avoiding eye contact.

"This'll be the last of these for a while. Back to water, juice, and Gatorade."

Gabriel grimaced, shaking his head.

"Come on, you've got to know what it's like to be on a training diet to keep your body like that."

"You're pretty much looking at it," Gabriel said with a shrug.

Jason looked up at Gabriel with concentrated focus, as if he were trying to solve a puzzle, then returned his attention to his beer.

"Can I ask you something?" he said.

"Sure."

"I've tried to be respectful about this mystery man of yours, but I'm going home tomorrow and I can hardly spoil your secret in LA. It's that Arturo guy, right?"

Gabriel poked at the salad with his fork without acknowledging the question.

"He was side-eyeing me something wicked when we were talking in the locker room," Jason said.

Gabriel looked up and shook his head with a sigh. He had seen this look before. "It's complicated," he said.

"I think people do," Jason said. "And I think they care about you, so they respect your privacy, but they also worry about you."

"And you?"

"I'm going home tomorrow and I think you need to talk to someone," Jason said. "You know what I really loved about this week?"

"Hmm?"

"I met this guy. He's like no one I've ever met before—he's smart, and he's sweet." Jason lowered his voice. "And he's sexy as hell."

Gabriel rolled his eyes and allowed himself the briefest of grins.

"And when he works? He's the baddest of badasses. He has this confidence that just amplifies everything. He owns the space he's in.

People want him, and he just lets it flow over him. It gives him power. But then, when he's not working, he's totally different—quiet, kind of shy. And I like that, too."

Gabriel looked away, down. He didn't have the strength to meet Jason's eyes.

"But he's got this world he hides from people where he just seems to give in, and I don't get it, because I know he's got this other side that could run the world. Where's *that* guy?"

"He's a character," Gabriel mumbled.

"How's that different from anyone else? When I'm on the field, I'm brash and in-your-face because that's who I need to be. I try to get in the receivers' heads. I talk trash like you wouldn't believe. I own it. I like to think I'm not like that the rest of the time, but I know that person's in there." Jason tapped his chest with his fingers. "He's there if I need him.

"You told me about how you and Miguel convinced the league to change up your character. You know what that tells me? That the confident, runs-the-world guy I see in the ring?" Jason reached over, and tapped Gabriel on the same spot, just above his heart. "He's in there. He's part of you, too. You just need to let him out, let him breathe."

Gabriel shook his head. It wasn't that easy.

"You have choices," Jason said.

"But Arturo doesn't."

Jason reached across the table and took Gabriel's hand. He dipped his chin, trying to get him to look up. "Is he worth it?"

Gabriel shrugged.

"He challenges me. He makes me a better luchador. I feel very… connected to him."

"You didn't answer my question," Jason said. "Do you love him?"

Behind them, a waiter dropped a tray of glasses, shattering them on the floor. Diners erupted in applause, but Gabriel simply sat up straight, looking forward as if waking from a stupor.

"Let me ask you something," he said. "You're out…"

"Since high school," Jason said, smiling.

"But the NFL—how? Has any out gay player ever made it in pro football? I know a couple have tried, and a couple have come out after they retired, but are there any active players...?"

"No," Jason said matter-of-factly. "Not yet. But there will be, and I've got as good a chance as any at being the first."

"Does it worry you?"

"Worry me? What? The talk? I can bring it with the best of them. And who knows? Maybe it'll change when I go pro, but so far all my teammates care about is whether I get the job done."

"I could never imagine not being honest about who I am," Gabriel said.

"Then why—?"

Gabriel knew from the very start of the conversation where this was going. *Why. Why do you stay with someone who can't—or maybe won't—acknowledge you?* He'd asked himself the same question dozens of times. He had yet to come up with a convincing answer.

Maybe it was love. Maybe it was the way that Arturo's touch could send his pulse racing. Maybe it was just habit. But whatever it was, he wasn't ready to abandon it, not yet.

"Your job? It's clear-cut. Chase the guy. Tackle the guy. Catch the ball. But this world? It's different. There's the sport, and there's the story. It's a performance. Miguel's taught me to respect that tradition, but Arturo's shown me what it *can* be, how to make it better."

"Gabriel, I didn't mean—"

"Of course you didn't, and it doesn't have to make sense to you. And whatever you and Ray, or even Miguel, think, this is the life I choose."

Gabriel went back to his meal, scooping salad onto his plate. He had nothing more to add.

The outburst quieted Jason. If he had been looking for the strong character in Gabriel to exert itself, he'd found it. Minutes went by before he could offer up a simple "Sorry."

"I know we've only known each other a week, but it just felt—"

"I know."

"I feel kind of protective of you."

"I don't need protecting."

★   ★   ★

BUILT IN THE SHADOW OF Arena México, Gimnasio de Campeones stood as a counterpoint to Gimnasio de la Ciudad. Modern and well-appointed, it was built and run by la Liga de Campeones not so much to train luchadores, but to keep their existing stable of wrestlers content.

League officials filled its weight room with the newest and most cutting-edge equipment. LC luchadores practiced at full speed in a modern ring in a room that replicated the space of the big arena.

For a young luchador weaned and raised in Miguel Reyes' tiny gym in the north of the city, Gimnasio de Campeones looked like a slice of heaven.

Gabriel had been squeezing in training sessions at Arturo's gym for several months, but always as a guest. The LC wouldn't complain about its competitor's rising star making use of its trainers and equipment, especially since the short term of his Triple L contract was an open secret in the wrestling community. And the fact that his former trainer was now an up-and-coming LC luchador was a strong lure to make sure he got accustomed to the new league's largesse.

He had taken days off after his league debut, claiming that his body needed to recover. Each of those days, he received a call or text from Arturo wondering when he was planning to get back to work and asking why he hadn't stopped by.

With Jason gone and guilt kicking in, Gabriel made sure that he trained with Arturo at the LC gym before he returned to Gimnasio de la Ciudad.

"Since when does it take you four days to recover from a match?" Arturo asked. He stood alongside a leg press machine as Gabriel worked out. In theory, he was supposed to be watching Gabriel's form and technique.

"I've just been busy and I didn't have another bout scheduled right away."

"Busy with Raymond's brother."

"Always so jealous," Gabriel sighed, finishing the rep. "Jason went back to LA, and all we did was go to a couple of museums and lunch."

"Good. Now maybe you can get back to work."

He marched over to the weight room, Gabriel on his heels.

"Hey, stop. What's this all about—the party? I asked you to go. I just about begged for you to go, and you just walked out. Now you're upset?"

"You never came over."

"And you never showed up."

Gabriel settled at a weight bench and raised his hands to the bar. "Spot me."

There was never much chat when they worked out together. They would simply go about their routine, alternating between lifting and spotting for each other. But Arturo had questions, and Gabriel had issues.

"You should work out here more," Arturo said. He kept his voice reserved, even though they were alone. "I miss our training sessions."

He offered a weak smile.

"You could have stayed at Ciudad. You could have worked it out with Miguel. I wouldn't have had to sneak around like this."

"Why would I want to go back there? Look at this place. Gabriel, that gym of yours is crap. You could get so much more out of the LC."

"I'm with the Triple L."

"Pretty soon you won't have to be. Think about it. We could be on the same parejas. We could be a team."

"And?"

"We could spend more time together."

"Really?"

"It would be good for your career. They may love you now, but then what? You've got nowhere to go over there. This league? They've got big plans: TV, syndication outside Mexico. They're in talks to tour Japan and to bring lucha leagues across the border. The LC isn't stuck in the past. In a couple of years, it'll be bigger than the Triple L.

"If I go on the road, you could come with me. We could be together."

"Aww, he *does* want me," Gabriel said, a sharp-edged tease. He nuzzled his lips behind Arturo's ear, whispering, "Sometimes, I'm not so sure."

Arturo's eyes darted from one side of the room to the other. They were alone.

"Of course I do. You know I do. Why do you think I'm trying to get you to jump leagues?"

"Oscar has been good to me, and I can't leave Miguel. He's done so much for me."

"So have I. You'd choose Miguel over me?"

"It's not like that. He's like… like a father to me. And I *am* with you." He stretched his palms across Arturo's shoulders and traced his muscles. "Let me show you. We used to always do it in the gym."

"We also used to close the gym."

Gabriel stood and stretched out his hand.

"The shower doors lock."

He nodded toward the far corner of the training center.

"Gabriel…"

"Shh. No one's here. There isn't a class until this evening. You said you missed this. You think I don't care. Come with me. Let me show you."

He led Arturo to the back of the center, to a room with whirlpools, saunas, and a row of wide doors encasing a bank of showers. Arturo looked over his shoulder, checking.

"I told you, we're alone. The guy at the front desk was locking up for lunch when I got here. He knew you were here, so he let me in."

He stepped forward, stretching his palms across Arturo's abdomen. Gabriel ran his hands up his chest and over his shoulders, drawing his face close enough for their mouths to meet.

"You think I don't want you?" Gabriel whispered against his lips. "Let's do it like we used to, right here."

Except it wasn't like their stolen moments at Gimnasio de la Ciudad, and Gabriel knew it. In Miguel's gym, he had always waited for his cues, for Arturo to make the first move. But he no longer saw Arturo as a figure of authority—in or out of the ring.

He reached for Arturo's hands, raising them above his head, pressing them into the tiled wall.

"What's gotten into you, Gabriel?" Arturo said. Breathless, he rolled his head back against the wall, giving Gabriel access to his chin, his neck, his shoulder.

Gabriel simply stepped back, keeping Arturo's hands in his, and pulled him into a shower stall.

"If anyone's left in here, they'll hear us," Arturo said.

Gabriel released his hands and turned on the water. He reached again for Arturo.

"No, they won't. I promise. I won't let that happen."

He kicked off his sneakers and pulled Arturo's T-shirt over his head, then dropped it on the floor. He couldn't get them undressed fast enough, alternating in rapid-fire succession from Arturo's clothing to his own. His hands traced a restless path down Arturo's chest, along his ribs and back, until they grabbed solidly at his ass.

He slipped his thumbs in the waistband of Arturo's warm-up pants, sank to his knees, and slipped the pants down his thighs as he buried his face in Arturo's hip.

And as his senses were overcome by the rush of steam, water, and Arturo's soft moans, Gabriel could have sworn that he heard the mumbled words, "Promise me."

★ ★ ★

THE WORLD CAN TURN ON a dime, or a pinhead, or on a knee turned at an ungodly angle between soggy grass and a 243-pound tight end.

Loyalties may not be forged from passion, but from the need to grow, to cultivate new audiences. And partnerships can come and go because of both.

The world turned upside down during Rivalry Week, that Saturday when the NCAA told fans of even the most lackluster athletic programs that they should care on principle about college's most storied contests: Auburn versus Alabama, Michigan versus Ohio State, UCLA versus USC.

For football fans, Rivalry Week was a daylong buffet of college games rising in the SEC in the morning and setting in the Pac 10 at night. For Ray Michaels, it meant weeks of research, staking out an American sports bar with strong satellite reception and cold beer, and nurturing friendships with willing bartenders who would make sure that the Bruins game would play on *his* television, uninterrupted. The Bruins versus the Trojans was not a game for a laptop monitor.

A casual football fan and an increasingly enthusiastic Jason Michaels fan, Gabriel tagged along to watch Jason's final regular-season college game. The matchup would determine not only the winner of the division, but also Jason's fate in the Heisman campaign. He would be challenged. The Trojans' receiving corps was unexpectedly strong, and hours before kickoff the Los Angeles Memorial Coliseum had been caught in the middle of an unseasonable November rainstorm that left the field sloppy.

Watching college football with Ray Michaels required a strategy. A bad play? A Bruins turnover? Keep quiet, ride it out. A touchdown? A great tackle? An interception by a certain free safety? Be prepared for high fives and hugs.

Ray poured his heart and soul into college ball, and no more so than when his brother suited up. He bobbed his head as he watched the first quarter, a *yes, yes, okay, yes* repetitive motion that traversed his body from head to shoulders to legs as the teams exchanged possessions, getting a feel for each other without either one breaking out in the slop of the Coliseum.

That changed—loudly—in the second quarter, when Jason lined up with the special teams unit to receive a punt on the Trojans' fifteen-yard line. USC's kicker had steered clear of Jason until then and paid a price when the UCLA star made a highlight-reel return, bouncing off defenders, stutter stepping until he found a clear field and room to build speed all the way to the Bruins end zone.

Ray leapt up, arms raised above his head in a victory "V." He spun around and hugged Gabriel, the stranger sitting behind him, and then Gabriel again, lifting him off his feet.

"That's my brother, right there! Oh yeah, baby!"

The teams chipped away at each other after that, exchanging field goals on the slow, muddy turf. Starting players who began the game with the buzzing energy expected of a rivalry game stumbled to the line of scrimmage, covered first in grass stains, then mud, then blood.

By late in the third quarter, the Bruins held a narrow lead, thanks in no small part to Jason's blanket-like coverage of the Trojans' receivers. There was little doubt, to Gabriel, Ray, or the network announcers, that he was locking down his spot in the Heisman race.

Ray pointed at the screen as the cameras closed in on Jason, lining up at mid-field.

"My brother, Gabe. He's gonna be a star."

"It looks like he already is," Gabriel said.

The Trojan quarterback pulled back to throw—a short out pattern to the receiver Jason had covered all afternoon in a zone blanketed by Trojan linemen.

It didn't look like more than a routine tackle at first, a tough hit that would leave Jason on his back while he caught his breath.

Except he didn't get up.

The network replayed the hit, repeatedly, in slow motion. Ray's face sank, looking increasingly somber with each slow-motion replay. It was painful to watch Jason's leg twist in on itself toward his back as he was leveled on the forty-yard line. When the feed returned to a live shot, players from both teams circled Jason Michaels in a halo of blue, crimson, and gold.

Ray watched in sullen silence as a paramedic crew lifted Jason onto a stretcher and hoisted him aboard a waiting golf cart that would take him to an ambulance just outside the stadium.

With a quarter left to play, Ray stood up, walked to the bar, and paid the tab.

★ ★ ★

THE RUMORS SPREAD RAPIDLY THROUGH the lucha libre community. The Triple L and the LC had entered into talks for a one-time event pitting their stables of luchadores against one another. Even before it was confirmed, *Lucha Semanal* ran a front page story guessing at the matchups.

But what seemed like a done deal between the leagues nearly collapsed several times on its way to the Arena México. The Triple L insisted on exclusive television rights. The LC balked and countered by demanding that its promotional team handle the marketing.

They had even dragged Miguel into the talks when they eyed several of his independent luchadores for undercard bouts.

"These league executives are all idiotas," he grumbled. He had never been on board with the promotion. The two empresas had different styles, even different audiences. But, he acknowledged, they each had something the other wanted and they were willing to cooperate with each other in order to secure it.

Ultimately, he proposed the solution that got both leagues to sign on the dotted line: a three-on-three parejas match, one league's técnicos versus the other's rudos. Two referees, one from each league, would officiate, and each league would promote the match as the conclusion to a long-simmering feud.

"They flipped a coin to decide which side each league would represent," he said. "The Triple L got técnicos."

"So—"

"So El Ángel is a part of it."

Gabriel slapped his hands together, wadded his palms into fists and punched the air, but Miguel sat quietly.

"What else?"

"And so is La Rosa."

"But you're not a Triple L luchador."

"True."

Miguel scratched his chin and pursed his lips.

"Oscar came up with a theme, something that's supposed to raise tension between the leagues, give them a reason for a grudge match."

"And that is?"

Miguel's face told the story. He hardly needed the words.

"You," he said. "Your former trainers, fighting over El Ángel Exótico—that's the grudge. That's why La Rosa will be in the ring."

"And Arturo," Gabriel said.

Miguel nodded.

"Yes. Oscar remembered your debut. So did the LC. They're going to pitch it as a feud between El Cadejo and La Rosa. They'll expect us to mix it up over you, then declare it a contract match."

"I have to defend my contract?"

Miguel waved it off, shutting him down.

"No, no, no. Don't worry. You're not changing leagues. You're not even in the bout, not officially. That was the big sticking point. The Triple L has to win. To get that, they had to give something up."

Miguel looked across the room, to a corner where Ray was caught up in a quiet video chat with his brother.

The words collapsed from Gabriel's lips as he unraveled the plan.

"Not Ray."

Through the convoluted trickery of lucha libre storytelling, The Dark Storm would ultimately be forced to retire. The leagues had worked it out. The bout would be evenly matched, a dead heat, with the rudos of the LC ultimately succeeding using dirty play. As they prepared to claim El Ángel Exótico for the LC, The Dark Storm would fall on the sword, offering to sacrifice his career so that El Ángel could stay with his mentor.

In real life, Ray was headed home to help his brother convalesce. His contract had been suspended with an offer from Oscar Chavez to help establish him as a new character in the burgeoning Los Angeles wrestling circuit.

"It was the only result that made sense," Miguel said. "His brother's injury was the linchpin. He needed to go home, and Oscar needed to sacrifice a luchador."

Ray looked up from his computer and caught Gabriel's eye. He acknowledged him with a half-hearted wave.

"And Arturo's on board with this? He hasn't said anything to me," Gabriel said.

"They're talking to him today, but everyone knows he's been trying to get you to jump leagues—"

"I swear I never—"

Miguel put his arm around Gabriel's shoulder.

"I know. Using their gym isn't the same as signing their contract. But he wants you over there, and he'll see this as an opening—and that's why he's going to agree to get in the ring with me again."

Whatever feelings he might have for Arturo, Gabriel wasn't sure he trusted him to stick to the script, especially if he were to face Miguel again. They had reached a tentative truce on the subject over time: Gabriel didn't bring up Miguel's name around Arturo, and, in turn, Arturo kept his temper in check. In hindsight, Gabriel realized that it hadn't solved anything, but at least he had gotten some peace. But he could not guarantee that the détente would hold once Arturo learned of the upcoming bout.

Ray snapped his laptop shut and tapped his hand on the lid before clambering to his feet.

"How is he?" Gabriel said across the room.

Ray forced a closed-mouth smile. He had been aloof since his brother's injury, but Gabriel had never seen him look so grave.

"Not good—he tore two ligaments and cracked his knee."

The short prognosis spoke volumes. Forget the Heisman or the first round draft pick. The possibility of Jason ever playing an NFL game may have ended on the forty-yard line of the Los Angeles Memorial Coliseum.

"Can he come back?" Gabriel asked. "What did the doctors say?"

"He's going in for surgery tomorrow, and they'll see. If Jason works hard—and he always does—he'll be in decent shape again someday."

"Football shape?" Gabriel asked, but he knew the answer. Safeties, wide receivers, cornerbacks—the speed positions all relied on strong, flexible joints, and Jason had damaged the entire support system for his knee.

It was all over the American sports blogs. He had torn his medial collateral and anterior cruciate ligaments. There was a hairline crack on the tibial plateau, just behind his kneecap. The prognosis for eventual recovery was good. He might even get into something approximating playing shape again. But he would be out of commission for months— right when the scouts were watching.

They wouldn't wait for him.

"You don't think he'll get a second chance?"

"He'd be lucky to get on a practice squad," Ray said. "He's done."

Miguel stood off to one side, staying out of the conversation, but clearly tuned in. He kept his head bowed and his arms folded. He didn't look enthusiastic about what he was hearing.

"I'm going home, Gabe. Jason's going to need me." He glanced over at Miguel, who kept his head bowed. "The timing works, I guess. Someone needs to go, and I need to leave. Oscar's worked things out, even got me a show in LA."

"A *show*?" Gabriel asked.

"Their word, not mine. Apparently, it's sort of lucha-meets-club-scene thing. Whatever, I'll take it, and the money's all right. I could use the work when I get up there. I'll stay here until the bout, but then I'm headed home. Jay's going to move in with Dad until I can get up there, and then we're going to get a place together, at least until he's able to get around on his own."

"So that's it for you here?"

"I'll come back to finish out my contract someday. You know, a miraculous comeback. I'll lose, I'll leave, and someday La Tormenta Oscura will be resurrected. Maybe it's time to go back to being The Cyclone. It's still a good name, yeah?"

"It's very you," Gabriel said.

For the first time since the third quarter of the UCLA versus USC game, Ray smiled. It lacked its usual effervescence, but it was a start.

"Come on," he said. He held his arms outstretched. "You know you want to hug me."

Ray had always been a hugger. Friends, family, opponents, bartenders—anyone he felt a bond with had hugged it out with Ray Michaels at some point. But this was different. Ray didn't let go, not right away. He reeled Gabriel in and held on.

"You should call him. He could use a friendly voice, you know? I think he'd really like to hear from you."

He patted Gabriel's back and let go.

Gabriel nodded. "I will."

Ray shoved his laptop into his backpack and slung it over his shoulder. He started to leave, and then seemed to think better of it. He turned. His face had a look of mischief about it.

"Send him a picture of you in your costume. That'll cheer him up."

★　★　★

THE EMPRESAS BEGAN THEIR PROMOTIONS immediately, peppering their events with the early strings of the storyline that would lead to the eventual championship match. Based on carefully cultivated tips, *Lucha Semanal* reported the rumors of dispute building between them. They followed up with breathless stories about the center of the conflict: the Triple L's popular young exótico, whose role in the conflict predated his professional debut.

LA BRONCA DE BRONCOS

There's bad blood brewing between the luchadores of the Liga de Campeones and the trainers of the Liga de la Lucha Libre. Could it be professional jealousy, a changing of the guard, or maybe something personal? They aren't talking, but it's clear that this has escalated from luchador versus luchador to an empresa versus empresa conflict over a rising star of the Triple L.

Broadcast from the jumbotrons at Arena México, the LC's luchadores openly taunted their opponents during the Triple L's weekly matches. In return, Oscar Chavez stormed the ring at LC events, grabbing the microphone from the announcer between bouts, declaring them traitors to the lucha libre code. He painted them as villains, trying to steal his league's talent, prompting the arena to drown in a sea of boos and catcalls.

Both leagues peppered the arenas with flyers advertising the Partido de Rancor, the first cross-league campeonato, which they promised would result in a shakeup of Mexico City's lucha libre circuit.

They scheduled the bout early on the Friday night between Christmas and New Year's Eve, when vacationing families would be visiting the Federal District for the holidays. The strategy worked; the few seats left by the day of the event were easily sold out to walk-ups. The event featured a huge undercard: indies, minis, luchadoras, trios—that gave the after-work crowd ample time to fill the arena, guaranteeing a loud and colorful backdrop for the television cameras.

By the time of the main event, the promoters had set up the crowd with a staged increase in volume, light shows, and pyrotechnics. Flames erupted from the pillars at the edge of the upper stage, near the entrance to the ramp from which the rudos of the LC and the técnicos of the Triple L made their entrances.

Ring girls lined the ramp to the stage, alternating space with La Rosa's bikini boys.

Amid thunderous heavy metal, red lights, and billowing stage smoke, the LC rudos took to the ring first: El Grande, who had signed with the LC shortly after his former partner changed his stage persona to The Silver Cloud; Johnny Rocker, a popular Texas-based rudo who had recently relocated to Mexico City; and El Cadejo, who captained the team and received the crowd's largest ovation. He flipped into the ring and pounded his chest, drawing a roar from fans of the LC and of the heels.

As was often the case, however, the técnicos had a loyal following inside the arena, a mass of longtime lucha libre fans that turned out to cheer on the heroes.

The arena lights exploded in warm yellows and brash pinks as the Triple L técnicos hit the entry ramp: The Silver Cloud, once again ready to face down his old partner; The Dark Storm, aligned with his longtime teammates; and La Rosa, set to once again square off against his former assistant.

Dressed in white wrestler's tights and his Ángel mask, Gabriel stood guard at the turnbuckle at the técnicos' side of the ring as the appointed assistant for the night. He had an assignment to fulfill: Look concerned and stay out of the way until he received a signal to rush the ring. Ray would push him back, keeping him out of the action.

The match started according to plan. The luchadores followed their script: The rudos rushed out to an early advantage, controlling the tempo and dominating their opponents. The Silver Cloud and El Grande quickly abandoned the ring for the ramp, where El Grande tossed the Cloud into the ringside seats. The Dark Storm and Johnny Rocker had been assigned to sit out the first minutes, which gave La Rosa and El Cadejo room to work the entire space of the ring.

El Cadejo strong-armed La Rosa quickly to begin an in-and-out series of nearly-there pins from which La Rosa escaped. He dove for the corner, reaching out for the Storm, when El Cadejo's new partner jumped into the ring and onto his back. El Ángel Exótico protested from the sidelines, but the Storm pushed him back before joining the fray.

He shoved at Johnny Rocker, forcing him off La Rosa, and buying time for the exótico to regain his footing as El Cadejo attacked. La Rosa darted away just as El Cadejo reached out to him, causing the rudo to fall into the padded ringside pit. He struggled to right himself and was forced onto his back when the Storm heaved Johnny Rocker over the ropes and into the pit beside him.

That served as the cue to bring the first round to an end. La Rosa and The Dark Storm looked at each other, made sure they were aligned, and then ran at the ring, leaping side-by-side, plancha suicida at the rudos below.

The first fall, as planned, went to the técnicos.

Gabriel breathed a brief sigh of relief. He hung on the outside of the ring, en la esquina técnica, and played his role, but it wasn't just a matter of appearance, or an act. He *felt* anxious and concerned because of the painful history between two men who both played enormous roles in his life, and because of Arturo's increasingly surly demeanor in the days leading up to the match.

But with a third of the bout on the books, Arturo had stuck to the script and shown no sign of veering into his dangerous improvisational habits.

The rudos were to ramp up the energy in the second round, to rebound after the insult of having lost the first round so decisively. They rotated the action in and out of the ring with the LC rudos attacking their opponents until the Triple L técnicos dropped from exhaustion or were chased from the ring.

As the round drew out, The Dark Storm and The Silver Cloud were sprawled at the feet of the ringside seats while El Cadejo leveled a series of head butts and flying kicks at La Rosa. With each successful attack, he turned to El Ángel Exótico, appearing to plead his case to jump ranks to the LC. Ángel, in turn, made a show of rebuffing his offer while buying time for his teammates to recover.

The wrestlers stuck to the script, but Gabriel could see something in El Cadejo's movements that he did not trust: a narrowing of the eyes and a jawline stubbornly set. He tried to make eye contact, hoping to somehow keep Arturo's well-documented temper in check.

El Cadejo was supposed to wrest control of the match from the técnicos in the second round. He was to attack La Rosa while the referee was distracted, a classic rudo trick meant to weaken the técnicos enough to leverage a pin when the referee returned to the action. He was supposed to strike with a roundhouse punch followed by a kick to La Rosa's gut.

As the referee faced away, El Cadejo spun back into La Rosa, landing his punch. But instead of directing a kick to the stomach, he aimed lower, leveling the exótico with an illegal kick near the crotch. He dove into a rana, using his legs to pin Miguel's shoulders and legs as the referee counted down.

Round two to the rudos. The match was tied.

Miguel rose slowly. He returned to the técnicos' corner, supporting himself by hanging his arms over the ropes until the action resumed.

"Let me in," Gabriel said. "You're hurt."

"I'm fine, and you're not wrestling today."

"Your forehead's bleeding, and you can hardly stand up straight."

Miguel pushed himself up and off the ropes.

"It's not your fight," he said and threw himself into the ring once more.

As planned, the Storm and the Cloud pulled themselves back to the ring as round three started, but La Rosa waved them off. This batalla was going to conclude in a one-on-one fight to the end.

He gestured to the Storm to return to the corner, to keep Ángel in place. He held up his hand to the Cloud, warning him away. Even the other LC rudos looked at him, clearly questioning the move, but they stayed put.

La Rosa charged toward the center of the ring, closing the gap with El Cadejo before the rudo could react. As he drew close, La Rosa flew at him, taking the rudo down with a flying kick to the upper chest. They fell in a heap with La Rosa sprawled across El Cadejo's back, but the rudo rolled out before his former boss could leverage his position into a pin.

The crowd noise exploded through the arena. Even if the luchadores tried to call out to their teammates, they would not be heard over the din.

El Cadejo paced, circling the ring slowly, his eyes never leaving La Rosa, who stood center, following the rudo's movement, looking for an opening.

Gabriel, following instructions, stood at the turnbuckle behind Ray, who blocked his access to the ring. This was to be La Rosa and El Cadejo finally settling a score that had been scripted weeks before.

But the dispute was real. It far pre-dated anything scripted by the empresas. The full house saw a great match, filled with tension.

Gabriel saw an old wound about to be exposed.

He nudged closer to Ray, trying to be heard over the crowd.

"This is going bad. You need to let me in there. I can stop it."

"Sorry, Gabe. Miguel wants you to stay put."

His pulse quickened. His head throbbed. Gabriel could not simply stand by.

"You know what happened before."

The Dark Storm stood his ground.

"Everything's cool. Don't worry. Everyone's on board."

Before he could finish the sentence, La Rosa sprang, launching his body at the rudo's chest, pinning him briefly against the ropes. El Cadejo slipped out, spun behind the exótico, and locked his arms behind his back. The referee began a count, but La Rosa lifted El Cadejo off his feet, flinging him to the floor.

As far as the arena was concerned, it was great theater.

Gabriel knew better.

He dove under the ropes and into the ring just ahead of Johnny Rocker, body-slamming El Cadejo, trying to separate him from La Rosa. El Cadejo spun around, glaring at El Ángel before backfisting him, knocking him to the mat. That gave Johnny Rocker space and time to leap onto El Ángel's back and pin him into the mat. He sat on his back, and the referee stepped forward, raising Johnny Rocker's arm into the air.

It should have stopped the match.

It should have sent a signal to the wrestlers to freeze the action.

It should have given everyone a chance to breathe, to cool down, to get back on script, for the announcer to declare a winner, and for the Triple L to sacrifice a member of its team. But this no longer had anything to do with empresas, or luchadores, or contracts—or scripts.

Arturo drove his body into Miguel, tying him up in the ropes. He grabbed Miguel from behind, flipped him upside down, and dropped his body into the floor, landing Miguel head-first.

He didn't stop with the piledriver. With Miguel dazed, Arturo rose to his feet and rushed to the nearest corner. He climbed the turnbuckle, faced Miguel, and leapt. The plancha wasn't an extraordinary move. It was legal, routine even, and practiced repeatedly from the early days of a wrestler's training to insure that he landed with his hands breaking the fall and his weight distributed so it wouldn't hurt his opponent. Arturo ignored it all and landed squarely on the back of the stricken técnico.

"No!" Gabriel shouted, pulling away from the dogpile of fighters. "Let him go!"

The referee pulled Arturo off of Miguel, and Gabriel rushed to his side. He looked up at Ray, back to the referee.

"We need a paramedic!" he shouted as he turned back to La Rosa's motionless body.

★ ★ ★

THE WRESTLERS LINED UP AGAINST the wall according to skill: a couple of professional luchadores to the front, a few serious amateurs filling out the middle, and one or two inexperienced newcomers bringing up the rear.

The instructor, older, thick-muscled, with close-shorn hair, barked instructions to his younger assistant, a skilled luchador who demonstrated each move for the class.

The assistant stopped beside one of the newcomers, a boy of no more than seventeen. It was his first time in the class. He had been warned: Do only as you're told; stay out of the way; don't get killed.

"Next time, you get yourself some proper wrestling gear," the assistant said. "No more of this sweatpants shit."

"Yes, Ángel," the boy said, the words rushing out on a breathy exhale. A look of relief spread across his face: He had been welcomed back to train in the gym. He turned to walk away when a hand grabbed his arm, stopping him.

"In here, it's Gabriel."

GIMNASIO DE LA CIUDAD HAD shut down after the accident. But the demand for traditional training remained strong among both professional and aspiring luchadores, in no small part out of respect for Miguel and the role he had played starting, nurturing, and guiding so many wrestlers' careers.

And the Reyes household needed the income.

With a blessing from Rosalinda herself, Gabriel worked with The Silver Cloud to reopen the business and get it back on track with regular training sessions. The Cloud, a veteran already thinking of stepping down from the ring, led the classes with Gabriel as his demonstrator. Gabriel handled the business of the gym, managing memberships and booking Miguel's indie teams.

He had secured permission to manage Miguel's wrestlers from the Triple L to ensure that it wasn't a conflict of interest, and Oscar Chavez had been accommodating. Whether it was out of guilt or because

Gabriel had not yet signed a contract extension was unclear, but Gabriel had watched carefully, paid attention, and discovered he had a knack for managing lucha libre events in the small markets.

When it became clear that Miguel would be returning to work, Gabriel negotiated a deal with the downstairs gym to merge and reorganize their space, moved the ring downstairs, and added workout space upstairs with the locker room and showers. It took some convincing at first—*why go to the effort to move the weights upstairs?* But Gabriel had the plan and the patter down and a crew of men with big muscles and bigger hearts to help him get the job done.

When they finished, he stood side by side with the Cloud, looking over the new downstairs lucha gym. Hands on hips, Gabriel took in the room's grimy gray-green walls.

"It could use some paint," he said.

"It's a gym, Gabriel. No one gives a fuck."

"They should."

He took it upon himself to reboot the room's look and feel and, with some help, overhauled it so that it felt new, modern, fresh—even if it was the same old place in the same old unfashionable neighborhood.

"*Now* it's ready. I'll give her a call and set it up."

★ ★ ★

PRIVATELY, THEY CALLED IT A grand re-opening. Publicly, they needed to treat it like any other day. If they hadn't, they might have had their heads lopped off with a quick thrust of Miguel's cane.

"Let's see it," he said, hobbling behind Rosalinda as they stepped into the remodeled gym.

He stopped dead in his tracks after he crossed the threshold to the open expanse of the wrestling center and saw the large wall painted in a brightly hued folk-art mural of the great stars of lucha libre: El Santo, Mil Mascaras, and others. And on the far side, near the entrance to the office, in a floral bodysuit and feather boa, La Rosa, arms raised in a pinup pose, flanked by two bikini boys, anchored the far corner of the mural.

"So I see we've moved," Miguel said.

"We weren't sure how you'd hold up against that staircase," the Cloud said. "Gabriel worked a deal to move us downstairs."

Miguel arched his brow and shot a look at Gabriel.

"You did this?"

"Rosa sketched out the mural for us, and another one for the boxers who work out upstairs so they wouldn't be pissed."

"So this was *you*," Miguel said, turning to Rosalinda.

"A team effort," she said, taking his hand.

Miguel was still recovering from the fracture to his L3 vertebra that had left him nearly paralyzed after the grudge match. For months, he had fought through physical therapy, regaining the balance and strength needed to walk, albeit with the assistance of a cane.

He would never wrestle again, but he made it abundantly clear that he intended to get back to work.

"What do you think?" Gabriel asked.

Miguel walked along the mural, inspecting the artwork. He lingered at the life-sized painting of La Rosa.

"I think I'll need a better office chair."

★   ★   ★

IT WAS AN ADJUSTMENT, BUT the system worked. Miguel gradually reclaimed management of his gym and of his independent wrestling troupe. He tried, often unsuccessfully, to stay out of the business of training luchadores and leading classes. He had become manager rather than trainer, leaving those responsibilities to the Cloud and to Gabriel, who continued to juggle their own wrestling careers with the gym's needs.

But he would not step aside when it came to training his top student. When Gabriel entered the training ring, Miguel would stand off in the corner, or pull his office chair from his office to watch, to coach, to correct, and to fine-tune Gabriel's evolving technical and performance skills.

He didn't need to demonstrate a flip to critique it.

"So what are you doing about character development?" Miguel asked.

"What do you mean?" Gabriel had worked with Miguel on the character of El Ángel Exótico since day one.

"I thought that's why you were training at that other gym," he said, pushing buttons. His quality time with Gabriel had diminished during his recovery. When they did see each other, Gabriel steered well clear of the subject of Arturo.

"That other gym was bad advice," Gabriel said. "I have everything I need right here."

Miguel laughed. "I'm not so sure about that. I hear Arturo's joining that LC group in Japan."

Gabriel cringed. He hadn't spoken to Arturo in months, but he couldn't help but follow his career. Mexico City was huge, but its lucha libre community was small and talkative.

"I haven't seen him. Like I said, I have what I need here. I'm good."

The breakup had been hostile and quick. Gabriel left Arturo within days of the accident, during his first real time away from Miguel's hospital bedside. He had made no effort to contact Arturo before he severed their ties other than a text saying he wanted to meet at Arturo's apartment.

When he arrived, Gabriel headed straight to the bedroom, where Arturo had given him a drawer in the vanity to store clothes. Arturo stood in the doorway as Gabriel shoved T-shirts and jeans into his backpack.

"It was an accident."

"Like running down a jaywalker is an accident," Gabriel had barked back. "You could have stopped. You didn't."

"It was part of the show. It just went too far. I landed wrong."

"I don't believe you. The match was over."

Gabriel had latched his bag and moved toward the door, but Arturo had blocked it.

"So that's it? You're just going to leave?"

"Yes. Move."

"Don't you think we should talk?"

"When did you ever want to talk before? Get out of my way."

Arturo stood his ground, daring Gabriel to push past him.

"That contract of yours is up. Think about your future," he'd said.

"That's exactly what I'm doing. Get the fuck out of my way."

Arturo wouldn't give up easily. He'd settled into the doorway, challenging Gabriel while pleading his case. "You and I are alike, you know. We're both ambitious. We want the same things."

It wasn't the first time Arturo had said this. And Gabriel had believed it, at least for a while.

"We may want the same things, but look how you go about it. Fighting, hiding." His voice dripped with disgust. "Why would I want to be a part of that? What reason have you given me? I should have been stronger. I should have ended this a long time ago."

"Don't leave me."

Arturo had never sounded so weak.

"This is the point where you vow to be better, right?" Arturo had shut his eyes as Gabriel brushed past him. "Don't bother."

"You haven't talked to him since?" Miguel asked.

"Not since you were in the hospital."

"Come here," he said. "Take my seat. I need to stand and get this blood flowing." Miguel stood up, precariously balancing his weight on the cane. He leaned in on it, beckoning Gabriel over.

"I hope you didn't do that for me. Don't get me wrong. I didn't like that you took up with him, but that's none of my business. You make those decisions for *you*, okay?"

"Why didn't you say something?"

"About Arturo? That's your business. He was a good trainer, and when I realized… I just think he must lead a very lonely life, doing things the way he does. I may not have thought he was good for you, but maybe I hoped you would be good for him."

"I don't see how you can defend him. He broke your back." Gabriel said. "That wasn't just some little foul."

Miguel said that it was time for him to retire from the ring, with or without the back injury that had left him hospitalized. "I just got pushed into it a little early," he said.

His time away from the gym had helped point the way toward its future. The Silver Cloud found his calling the moment he took over instructional duties at the gym, and so sealed his plans to retire.

"Ends up, he's a pretty good teacher and he likes it," Miguel said. "He says it's nice to finish the workday without freezing his balls off in an ice bath."

"I didn't realize he wanted to quit," Gabriel said.

"It's been on his mind for a while. The question for me is, ¿Y que será de Gabriel?" He reached out, grabbing Gabriel by the forearm. "Hmm? What about Gabriel?"

"What about me?"

"Your career is taking off, but you've scaled back your bouts to work here."

"The Cloud needed help."

"And now he doesn't," Miguel said. "Don't get me wrong. I appreciate what you've done. But you need to get back to it. The fans love you. You're a star. You also haven't signed an extension yet."

"I know—"

"Why are you hesitating?"

"We needed to keep this going—"

"And that's my point. If you were putting yourself first, would you have done that?"

"I owe this gym," Gabriel said. "I owe you."

"You don't owe me a thing. Now, let's look at this as an opportunity, okay? Do you want to stay with the Triple L?"

Gabriel shrugged. "Oscar's been pretty good to me."

"But? Are you thinking about going over to the LC?"

"Never."

Miguel took a few cautious steps and then a slow lap of the room. He stopped in front of the mural, studying the painting of La Rosa.

"You know, when you first walked into this gym, you were so full of yourself, coming in here and knocking Raymond on his ass. Sneaking into the locker room at the Coliseo and then talking your way into class. It was arrogant."

"Hey!"

"But you backed it up and you knew who you wanted to be. That guy? What does *he* want to do next?"

The easy answer to Miguel's question would be to re-up with the Triple L, and he could have done worse. Oscar Chavez would happily re-sign him to a long-term contract. But the past months had left Gabriel with time to question his future, and whether the league should be a part of it.

"Maybe's there's something else? A chance to call the shots, maybe?"

Gabriel would never get used to Miguel's uncanny knack for reading his mind. He narrowed his eyes. He hadn't even decided whether to broach the subject with Miguel.

"You talked to Ray," he said.

Miguel turned to him. "I talked to Ray."

"I don't want to leave you alone."

"You won't."

"It's everything you hate."

"So what? It's not my career. I trained you well. Maybe you can teach them a thing or two. Maybe it's time for you to spread your wings."

Gabriel shut his eyes and took a deep breath. He exhaled slowly as he got his head around the thought of moving on. He hadn't expected Miguel to encourage it.

"I don't know. It was just an idea."

"You don't have to make up your mind today, but you know what I think? I think you should at least consider it."

★ ★ ★

GABRIEL DARTED IN AND OUT of the Zocalo crowds on the cloud-swept Sunday morning. He had an errand to run, a quick stop at the gym, and he had told his aunt and uncle that he would meet them at the Cathedral in time for the eleven a.m. service.

The city had already awakened, and he ran a gauntlet of families walking to church, of tourists bartering with tour bus operators, of street merchants hawking toys, rosaries, and Virgin Mary statuettes.

Gabriel nearly tripped over the feet of one of them, an old woman huddled alongside a planter watching the crowds pass. She offered passersby a view into their futures and insight into their pasts for twenty pesos. She looked frail, with weathered skin and a hump in her back, but her eyes were bright and alert.

"Boy, do you know what's in your cards? I can tell you. Twenty pesos."

"No, thank you," he said, slowing his gait.

She stared at him for an awkward moment and then reached out her hand.

"Clouds are following you, boy. Let me see your palm."

Gabriel shook his head and kept moving, but the woman grabbed his hand and turned it over. She touched his palm, tracing the lines with her fingers, and then looked up into his eyes.

She looked as if she knew a secret.

"They speak to you. You should listen," she said.

Gabriel yanked his hand away. He looked back once as he fled toward the front steps of the Cathedral and his waiting aunt and uncle. The woman was still watching him. He felt her eyes follow him long after he had turned the corner to the church gates.

★ ★ ★

"I've lied to you."

He had spent most of brunch pushing his eggs around his plate, circling in one direction, then the other.

"What do you mean? You told us about the wrestling ages ago," Fernando said. "We've been to your matches. We're fans!"

"Sweetheart, what are you talking about?" Alma said. Her voice was laced with patience he considered undeserved, just as it had always been.

Gabriel looked down from the luncheon terrace of the Gran Hotel de la Ciudad to the expanse of crowded Zocalo, to the enormous Mexican flag that dominated the landscape. It snapped loudly in the breeze.

"About school, about how I was using my time. Where I went at night. Everything."

Fernando concentrated on his plate, on striking the perfect balance of eggs and roasted tomato on his fork. "Did you miss confession this week or something?"

"We assumed you had a boyfriend," Alma said. "We knew you'd tell us about him when you were ready."

It opened like a floodgate: the dropped classes; Arturo; his plans for a life that involved neither courtrooms nor boardrooms; how lucha libre was his occupation, not his hobby; how he needed something more. How he had prayed for their forgiveness.

"I'm sorry. You took me in. You treated me like a son. I owe you better."

"What brought this on, mijo?" Alma asked.

Gabriel pushed his plate away.

"I'm leaving."

Gabriel rested his head against the window of the 737 as it descended into the Los Angeles basin. With the San Bernardino mountain range to the right and the Pacific to the left, a concrete valley spilled out in front of him like mirrored images of the Mexico City sprawl, laid out side by side by side.

The new landscape provided relief, and the flight was an escape from a world he loved but needed to break free of.

His passport declared him an American, but the only connections he had were his birth certificate and the friends who had returned to Southern California months before. His life had become rooted in Mexico—in school, family, church, and his adopted family of luchadores and trainers in the arenas and gymnasiums of the Federal District.

Between Oscar's flexibility and Miguel's caginess, he had pushed limits and traditions as far as any luchador had ventured. He had redefined exótico for himself, and possibly for those to follow, but he'd known that he had reached a limit that he suspected he would never push past, so that he would never reach the goals he had once set for himself.

Not in the Mexican leagues; certainly not in the Triple L.

He needed to recalibrate. He needed to set his sights on the lofty ambitions that once drove him. Miguel had been right. To play by a different set of rules, he'd need a chance to write them. And to do that, he couldn't sign an extension of his existing contract.

He'd expected pushback. He'd got it, and more.

Oscar and the other executives of the Triple L hadn't been anxious to lose their rising star, and had fought Gabriel's decision to leave—first with incentives, then with threats that he would never appear on a league fight card again.

"If you go in there and tell them that you won't renew your contract, they'll see it as the end," Miguel had said. It was no surprise that Miguel had anticipated this, planned for it, and mapped a strategy that would let Gabriel walk away without slamming the door shut behind him. "What we need to do is give them the chance to think it's just the beginning."

"And how do I do that if I don't come back?"

"Through the global economy," Miguel had said. He'd winked. "And you think you're the only one with the fancy education?"

It may have earned a reputation as the liga tradicional, but the Triple L could also feel the heat caused by the cross-platform branding of the LC—the television network, the music deals, the fashion line, the outreach to overseas markets while drawing new talent and new fan bases to its flamboyant brand of wrestling.

The Triple L needed to step up its game in order to compete, Miguel had said, and El Ángel Exótico could be the perfect brand ambassador as the empresa teamed up with US promoters to dip its toes into new markets, new venues, and new business strategies.

"I don't understand why you would do this," Gabriel had said.

"I already told you. If you still have those goals you walked in here with, your best chance to reach them is there, not here."

"There are traditional leagues up there, indie leagues," Gabriel had said.

"You do that, then you might as well stay right here. Besides, you won't have Oscar on your side—and it pays to keep Oscar on your side."

Oscar Chavez already had ambitions for exporting lucha libre north, and had invested in a new venture by American promoters to carve a niche for Mexican wrestling in the US entertainment lexicon. Though it was already popular on Spanish language networks, they'd wagered that it could break through with English-speaking fans.

It just needed a gimmick.

Ray had served as a trial balloon, a US born-and-raised luchador in a new, American take on lucha libre. With live music, photo booths, burlesque acts, wrestling, and fully stocked bars, Lucha Bang had the kind of buzz publicists dreamed of, and regularly sold out its pricey tickets to audiences of couples, hipsters, and sports fans from San Diego to Seattle.

But even as it gained popularity, Lucha Bang's promoters had their eyes on another, so-far-elusive, audience—and they were willing to spend generously to secure it.

Lucha Bang's promoters wanted a cut of the lucrative west coast gay market, and they intended to attract it with Mexico's hottest young exótico. All it would take was willingness to part with a greater share of their business and a luchador looking for a new life.

★　★　★

LOS ANGELES GREETED HIM WITH a bear hug and a yelp that could be heard from one end of the Tom Bradley Terminal to the other.

"Gaaabe!! Over here, man!"

Ray towered front and center among the waiting friends, families, and limo drivers in the baggage claim. He waved his arms in the air, as if for some reason Gabriel couldn't already see him.

"How ya doing? Damn, it's good to see you!"

He wrapped Gabriel in his arms and lifted him off the ground in an uncomfortable but familiar greeting. He grabbed the largest of Gabriel's bags.

"Welcome to the City of Angels."

Gabriel thought that few cities could have traffic worse than Mexico City, where cabs routinely turned right from the left turn lane to cut off gridlocked traffic. One glance at the condition of the late-afternoon freeway convinced him it had competition.

"Oh, hell no. We're not getting caught in that," Ray said. "We'll cut over on La Tijera. I swear, one fender bender and the entire 405 gets fucked up." He grinned. "It pays to have a driver who knows the neighborhood. Besides, this way I can give you the tour."

He drove past mini malls and sardined tract homes in the shadow of the airport approach, through the oil fields of Baldwin Hills.

Gabriel killed time, asking about the city, the family, the beach. "Is this where you grew up?"

"Yeah, just over that way a little bit, near the old race track. We've still got an aunt over there, but my dad and stepmom moved a few years back."

He felt Ray glancing over from time to time. "What?" Gabriel asked.

"Jason. He's doing okay. Not a hundred percent yet, but he's wrapped his head around this thing and he's not letting it get him down. Just in case you wanted to know."

Gabriel smiled to himself. Ray had always tried to play matchmaker. "You think he'll play again?"

"Doubtful. Never say never, especially with my little brother, but the deck's pretty stacked, you know?" Ray said. "What about our man Miguel?"

"He's doing okay," Gabriel said. "Not a hundred percent yet, but he—what did you say—wrapped his head around it? He was anxious to get back to work, even though the work has changed. If we're not careful, he'll be running his own empresa in no time."

"I don't know. I kind of think he has been all along," Ray said. "Even though he doesn't call himself a manager—"

He let his sentence drift into air.

"So, Jason would have come, but he had PT this afternoon. I thought we could meet up for dinner somewhere near the loft."

Ray smiled and reached over to turn on the stereo. "I think you're going to like it here."

The landscape shifted rapidly as they hit downtown, beyond the Staples Center and financial district, to the new museum corridor, and past Skid Row to a neighborhood of aging warehouses and late model BMWs. The streets were alive with consciously casual pedestrians, and eclectic ground-to-roof street art covered the brick and concrete buildings.

Gabriel took in the paintings with wide-eyed wonder: pop art, free forms, re-creations of classics—the Mona Lisa painted on a tin shed. The street was its own color wheel.

"It looks like the university district," Gabriel said. "The city allows this?"

Ray shrugged. "Leave it to Jason. Most jocks live in the Marina or the South Bay, but Jay had to get himself a loft in the Arts District." Ray sighed dramatically. "No infinity pool."

The area pulsed with bright reds and vivid indigos, full of a vibrant sense of rebellion, on the fringes of fashion and pop culture. They were less than an hour into the city, and Gabriel could already feel its heartbeat.

Ray pulled up to the loft complex, a converted warehouse now inhabited by young professionals who could afford it and artists who could find roommates. It overlooked a rising sun twenty-four hours a day: an electric-hued painting that covered the wall of the neighboring building.

"Let's dump your bags. We're going to meet up at Wurstküche."

"Worst *what?*"

"Beer, brats. Trust me," Ray said.

GABRIEL SPOTTED HIM INSTANTLY, TUCKED in at a corner table, sipping an amber ale and strategically positioned to watch Sportscenter on the TV behind the bar. Jason looked as though he could still take on an entire receiving corps—his build was as carved as ever, but it was hard to miss the brace that still buttressed his left knee.

Jason looked up, slid from the booth in an uneasy movement, stood up gingerly, and opened his arms wide to greet him with a hug.

Ray dropped two menus on the table. "I'm going to go get in line. Text me what you want," he said, leaving them behind.

"Ray loves this place. Be prepared for sausage jokes," Jason said. He eased himself back into his seat. "It's good to see you."

"Same," Gabriel said. "Thanks for letting me crash."

"Stay as long as you like. There's plenty of room, and Ray's finally starting to make noises about getting his own place."

"Finally?"

Jason dropped his voice to a conspiratorial tone. "I love him, but he's got to go. He won't let me do anything for myself, and it's driving me crazy. He sleeps in when I have to be up. And he sings, constantly. I'll have no peace until he moves out."

Gabriel reached across the table to clasp hands. He held on and squeezed. "How's the leg?" he asked.

Jason released his hands, picked up his beer, and kept his eyes low.

"Getting there," he said. "It shook me up. It still does." He stalled, sipping at his beer and looking up at the televisions.

"It was always going to be football, you know? Ever since Pop Warner. Now it's gone. Just like that." He waved his hands in the air like a magician. "Everyone says it can be gone in an instant, but you never expect to be the one.

"Dad insisted that I get insurance during my junior year in college. He thought I needed a policy to protect my potential earnings in the event of a catastrophic injury. I thought he was crazy," Jason said. He looked down at his knee, pieced back together and still held tight with brackets and Velcro. "Thank you, Dad. That damned policy is my lifeline."

Like so many aspiring NFL players, Jason had hoped to play for ten, maybe fifteen, years and then coach or get a spot in a broadcast booth.

The future had seemed bright, simple, and distant. But coaching jobs and broadcast gigs don't happen straight out of college.

"I'm working on it," he said. "I took a break from school until I figure things out. I'm just not quite ready to go back. I tried, but—"

Jason's phone buzzed on the table with a message from Ray: *Buffalo or rattlesnake?*

Jason shook his head and tapped out: *Don't you dare. Turkey. Peppers.*

"Make it two," Gabriel said. "And until then?"

"In the meantime, I hang out with Ray, and the wrestlers, and the strippers."

"What?"

"Oh, you just wait." Jason said. "And what about you? Last I heard, you were running the gym. Ray was worried that you were going to quit wrestling."

"No, I just got really busy—"

Jason stopped him mid-sentence with a wave at the air.

"That's not what I was asking," he said. "Did Arturo—?"

"We're done. I've seen him at the arena, but we don't speak. I think the empresa's sending him to Japan."

Jason forced a stoic nod, but it was hard to miss the smile starting to crease his lips.

"And you?"

"What?"

"Is this a visit? A tour? Ray's been a little vague."

"I'm still figuring it out," Gabriel said. "I needed a change, something more. I think maybe I was Miguel's Ray. You know, it was time for me to leave?"

"I doubt Miguel wanted rid of you," Jason said.

"No, but he wanted his gym back."

★ ★ ★

WHEN IT WAS OPEN, BUSINESS at the Pyramid Theater in Hollywood was conducted largely in the dark. And by the looks of it, that was probably a good thing.

Built in the 1930s, the theater had seen better days. The floral lobby carpet was torn and stained. Over the years, the grungy grout between the aging bathroom tiles had obviously absorbed a wider variety of fluids than had been intended. The floor around the bar gripped shoe soles like vice-grips. The curtains had absorbed the acrid scent of weed that crowds had never worked hard to hide.

But when the lights went down, the cavernous theater rose to life, from the pyramid-shaped wall sconces to the booming sound system that had been installed for salsa club nights, occasional concerts, and the regular visits from the Lucha Bang troupe and its entourage of musicians, bouncers, and burlesque dancers.

"This is where we wrestle?"

Eyes wide, Gabriel took in the gilded ceiling and the velvet curtains stiff with stains. "It looks like an old dance club."

Ray slapped him on the back. "It *is* an old dance club. Welcome to LA lucha—it's a little different than what you're used to."

The foyer walls, covered in framed photographs and programs from the Pyramid's heyday, brought the aging theater's history to life.

Over the decades, it had been converted from live theater to movie house and back again and then sat dormant for years until an investor snapped it up on the cheap and turned it into rental space for special events. It had slowly come back thanks to an investment in sound, booze, and salsa music, which had a dedicated following in the city.

When the promoters of Lucha Bang had first begun to sniff around the city for a home base, it had seemed they would settle on a traditional sports venue. The Olympic Auditorium, for decades home to the city's wrestling and boxing events, had shut down after being purchased by a local church. The Staples Center and the Sports Arena were too large and too costly for the fledgling lucha league, and promoters had wanted something different, a trendy vibe that would attract more than just wrestling fans.

Lucha Bang needed to be edgy, an experience.

They had looked instead to the theater and club spaces dotting the city. Most of the old theaters of Hollywood had already undergone renovation: the Egyptian, the El Capitan, the Chinese. And, through historic preservation efforts, the downtown spaces were largely committed to remaining theaters. When Lucha Bang promoters saw the ad for a reggaeton concert at the Pyramid, they'd known they had a match.

"You wouldn't believe some of these old movie houses that have been restored," Jason said. "They're beautiful. You'd love them."

Gabriel walked the space, became familiar with it.

"And this one has *not* been restored, right?"

The room was abuzz with energy. A crew noisily installed the wrestling ring, while another assembled the rigging on a trapeze-like device, a gold hoop.

"What's that?" Gabriel asked.

"That?" Ray said, smiling, "That means we're sold out."

THEY WOULDN'T BE ABLE TO work out in the theater, at least not right away. While the crews finished installing the ring and rigs at the Pyramid, the luchadores prepared offsite at a nearby boxing club.

The new wrestling troupe was already assembled when Gabriel arrived: the Bam Brothers, rudos from East Los Angeles whose costumes of torn T-shirts and camouflage pants looked more thrasher rock than lucha libre; CaCa, a mini dressed like a parrot whose gimmick involved fake bird droppings, and his wrestling partner, Super Hiss, whose Lycra costume was covered in a snakeskin print. Gabriel's opponent arrived last, burrowed into a dark, oversized hooded sweatshirt and warm-ups.

The wrestler unzipped the sweatshirt and removed the hood to reveal a curvy and intimidatingly fit woman with dark hair and a rock-solid scowl. Standing about five-foot five, she had the cut frame of a lifelong athlete and the attitude of a CFO.

She walked up to Gabriel and held out her hand.

"You must be Ángel," she said. "I'm Lola, but in the ring, they call me Electra. I'm your rudo."

Gabriel had never seen a luchadora square off one-on-one against a luchador, and the prospect of fighting a woman left him off balance. His words tripped on his lips.

"Gabriel," he said, taking her hand. "I mean no offense, but there's got to be a mistake."

"And here we go," Lola huffed. "Are you saying that no one told you I was going to be your first opponent?"

Ray stepped behind Gabriel, clasping his shoulders in his hands.

"You don't want to hold back against Electra, Gabe. Lola here used to be a serious boxer—the light welterweight champ."

"Two years running," she said, finishing the sentence.

"She's badass, Gabe. She can hold her own."

"Damn straight," she said, slapping Ray's outstretched palm. "And if the Olympics gave half a fuck about women boxers, they would have expanded the weight classes, and I would've gone to London."

"Gabe here's a legit flyer, Lola, a true luchador. None of the tackle-and-sit shit," Ray said.

Lola waved him off and circled Gabriel.

"I've seen you wrestle before—last year in Mexico City, at the Coliseo. I think you'd just signed on with the Triple L. You put on a *show*. I liked the wings. It'll be an honor to try to kick your ass—even if I have to take a dive."

"I'm not sure I'm comfortable with this," Gabriel said. "I don't want to hurt you."

Lola set her hands on her hips, shifting her weight to one side. "Oh, please. You wouldn't stand a chance. Now, are we going to get to work, or not?"

Promoters pitched the match as a battle of the sexes. Lola was the wronged woman who didn't believe that a man more glam than she belonged in the ring. Gabriel's role was simple and familiar: glamorous, aloof, and tougher than the fans would expect of a man dressed in shiny thigh-high boots, glitter eye makeup, and a mask.

Gabriel held back on his first kick, scarcely launching himself from the ropes and landing softly. Lola took instant advantage. She kicked out and flipped Gabriel on his back. Straddling his chest, she grabbed his hands, then pressed her body forward, pinning his wrists alongside his head. Her breasts settled uncomfortably close to his cheeks, and rather than kick himself out of the pin, he turned his head away, losing any chance at leverage.

"Don't get any ideas, Ángel. They're already spoken for."

"I wasn't—" Gabriel stammered.

Lola stood up, laughing, and held out her hand to help Gabriel up from the mat.

"I know, I know." She turned to look at Ray, then back to Gabriel. "You call that a legit flyer? And you? You want to really show me what you got now that our introductions are out of the way?"

Inhibitions slip away slowly when a man is raised to treat women like "ladies," but a beat-down can speed up that process. After his second fall, Gabriel picked up speed. After the third, he tapped into the aggression that had earned him a reputation not just for his costumes or glamour, but also for his ability to out-think and out-maneuver the rudos of Mexico City.

"Let's see your tijera, your helicopter-into-a-head-scissors," Lola said. "That's your signature. Use it."

He launched, kicking his right leg toward her throat, locking on and whirling her around and down to the mat.

He stood and helped her up.

"That's more like it," she said. "Now, let's talk about the match."

He outlined a plan for three rounds. She stopped him.

"Just one, Ángel. We play one round to the takedown."

He looked at Ray, puzzled. Ray simply shrugged. "Like I said, man. Welcome to LA lucha."

"Don't worry. You're the headliner. We can run this thing long."

They mapped out the bout. Ángel would lay off at first, much as Gabriel had done. He would play the gentleman, and Electra would make him regret it through a series of kicks to the chest and abdomen that would leave him gasping on the mat. He would recover when she turned her back, posing and mocking him before the crowd. He would gather his strength in the corner, then roar out, propelling himself off the ropes, taking Electra down. She would fall from the ring; he would dive after her and pin her in front of the ringside crowd until she gave up, loudly vowing revenge.

"You've got talent," Gabriel said as they wrapped for the afternoon. "Why haven't I heard of you before?"

Lola slipped her arms back into her sweatshirt.

"Because I'm a Greek-Mexican luchadora from Pomona," she said, pulling the hood over her head. "If you want some ring time in the theater tomorrow before the marketing people get us, I'll be there early."

GABRIEL AND JASON CAUGHT THE Red Line to Hollywood in the mid-afternoon. The theater was a manageable walk from the Hollywood and Highland station for Jason, and the subway was faster and cheaper than fighting the Hollywood Boulevard crowds and the gouging prices of summer parking in the tourist zone. Ray, who had errands to run, promised to drive them home after the match.

"I can't say this is my favorite part of town," Jason said, sidestepping a sidewalk performer dressed in a mangy Sponge Bob costume. The stretch outside the Chinese Theatre had them all: the superheroes, the bad guys, the children's characters, all angling for a share of the tourist dollar, posing for pictures—whether you wanted them to or not.

"They're just trying to earn a living," Gabriel said. A woman dressed as—Gabriel wasn't quite sure, but she resembled a fairy—shoved a five dollar bill into a bedazzled bag jammed with tips. He did a double take. "Maybe I should come here as El Ángel."

Jason smiled, bumping arms with Gabriel as he tried to keep pace.

"You'd make a killing. It's different, though—not what you're used to. It threw Ray at first, but that only lasted until he saw the strippers. He adapted pretty fast after that."

"Ray is nothing if not adaptable," Gabriel laughed. "To be honest, I'm still working this out. My coach believed in tradition. He bent that to help me shape my character, but this feels more like the LC, you know? And Miguel hated the LC. I'm still not sure why he went along with this."

"Maybe he thought you needed a break, something new," Jason said.

"Is that why you spend so much time with them?"

Jason kicked at the sidewalk as they waited for a crosswalk light to change. "Maybe," he said. "You know, the second I felt my knee snap, I think I knew. But I told myself I could fight it. It wasn't until after surgery that it all sank in—everything I'd worked for was done, gone. I could have stayed at school, hung out with the guys. But I just couldn't. There wasn't a place on that campus that didn't remind me of what I'd lost, so I took a break. Ray had me tag along here one day, and it just stuck. I've been helping out with their strength training. It's therapeutic."

The wrestlers of Gimnasio de la Ciudad had always joked that Ray was their savant, the guy with a sixth sense for what people needed and who could gently push them in that direction—or, in some cases, shove them. Whether Ray knew what he was doing or just had well-tuned instincts was a mystery.

Gabriel looked at Jason, who had gone silent as they crossed the street. He seemed distracted, measuring what to say.

"Jason?"

"They're going to love you, you know. That combination of tough and…"

"Tough and what?"

Gabriel grinned. He bumped their shoulders, egging Jason on.

"You're going to make me say it? Fine. Tough and… an exótico."

"By definition," Gabriel said.

"And smart."

"I don't think that's part of the character."

"Oh, yes it is," Jason said. "You can see it in the ring. The intensity. And I'm not done, so quit interrupting."

"Fine, fine," Gabriel laughed.

"Handsome. Sexy. Strong. Authentic."

The sidewalk crowds thinned after they cleared Hollywood and Highland. As they walked side by side, Jason hooked their pinky fingers together and leaned close.

"Beautiful," he said.

"Jason…"

"They're going to love you, Gabriel."

Gabriel hoisted his backpack higher and let it settle comfortably on his shoulder. He stretched his hand, let their fingers fully intertwine, and held on tight.

★ ★ ★

THE PYRAMID SPRANG TO LIFE in the hours before Lucha Bang.

Crews decorated the foyer and bars with kitschy black velvet art and positioned black lights to showcase their designs: sugar skulls, the god Tonatiuh, a jumpsuit-era Elvis. Near the foyer doors, just inside the metal detectors, stood souvenir stands with T-shirts, luchador masks, and CDs from the evening's scheduled bands. A photo booth was decorated to look like a tomb.

Gabriel shook his head.

In the days leading up to his bouts in the Mexico City arenas, he had spent much of his time in the practice ring, working out storylines and fight choreography with fellow luchadores. In Los Angeles, those moments were shared with a series of lighting, sound, and costume checks.

The ringside seating—folding chairs that could easily be moved out of harm's way as luchadores dove from the ring—had been set with precision. Upstage, a platform was ready for the event announcers, with a side stage for the evening's band. Downstage, the platform extended forward into the crowd to create a space for luchadores to pose and strippers to strut. Toward the back of the theater, glasses crashed as bartenders set up their stations for the night.

Gabriel leapt to the stage, set his bag aside, and climbed into the ring. He circled the space and began the familiar routine of testing the turnbuckles and letting his body softly bounce against each side, testing its give.

"Glad to see you learned something from me," a voice boomed from the back of the theater.

"Always test the rig," Gabriel said. "You're early, Ray."

"I know your habits. I figured you could use a friendly face around here." Ray glanced over at his brother. "But I see that's been handled."

"Lola said she'd be here early—"

"Right here." In black leggings and a red sports bra, Lola emerged from backstage. "They want us dressed for lights and pictures in two hours, and I'm gonna need some time to get ready. Want to run through this?"

They walked and talked through the match, mimed the vaults and more violent takedowns, but focused on the choreography and timing. Lola was the picture of concentration, intent on details: the falls, the drops, the pins.

Her single-mindedness left Gabriel in awe. Every crash behind the bar or shout of a crew member distracted him, but nothing shook Lola until the crew tested an overhead rig, an apparatus for one of the burlesque performers.

They were still in the ring when Lola began to look over her shoulder. Behind her, a leggy redhead was lowered to the stage aboard an oversized gold ring. Seated elegantly askew, she looked like a retro bombshell, like Ann-Margret, in a shimmering green corseted gown, thick feather boa, and stiletto heels.

Lola's eyes didn't leave the rig. Neither did Ray's.

Jason leaned across the ring to Gabriel's shoulder. "Ray's got it bad," he whispered.

"Apparently so does Lola," Gabriel replied. "Who is she?"

"Fanny Vice. And I hate to tell you this, but they probably sold more tickets for her than they did for you."

Her music echoed across the empty hall: a classic striptease tempo, heavy on the horns, heavier on the drums.

She stretched and posed on the ring, arched her back and kicked up her heels, and moved like a child on a swing set. When she slowed, she slid seductively to the stage and touched down with a saucy wink and a pointed toe.

She performed a slow striptease for the benefit of the lighting and sound technicians. Her act was heavy on the tease, but not shy about the strip. She took over the runway, bumping and grinding her way across the stage as the crew adjusted lights for her routine. Once down to g-string and pasties, she retreated to the swing, which was now adjusted to rotate freely.

Fanny's striptease became a trapeze act. They hoisted her above the stage, where she swung, then dropped, supported by her outstretched arms. The swing began to spin, gradually increasing its speed until she extended her pointed toes, forcing it to slow. Fanny jumped off, striking a pose until a detached voice from the back of the room called out, "We're good." Only then did an assistant rush to the stage and wrap her in a light floral kimono.

"Thanks, honey," she said.

She turned her head, peeking over her shoulder, and glanced back to the ring, where all action had come to a halt.

"Don't stop for me," she said.

She stepped up to Ray and wrapped him in a hug, kissing his cheek. She nodded to Jason and reached her hand out to him. When she unfurled herself from Ray's arms, she stepped close to Lola, ducked her cheek alongside the luchadora's face as if whispering something in her ear, then pulled back with her blue eyes locked on Lola's face before she kissed her.

"And you must be the new guy," she said. Her voice was gently teasing, soft and breathy. "Hello, new guy."

Even draped in a silk robe with her hair disheveled, she was stunning, with high cheekbones, porcelain skin, and ruby lips.

Gabriel extended his hand. "Gabriel."

"And here I thought you were just another angel." She winked. "I'd better get myself dressed again. Clothes on, clothes off!" She clapped her hands like a flamenco dancer. "Lola?" She held her hand out, waiting for palm to meet palm. "Let's go get you dolled up."

They left hand in hand, sucking the air out of the room.

Jason looked at his brother and chuckled. He raised his hand in front of Ray's face and snapped his fingers.

"Over here, Ray. Earth to Ray."

Snap. Snap.

"Damn," Ray said. He exhaled; he puffed his cheeks out like Dizzy Gillespie's, and his eyes were slightly glazed.

"I think that ship's sailed, Ray," Gabriel said. He looked at Jason. His voice softened. "I should probably get ready, too. Are you going to stick around?"

"I'll be right here," he said.

HE'D CONSIDERED ALTERING HIS COSTUME when he came to Los Angeles; he'd ditch the revealing trunks and switch to traditional wrestler's tights.

The promoters would hear nothing of it.

Too traditional.

Nothing about El Ángel Exótico was traditional, he'd assured them.

More exótico, less macho, they'd said.

He'd tried to convince them that the simple act of wearing tights would not alter the fact that his character was gay.

We signed El Ángel Exótico; we want El Ángel Exótico.

If the US lucha libre leagues were supposed to free him, he had yet to see it.

So he dressed in the familiar gold and white costume: the trunks, the thigh-high boots, the wing-inspired cape. He dusted his eyelids in glitter, lined his eyes in gold pencil to bring out the amber in his irises, and tucked tufts of wavy brown hair under his mask.

"Could you lace it for me?" He looked into the mirror to where Lola sat, transformed into Electra, her stage persona.

She was dressed in midnight purple, a two-piece luchadora ensemble with trim across the chest that looked like a leather breastplate, cut high to expose her toned torso. The tights were cut to match, with matching accents. Her dark hair had been teased wide, making her resemble a combat-ready Sophia Loren.

The final touch, a barely-there mask, covered her from forehead to nose, but left enough room to see Cleopatra eyes.

She'd been transformed.

"You look beautiful—and a little scary," Gabriel said.

Fanny nudged in front of him and adjusted his mask.

"They said you were glam, but *whoo*," she said in an exaggerated exhale. "I like the liner. It brings out your eyes. Nice touch. And if you ever want real wings, I can hook you up. I've got great connections for feathers."

Dressed in character, the entire ensemble met on stage to pose for photographs with sponsors and fans who had purchased pricey VIP packages. The photographer had set up a portable studio to shoot portraits of each performer after the guests cleared—headshots for promotions and wide shots where he encouraged them to "play it up" in character.

El Ángel Exótico squared off against Electra for the camera, then mugged in a back-to-back pose with Ray, who was costumed as his new persona. He had swapped the blue La Tormenta Oscura costume for a new costume and a familiar name: As the Cyclone, he wore dark brown pleather luchador tights trimmed in dark blue and copper, which gave the illusion that he was nearly naked.

He struck a muscleman pose and gabbed away, showing off his new costume.

"I was even able to keep the weather theme," he said.

"One more set, okay?" the photographer asked, waving Ray away. "Let's get the angel on his own."

Gabriel stood in front of the backdrop, thinking. He raised his arms, lifting the cape like wings, like the Angel of Independence statue. As the photographer fired away, he raised his chin and shut his eyes, soaking in the warmth of the lights.

He snapped back to attention at the sound of heels clacking across the wooden floor. Lucha Bang's publicist clutched a tablet computer to her chest with a schedule that would not be ignored.

"We'll need everyone out back to get set up for the arrivals. Can you all follow me?"

They staged the performers' entrances like a parade that ended at a red carpet movie premier. Collector cars—a mix of old and new, high-performance sports cars and custom cruisers—lined up in a parking lot behind the club, preparing to drive up slowly, to a cascade of studio lights and cameras hired by Lucha Bang.

The promoters put their two stars together in the last car, a 1963 metallic red Impala convertible, a prize-winning lowrider. The plates read "CHRYBOM."

Gabriel helped Fanny into the car. They climbed atop the back seat and waited in line as car after car slowly rounded the corner to the front of the Pyramid, where cameras and fans awaited.

Fanny settled in, legs crossed elegantly so the slit in her dress fell back, exposing sheer black thigh-high stockings.

Gabriel kept his eyes on Fanny's face. She laughed.

"It's okay to look. That's kind of the point."

He shook his head and sighed.

"What's wrong, angel?" She had a voice that could reach into his soul: breathy, empathetic, a bit hotter than he cared to admit.

"Nothing," Gabriel said. "This is all just a bit different. I'm adjusting."

"I thought you were some big star down in Mexico."

"I don't know about that," he said.

"I do," she said. "Don't be humble. Lola's told me all about you. Made me watch you on YouTube. She's been studying video. You're used to crowds and cameras—you play to them, and you do it well. So tell me, how could this be new?"

"This." He pointed to the line of cars. "We didn't do anything like this. We'd pose for the camera and run down a ramp, but that was it. No cars, no strippers—"

"It's all just show, sweetie. And please, I'm a burlesque artist." It was the softest of admonishments, but the point landed.

"Sorry," he said. "Your act is very good."

She laughed. "Honey, do you have *anything* to compare me to?"

Their car stuttered and lurched. Fanny yelped.

"¡Agarrate cavrona!" the driver laughed, triggering the low rider's low-end hydraulics. The car hopped and danced, rocking left and right as it crept toward the theater. Gabriel put his arm around Fanny's waist to steady her.

"Do you do all the shows?" he asked. "Do you go on the road with them?"

"Oh, hell no. Fanny Vice does *not* do Fresno. Besides, this is just my short-term plan. Another five years on stage, and I'm done."

She outlined a series of investments, from hedge funds to flipping starter homes in the Inland Empire.

"Fanny may retire from dancing, but it doesn't mean that her brand dies. I've got a lingerie line in the works, and let's just say I'm in talks to represent a brand."

She hadn't always been a stripper. Before she bought her first tasseled pastie, Fanny Vice had been Bonnie McCreary, a Cal business major with a 3.81 GPA. She had prospects. She had student loans. She also had friends who had dragged her out to a strip show in San Francisco for her birthday, she said.

"Most of the dancers were pretty conventional—pole artists, lap dancers, hair flippers. But there was this one, she was older than the others, and she did a good old-fashioned Sally Rand fan dance. She was probably in her early forties. She didn't have a perfect body. She didn't grind. It was a strip *tease.* I chatted her up afterward. Next thing I knew, I was learning the art of burlesque... And I *love it.*" She gave him a hard look, as if she could see straight through his mask. "Do you love what you do?"

Gabriel nodded. "Always."

"Then question less, enjoy more," she said.

NO MATTER WHAT RESERVATIONS HE may have had about the format, Gabriel had to concede that they had been right: Miguel and Ray, the local promoters, even the Triple L—they had all insisted that the City of Angels would embrace him and his new brand of exótico luchador.

Fans who had only seen him wrestle on television, on the syndicated shows that cut matches down to minutes, lined up long before the doors opened to secure ringside and aisle seats. Fueled by beer, cocktails, and drugs shared in dark corners of the hall, they sprang to raucous life when a video package showing El Ángel Exótico's Coming to America story played out on overhead monitors: highlights from the Triple L; footage from his airline commercial showing him walking through Mexico City International in costume; his arrival at the theater with Fanny Vice aboard the CHRYBOM; and finally, a live shot of him backstage, arm stretched high over his head, slowly limbering up before the bout.

And as the first bars of his introduction music played, women and men screamed as one.

He'd grown accustomed to it in Mexico City. He hadn't expected it in Los Angeles, not yet.

He stood at the back of the theater, near a stage door that led to the dressing rooms. He took a long breath, drawing it deep into his abdomen. He closed his eyes and raised his hand to his chest and crossed himself. He reached for the chain around his neck and lifted its cross to his lips. He opened his eyes to the camera, which had closed in on the face of El Ángel Exótico—the beautiful, arrogant, untouchable técnico.

Without hesitation he stormed the room to an assault of backbeat, follow spots, and smoke bombs. He made a beeline for the ring.

Gabriel allowed himself only the slightest break from character, when he spotted Jason in the ringside seats. Hearing his wolf-whistle as he entered the ring, Gabriel leapt atop the turnbuckle, looked directly at Jason, and blew a slow, exaggerated kiss off his fingertips.

The crowd approved, loudly. Jason beamed.

And for the first time in months, pre-match excitement electrified his body. He nodded almost imperceptibly toward Lola, which was her cue to attack.

GABRIEL SANK INTO THE FOLDING chair, rolled his head back, and exhaled. The Pyramid hadn't quite cleared, but the performers of Lucha Bang were ready to call it a night and claim the bar for themselves before it shut down once and for all. One by one, they had stepped up to congratulate him, to shake his hand, and tell him to join them for drinks at a bar down the street.

Fanny was first, waiting just offstage as he finished. He assumed she was waiting for Lola, but instead she pulled him into a hug, told him he was beautiful, and kissed him on the cheek, leaving a trail of garnet lipstick.

Stripped of masks, Lycra, and sequins, their characters cast aside for the night, the troupe resembled Miguel's ragtag ensemble of traveling luchadores. They teased and joked, showing a familial bond born of time spent together in gyms and buses up and down the West Coast.

Lola, already changed into torn jeans and a black tank top, mussed his hair as she walked by. She looked back over her shoulder and curled one corner of her mouth in a half-smile.

A hand grabbed his shoulder and dug in. Then on the other side, the shock of an ice-cold beer can rolled along his neck.

"Thought we'd get started a little early—like the old days," Ray said.

"In the old days, there would have been a tub full of beer in here." Gabriel said, popping the can open. "Where's Jason?"

"Are we there already? No, 'Thank you, Ray'? No, 'How thoughtful of you to get me a beer, Ray'?"

"Pretty much, yeah."

"Fine. He said he didn't want to get in the way. He's at the back bar. I'm also supposed to tell you that he bought the beer, not me."

"Well, you did bring it to me."

"That I did. And Gabe?"

"Yeah?"

Ray grabbed both his shoulders in his hands and pushed. "It's good to have you back, man."

Just as Ray had assured him, Gabriel emerged from the dressing room to find Jason sitting at the bar, sipping a Heineken, and chatting with one of the bartenders as she racked glasses and inventoried bottles. He was backlit, haloed in a shimmering light.

Jason's insurance carrier had officially declared him disabled, but it wasn't obvious to the naked eye. The one-time NFL prospect still looked ready to take the field. His leg may have been irreparably damaged, but his body was still a well-tuned instrument.

How he'd ever said no to Jason Michaels, Gabriel would never entirely understand. Now, after only a few days together, they had fallen into an easy rhythm, a give-and-take of conversation that had a familiarity that seemed to be built on a foundation of years of intimacy, not weeks. It also had an electric undercurrent, an urgency, buzzing under Gabriel's skin every time Jason drew close.

He had tried to tell himself to be patient, not to rush into anything, to let this *thing* breathe.

And the sight of Jason, awash in the bar's golden light, reassured him that patience was a waste of time.

"Hey, rock star. How long have you been standing there?" Jason rose from the bar and wrapped Gabriel in a brief hug. "You get your beer?"

"Raymond followed your instructions to the letter."

Gabriel's attention drifted, slipping from the green of Jason's eyes to his lips. They were full, creased in a smile, and hopelessly distracting. He stepped closer and kissed him. Jason's lips were everything Gabriel had imagined—warm, firm, welcoming.

"I just wanted to get that out of the way," Gabriel said.

"Out of the way?" Jason rolled his eyes upward, as if inspecting the ceiling. "I might have been thinking about doing that for a while, too. Like, months…"

It was more than Gabriel could take. He pulled Jason into his arms and kissed him again, harder this time, silencing him with an open mouth that pressed for more, licking at Jason's upper lip for an invitation in. He wrapped an arm around Jason's back, pulling him into a locked embrace.

They were interrupted by laughter, a wolf whistle, and a raucous round of applause that erupted from across the room. Leading the heckling? Ray.

"It's about time," he shouted across the hall. "Now, can you break it up so we can get out of here?"

"They want to buy me a drink," Gabriel whispered.

"Or five," Jason said.

"Come on, fellas. We promise not to tie you up for too long," Fanny laughed. "Unless, of course, you're into that."

Jason's fingers tangled with his own and gave his hand the slightest tug.

"Let's go," he said.

They promised each other they'd keep it short. One cocktail, sipped slowly enough to make it last a while. They knew this crowd; they'd be distracted soon enough. After lingering over Old Fashioneds, they could disappear into the night.

They idled in each other's orbit from the moment they left the Pyramid. Their hips brushed together as they walked down the block to a bar favored by locals and easily overlooked by tourists. Their shoulders bumped over cocktails. Their fingers occasionally drifted down as they stood, providing the lightest reassuring touch to a forearm, a waist, a wrist.

They let the conversations drift over them: Lola, swapping gossip with Ray and Jason about the Olympic team; Fanny, telling Gabriel about an artist she wanted to introduce him to; Ray. God only knew what story or joke he had shifted to from one moment to the next. They nodded. They smiled. They glanced at each other, knowingly.

Nearly two hours in, Gabriel felt the warmth of a hand splayed on his lower back and the intimate pressure of eyes searching for a cue. He set aside their empty glasses and led Jason out of the bar with a quick nod to Ray as they slipped out the door.

He knew that the moment they cleared the threshold, the city would be theirs.

It was a secret Gabriel had quickly unraveled, how Los Angeles shrinks at night; that the metropolis rolls up its darkened sidewalks before last call, reluctantly turning the streets over to those who live on them.

Three steps out of the bar, just beyond its shaded windows, he gripped Jason's hand and used it for torque, turning and pressing him against the building's stucco façade.

"Was that a wrestling move?" Jason asked. His words escaped in a breathless release as Gabriel nodded yes, an automated motion as he tipped his head and stretched his torso to reach Jason's lips. Tired of waiting, tired of polite gestures, he surged forward and unleashed months of pent-up frustration, want, and attraction denied.

There was no need to ease into the moment. He slid his tongue along Jason's sweet lips in a welcome request that was answered with an open mouth.

He could still taste bourbon on Jason's tongue.

Gabriel released his hand and slid it down. His thumb was drawn to the sharp angles of Jason's face. He followed along with his mouth, tracing a path to Jason's cheek, to his jaw, to that small spot behind his ear that elicited a soft moan from somewhere deep inside Jason's chest.

"Jason…"

Gabriel's mumbled whisper was cut off by the demanding horn of a black Chrysler 300 with an illuminated U in its windshield.

"Ray's gift to us," Jason said, catching his breath. "He said he'd spring for a ride home. He said something about staying with the girls tonight."

Gabriel exercised restraint as they hit the 101 South. At least he tried. His hands had other ideas, drifting to Jason as if by gravitational pull. Fingers aligned. Palms reached for knees, then higher.

He toyed with Jason's zipper, palmed at his crotch. Jason's gasp sent tremors down his spine. He glanced up toward the rear view mirror. The driver kept his eyes on the road and the stereo volume loud enough to block out Jason's rhythmic mumble, "Shit. Shit. Shit."

He shadowed Jason as they stumbled from car to loft. He was close enough to touch fingertip to spine, to caress his neck as Jason unlocked the door and threw it open.

He stopped mid-threshold to kiss him again, to bury his face in Jason's neck, where the rich scent of his cologne still hinted of leather, oak, and moss. Jason trembled and stumbled over his words.

"Do you want a drink?"

"Really?"

"… trying to be polite…"

Gabriel touched his fingertips to Jason's mouth. He traced the outline of his lips, cutting him off. "I don't want a drink. I don't want polite."

He cradled Jason's face in both hands, reeling him in while turning their bodies, allowing the door to shut behind them. His back to the wall, Gabriel rolled his head, inviting warm lips to map his neck, asking a tongue to circle his Adam's apple and a hand to slip down the placket of his shirt until it gripped and pulled the fabric free from his waistband.

Jason ran his palm around Gabriel's waist and up, charting the notches of his spine. He burrowed deep in Gabriel's shoulder, mouthed at his neck, murmured unsteady words of need and want, of having wished this from the start.

He tried to kneel, slowly, cautiously, reverently. He flinched as he put weight on his injured leg, shut his eyes and drew a deep breath, and looked up at Gabriel.

"Your knee. Don't—"

"I want to," Jason said. He unbuttoned Gabriel's jeans with a quick slip of the fingers and reached for the zipper.

"Stop."

Jason looked up. His lips were parted; his breathing was ragged.

"Stand up."

He helped Jason to his feet, kissed him gently, and took his hand.

"I'm not trading that for you hurting your knee any more than you already have," he said. He placed a soft kiss on Jason's jaw. "Take me to bed."

Jason turned Gabriel in his arms, pointed him down the hall, then wrapped his arms around his waist and nuzzled his neck as they walked in unison, with Jason's every step mirroring Gabriel's movement.

Fingers raced upward as they moved as one down the hall, unbuttoning Gabriel's shirt then slipping down again.

"Gabriel?"

Lips captured his ear lobe. A hand reached down his briefs. He could answer only with a cascading moan, an acknowledgment without words. He dropped to the bed, pulling Jason with him.

"Gabriel, fuck me."

Eyes open, Gabriel hesitated, and the sudden silence opened the door to the question.

"Unless you don't... In which case, I'm good with it, either way, I swear," Jason said, his body tensing.

It wasn't that Gabriel lacked want. Far from it. The want had built for months, even if he had suppressed it.

He had just never been asked before.

"It's not that. I just haven't..."

Jason sat up; the moment was interrupted. "We can slow down," he said. "We don't have to..."

"No. Oh god, no. I just... haven't... Arturo didn't really like..."

"Say no more," Jason said. His hand drifted down Gabriel's side until it settled on his hip. "Just tell me—what do you want?"

Gabriel propped himself up on an elbow and looked into Jason's eyes. He had little doubt that this man would do anything he wanted. All he needed to do was ask. He rolled Jason onto his back and kissed him deeply.

"This," Gabriel said. "I want this."

JASON TRACED THE GOLD CHAIN with his fingertips, following the delicate line to the base of Gabriel's neck.

"I like your cross," he said, rolling it between his fingers.

"I've had it as long as I can remember," Gabriel said.

Jason pushed himself up from the bed and leaned across Gabriel, reaching for the nightstand. He opened the drawer and pulled out a small jewelry box.

"I've been bad," he said. "I started taking it off for football, then I just got lazy."

He opened the box and pulled out a chain that held his own gold cross, yellow with white inlays, on a gold chain. "I used to leave it on twenty-four seven."

"Do you still go to church?"

Jason shook his head. "I used to go every week. We met at The Forum—the old arena where the Lakers used to play? Those services, they were like concerts. There was music, and the old ladies were talking back at the preacher, giving him encouragement, you know? Making sure the Lord heard it. And at the end of the service, you left that arena singing to yourself and believing 'The Word.'"

"And now?" Gabriel asked.

"Not so much. I got into college and fell out of the habit. Saturdays were game days, and Sundays I just felt kind of beaten up." He kissed Gabriel's cheek. "You?"

"Every Sunday, or my aunt would bust into my room, grab my ear, and drag me there herself. You don't miss Sunday service in that house, or confession."

Jason's eyes brightened. He flashed his thousand-watt smile. "Confession? Oh, I'd like to hear that."

"The only people who say that haven't had to say twenty Hail Marys," Gabriel said.

Jason kissed Gabriel's cross, then dotted kisses up his neck until he reached his lips. He traced lazy circles across Gabriel's chest with his fingertips and accented each thought with another soft kiss.

"You know, the cathedral's just up the street," he said.

"Cathedral?"

"Our Lady of the Angels. It hangs right over the freeway. We drove past it last night, but I don't think you were paying close attention."

Gabriel buried his face in his hands and shook his head, briefly reliving the backseat moment. He pulled his hands away and curled into Jason's side.

"We used to go to the cathedral every Sunday," he said. "Most people went to the basilica up the hill, but my aunt and uncle, they always insisted on the cathedral."

"The one built on top of the ruins?"

"They're all built on top of ruins," Gabriel said, shrugging. "They're built *from* ruins."

"We should go Sunday. We can get brunch after, check out downtown, maybe go to the MOCA. You'd like it."

Gabriel made absolutely no effort to bite back his grin, to play it cool, to hide what he was feeling.

"You have my whole day planned," he said.

Jason set the jewelry box back on the nightstand, rolled back into bed, and pulled Gabriel on top of him. "And you had my night planned, but I'm not complaining."

THE ROAD BETWEEN MEXICO CITY and Puebla isn't quite the same as traveling up the I-5 corridor. In Mexico, a road trip lasted a day, or a night. In the US, it lasted for weeks at a time, as the Lucha Bang troupe piled duffels of belongings into buses and shared food, transportation, meals, and the occasional bed in a series of generic motel rooms up and down the West Coast.

Roadies would set up the show a few days in advance—enough time for the wrestlers and dancers to get in a workout and sense the feel of the new surroundings. After an evening performance, or maybe two, they would strike the stage and board the buses for a late night ride to Fresno, San Luis Obispo, and a series of college towns.

Gabriel would try to sleep, but the cast and crew often had other things in mind: card games, movies, gossip, music, or reassuring handholding as they suffered bouts of homesickness.

"I'm starting to think I was little spoiled, working with Miguel."

Ray lifted the brim of the baseball cap he'd pulled over his eyes as he tried to catch a nap on a late night leg between Tacoma and Portland. "You're just figuring that out?"

He grinned, then yanked the cap back down over his face and folded his arms across his chest.

Gabriel leaned his head against the window of the coach and let the vibrations of the road sink into his skin. He couldn't sleep, again, and the hours between cities had become his catch-up time: on books; on league news from Mexico; or on texts with Miguel, or his aunt and uncle, or Jason. Toward the front of the bus, a group played cards, but he stayed away. He had learned a quick and costly lesson that Lola wasn't just a tough fighter. She was also a brutally deceptive card shark.

Often, he drifted off, watching the scenery fly by, letting his mind drift.

"They added a stop in Phoenix, right after the Vegas shows," Gabriel said.

Ray rustled beside him. He pulled the cap off, and stretched, and straightened up in his seat. He sat for a solid minute before responding.

"Is this your first time back?" he asked.

Gabriel focused on the passing trucks. He nodded as he watched the come-and-go light show.

"I haven't been there since I was ten."

As a child he'd had plenty of cause to question his aunt and uncle's edict against travel back to his birthplace. But that dissipated in time, as age and priorities shifted. Mexico City had been enough, for a while, and a visit to a gravesite wasn't likely.

The night owls—Lola, the minis, a couple of dancers—were deep into their regular poker game. Somehow, Lola kept lulling her companions into hand after hand of low stakes hold 'em on the tray tables of their tour coach, even though they must have known they had little chance of winning. Occasionally, shouts or a group moan would rise from the impromptu card game. Lola had won another hand.

"Are you going to go visit them?" Ray asked. His voice was unusually hushed, masked by the loud hum of tires on blacktop and the din of the late-night poker game.

"Huh?"

"Your parents."

It wasn't that Gabriel had not considered it. He had thought about nothing but the possibility of his first visit to his parents' gravesite since hearing about the schedule change.

"I don't know. It's outside of town—"

Ray rested his hand on Gabriel's forearm. "I can rent a car," he said. "I'll go with you."

It was something he hadn't considered in years, certainly not since he was old enough to make it happen. And now that it was a real possibility, Gabriel was frozen by the prospect. What would he do there? Leave flowers or a token to decorate their graves? Reflect?

As if he wasn't already doing that.

"It's important to be with family, Gabe. I'll stay out of your way. You've got plenty of time to think about it."

★ ★ ★

THEY LEARNED TO RELY ON each other both inside the ring and out of it.

Night after night, Lola challenged Gabriel's skills in the ring, put him through his paces, even if the ending had been scripted long before. Before each bout, they would review their plans and make adjustments, and she would still throw in something new. She would say that it was to keep Gabriel on his toes, to make sure he didn't get lazy.

There was no doubt about it, Lola was a beast.

She deserved to be a star. Instead, they played her as an oddity, the buff luchadora with a bad attitude, ready to take on any man. She could certainly put on a show.

The patented fire in her voice, the bravado, was something she turned on and off. The badass fighter who dominated the ring and controlled interviews as Electra was noticeably absent when Lola was left to her own devices.

He figured it out just two stops into the tour, in a cramped dressing room of an abandoned J.C. Penney that doubled as a country-western dance hall on Tuesdays and Thursdays.

Most of the performers had already changed into their alter egos, but Lola lagged behind, dressed in costume, but her hair still pony-tailed and the only color on her face the telltale hints of red ringing her eyes.

"You need help?" Gabriel asked.

Makeup spilled out in front of her. She looked and sounded lost. "Bonnie usually does this," she said.

"Never in Sacramento, right?" Gabriel said. It failed to lighten her mood.

"Or Fresno, or Tacoma, or Portland," Lola said. The self-described tough bitch sounded painfully vulnerable. "I never had to do this shit when I boxed."

"I had a hard time at first, too, even with the mask," Gabriel said. "They told me I needed to be glamorous, to do my eyes and lips. I'd never done anything like that before. I'd never wanted to. I figured if I wore a mask I wouldn't have to wear makeup."

"And?"

"And I was wrong."

He stood behind her and bent over her shoulder until they were cheek-to-cheek. "My coach used to do this for me, then I had to learn to do it for myself."

Miguel hadn't tolerated being Gabriel's makeup artist for long. He'd coached, and he'd expected Gabriel to learn, just like every other facet of the lucha libre game. Gabriel had been forced to learn the art of the smoky eye and pouty lip from early on. He touched her cheek to turn her face toward his.

"Let's see."

He touched up, and contoured, and powdered. He borrowed an electric-purple shadow from one of the dancers, and combined it with shimmering gunmetal gray to coordinate with her costume.

"And lips?" He dug through the makeup supplies and fetched a lipstick and coordinating pencil.

"Blood red. Pout for me."

That she could do.

He gently turned her shoulders until she faced the mirror.

"Look how beautiful you are. Look how *tough* you are. Now the only question is the hair: Scary Spice or Sporty Spice?"

"Scary," she said, grinning. "Definitely Scary Spice."

As he teased out her hair, she met his eyes in the mirror and mouthed *thank you.*

"One more city, and I get my girl back," she said. "What about your man?"

Her former hometown had always been good to Bonnie McCreary, so it made sense that Fanny Vice would return to the Lucha Bang stage in San Francisco and stick around through Las Vegas.

Jason was another matter.

"Back to school," he said. "I won't see him until we're back in LA, and they've added some extra stops."

They had made do with texts and, when their free time aligned, calls. If he got especially lucky, Gabriel would grab a seat alone in the back of the bus on a late night ride, plug in his headset, and quietly get Jason off over a mobile video app. It was less than ideal, a lot less.

"There you go," he said, moving out of the way so Lola could check her reflection in the mirror. She bit back a smile, but it was clear she liked what she saw.

"I can teach you if you'd like."

She gave his cheek a quick kiss on the way out the door.

"I'd rather have my regular makeup artist back."

★ ★ ★

THEY DROVE IN SILENCE FROM the Sky Harbor rental car lot to South Tucson.

The relatively short distance between Las Vegas and Phoenix meant time off for the cast and crew of Lucha Bang. The wrestlers and dancers had opted to stay in Las Vegas for the day, but Gabriel and Ray hitched a ride with the crew bus carrying Lucha Bang's set pieces and portable ring. Once they rented a car, they hit the road again, ninety minutes deeper into the desert.

Gabriel clutched his backpack and let his head bob silently along with the road. Ray played aimlessly with the radio dial until he gave up fifteen minutes out of town.

"You want to stop for flowers?" he asked.

Gabriel watched the road.

"There should be a market just down the street," he answered. He wouldn't have been able to find the cemetery without the help of his aunt, but he retained a hazy memory of flower stands in the parking lot of a nearby market. The market was gone, replaced by a discount shoe store and a sandwich shop, but the flowers remained.

They followed the line of palm trees into the Catholic cemetery, where the road narrowed and wound itself around monuments and tombstones until they found a tree-lined corner near the back.

"This is it," Gabriel said. "It's around here somewhere."

Ray pulled to a stop and shut off the engine. "You sure this is the spot?"

"My aunt gave me the directions, and it's in this number range."

"Do you want me to stay?" Ray asked.

Gabriel shook his head and opened the car door. "No need. I'll be fine."

"All right then, you're on your own. I'm going to go get a coffee, and you text me when you want me to come back, okay?"

"Yeah." Gabriel climbed out of the rental and grabbed the flowers off the floorboard. "Ray? Thanks."

"You bet, buddy."

It struck him as odd—he couldn't bring himself to think *funny*—how all the graves represented so many different lives: mothers, fathers, lovers, children. But after a few years, they all started to blur together. What had been the new section of the cemetery at the time of his parents' deaths had long since been declared full, and the grass grew in a consistent mottle of brown and green in the days between maintenance.

Each memorial plaque in the section had the same patina and the same format: a simple bronze rectangle, topped by a cross.

Even the tombstones followed a particular pattern and style, as if the Tucson diocese had been running a flash sale.

He counted out the spaces and looked for the numbered guides at the end of each row until he found it: a smallish tombstone in gray granite with "Romero" carved across the top. Below it, two rings interlinked.

Luis Angel and Maria Gabriella Contreras
Loving Father. Loving Mother.

He dropped to the grass and sat in front of the marker, where he spent a half an hour in motionless solitude.

He remembered the backpack and the items he'd brought: tracing paper and a charcoal pencil. He brushed the grass away from the marker and rubbed at the stone, copying the inlaid rings, then rolled it up and replaced it in his bag.

As a child mourning the loss of his parents, he hadn't understood why so many graves were brightly decorated with flowers, balloons, flags, and memorabilia. But after taking time out each year to honor the dead in Mexico City, he'd come to understand the importance of the ofrenda.

He set the flowers—traditional marigolds laced with freesia, his mother's favorite—at the base of the marker, a vivid collection of yellows, reds, and purples.

He pulled items methodically from his backpack, organizing them at the base of the marker: the worry doll his mother had made for him in his youth, which he had clutched so tightly throughout their funeral Mass and had kept as a personal talisman; a card with a pop art print of El Santo that he'd found at the Lucha Bang souvenir stand; a tiny rainbow flag that he planted in the soft grass; and a prayer candle.

He pulled the last items from the bottom of the bag and set one on either side of the marker: two wrestler's masks. The first was a professional mask—white with gold-winged trim, a cutaway jawline, and a cross centered down the laces. The other was considerably smaller—a red and white child's mask, trimmed in silver.

He kissed his fingertips and set them on the grave marker, then settled on the grass to tell them his story, to fill in the gaps.

He was self-conscious at first, embarrassed to talk to grass and stone, so he started simply. He spoke of school, of museums, of sport. Of his aunt and uncle's dedication to his education and to church, and how they had been kind and loving, even when he hadn't earned it. And he spoke of arenas, and the people within them: the luchadores who had shaped his life as much as any family; the luchadores who had become family; of his successes and his failures.

"I thought maybe I'd found it, but now I'm not so sure," he said. "How do you know the difference between happiness and... drifting?"

He leaned back in the grass and listened to distant traffic and to a mockingbird antagonizing a small hawk that had landed too close to its nest. It was as good a time as any to listen to the world, and he was grateful that Ray knew how to nurse a cup of coffee.

★　★　★

"Wouldn't this be easier if you just moved in?"

Jason stretched out on the couch with the television on, as Gabriel put a handful of fresh T-shirts, jeans, and underwear in the dresser drawer—the one reluctant sign of domesticity he had allowed himself in Jason's home. He had been here before, with a drawer in an apartment, and he wasn't ready for more, not yet.

Besides, he was gone often enough that the drawer gave him weeks of use before the contents had to be replaced and washed.

They'd had the conversation before. It wasn't even much of a conversation, just the suggestion, repeated every month or two.

But it had all happened much too fast for Gabriel to take that next step, even if he did spend half his nights in Jason's loft. And he couldn't abandon Ray, his roommate on and off the road.

They'd found a reasonably priced two-bedroom apartment in North Hollywood—no beach, no infinity pool—but the rent was manageable on their inconsistent earnings. It wasn't an excuse that he would be able to use much longer. Their circumstances were changing, quickly, for the better.

Ray had taken a day job as a trainer in a swank gym that catered to customers seeking the appearance of perfection. He was happy to oblige and, between his training skills and his engaging nature, had become the gym's go-to trainer. He could more than afford the apartment on his own.

"I'm never around," Gabriel said.

"That should make it even easier," Jason responded. He grabbed a handful of popcorn from a bowl on the coffee table and kept his attention fixed on the screen.

Gabriel crept up behind him. "And what would Ray do?"

"Ray can handle... *Ooooph!*"

Gabriel vaulted over the couch, landed on top of Jason, and sent popcorn flying.

"You were saying?" Gabriel said, laughing and resting his forearms across Jason's chest, using them as a pillow.

"You're heavier than you look," Jason said. He wrapped his arms around Gabriel's waist and turned him so they were on their sides, face-to-face, nearly toppling off the sofa. "Ray can afford his own place now." Jason kissed him, an attempted distraction that Gabriel wasn't about to fall for.

"And so can I."

He had become the star of the Los Angeles lucha libre scene and the face of Lucha Bang, which had led to other offers. It hadn't hurt that Bonnie had put in a few good words here and there. He landed a low-profile commercial for a fast food chain that wanted a generic luchador in its ads, and a high-profile photo shoot for an athletic wear start-up that was interested in his body, rather than his mask.

The Triple L, which still owned the rights to his character, flew Gabriel to Mexico City to shoot promotions for Triple L TV, its American television start-up. El Ángel Exótico also landed a tequila ad and additional spots for the airline that had already hired him once for its "Spread Your Wings" campaign. Though the league got its cut for the character use, Gabriel's share of the royalties contributed to an increasingly comfortable income.

"As much as you're gone, does it even make sense for you to get your own place?"

"That's why I stay with Ray," Gabriel said. He tried to sound playful, with a teasing lilt in his voice, but Jason didn't laugh.

He kissed Jason's cheek.

"Give me time, okay? I don't think *we're* ready," he said. He drew their foreheads together. "But I hope you keep asking."

He kissed Jason again, harder this time, a check to make sure his words stuck. They must have. Jason tangled his fingers in Gabriel's hair and wrapped his leg over Gabriel's hip to pull him close. If it hadn't been for the sound of keys in the door, Gabriel was fairly certain he would have bought himself another month, at least. Instead, he rolled off the couch and onto the floor, leaving Jason flat on his back.

Ray stepped into the loft with a marked bounce to his step, a man on a giddy mission. He had a surprise, a night on the town for the three of them.

He just didn't say which town.

"What's the plan, Ray? Dodgers?" Jason asked.

"Nope."

"Some new club only you've heard of?" Gabriel asked. It wouldn't be the first time.

Ray laughed and pulled three tickets out of his wallet. "Lucha libre," he said, nodding with self-satisfaction. "I found a Groupon."

"What? We're off tonight. We are *not* going to lucha libre."

"*Lucha Extrema,* my friend—a cage match." He let the last words sit for a while, hanging on the A's for emphasis. "Pico Rivera, baby."

Gabriel grabbed at his temple and ran his hand down his face until he had covered his mouth. From the start, he had successfully avoided extrema matches, just as Miguel had cautioned.

He had always followed his mentor's advice about keeping a safe distance from dangerous underground matches. Over time, Gabriel recognized the purpose behind Miguel's caution: the scar down his back, the other on his thigh. When Gabriel got up the nerve to ask, Miguel told him about having once fought in an extrema match. It had landed him in surgery for a collapsed lung and resulted in stitches along his arm and shoulder, where he had been slashed by razor wire.

Gabriel remembered the scars from the first time he met Miguel in the dressing room at Arena México, and that had always been enough to keep him far away from the matches.

"It's not like you're booked to fight in it, Gabe. We're just going to go watch. C'mon. No one's going to recognize us."

Gabriel and Jason looked at each other. Jason shrugged.

"He's your brother," Gabriel said.

"He's your roommate," Jason countered.

Lucha Extrema had a reputation as a rogue offshoot of legitimate lucha libre. Usually found in border towns where lucha leagues didn't bother to travel, the matches were built on a foundation of blood. Though its promoters pitched it as lucha libre's answer to ultimate fighting, it was also the domain of the desperate, of luchadores who couldn't be booked for a match elsewhere.

The Pit had all the charm of its namesake. Dank and dark around the edges, illuminated by overhead fluorescent tubes, it looked like an arena on wheels, ready to pick up and flee at the first sign of the police, or Alcohol and Beverage Control, or the county health inspectors.

Gabriel had heard of The Pit, a former packing plant that had been converted into a boxing club until its fighters had jumped ship. Some had moved on to professional clubs, some to the rapidly growing world of mixed martial arts. It had been picked up by a small-time promoter a couple of years later who had tried to run a discount Mexican league—all lucha, no frills.

But Los Angeles audiences expected frills, even if they had discount coupons.

Close to bankruptcy, the promoter had moved further and further to the fringe of traditional lucha libre. He rigged the ring so he could remove the ropes and replace them with chain-link fence, making a cage that could be dropped over the wrestling surface. Inside, he littered the mats with tacks and even broken glass.

Fans with a lust for blood and beer began to trickle in.

Jason reached for Gabriel's hand. Gabriel turned and shot him a warning look. It was one thing to be a comfortably out couple in the Arts District; it was another at an extrema match in Pico Rivera.

"I have no idea why I let you talk us into this," Jason muttered, glancing at Ray.

"Says the big, bad Bruin." Ray laughed and surveyed the half-empty arena. "Looks like we've got our choice of seats. Want to go ringside?"

Gabriel and Jason answered in unison, a quick and absolute "No!" They sat back several rows, away from flying debris and the rowdiest of the fans.

It started out simply enough: a luchas de apuestas between two young luchadores in an awkwardly choreographed brawl. One was enmascarado, wearing a plain blue mask and matching wrestling tights; the other dressed in fatigues and wrestling boots. He wore his dark hair long and wrestled without a mask.

The match featured no discernable story other than it was mascara contra cabellera: the loser's mask or hair would go to the winner. And while neither wrestler exhibited particular finesse in the fine art of lucha acrobatics, the enmascarado possessed some skills, throwing himself at his opponent and rolling out of attempted pins with relative ease.

At the end of the third round, he had locked his opponent's elbows against his back and his face against the mat. The referee raised the luchador's hand above his head and pulled a chair into the ring for the loser. He handed the winner an electric razor.

"Here we go," Gabriel said. "Time for the haircut."

The enmascarado raised his arms in the air and gestured to the audience, encouraging catcalls and rhythmic clapping, as he locked his opponent's head in place by reaching an elbow around his neck. With the crowd's jeers and boos playing as a soundtrack, he shaved the loser's hair in long strips, holding each aloft before tossing it aside.

The fans went wild.

"That ever happen to you?" Jason asked.

"You don't claim the hair of a masked wrestler. You claim the mask," Gabriel said. "And no one's taking mine."

"It's the ultimate insult," Ray explained. "You lose a mask match, and you lose more than your mask. The winner claims your identity."

They discussed the masks almost reverently. Even Ray dropped his voice to a pious murmur.

"The mask is sacred," Gabriel said. "Pull off your opponent's mask during the bout and you're disqualified. It's only removed if you've lost a betting match."

"And then you have to start over," Ray added. "It ends careers, man."

As they spoke, the jaula was lowered to the floor, covering the ring. A crew sprinkled debris from buckets onto the mat that looked like broken glass, screws, and nails.

It was announced as a trios cage match. Theoretically, two teams of three would square off. Realistically, it was a mass of bodies fighting each other. They showed little skill, training, or care for lucha traditions. The wrestlers focused on driving their opponents to the floor and avoiding the debris strewn across the ring.

They ignored many of the customary rules of lucha libre. Referees didn't bother to break it up when a wrestler was pinned against the cage, and a blind eye was turned when a fighter kicked an opponent in the groin.

Wrestlers were bloodied in short order. Two were eliminated.

The action sucked Gabriel in despite his better judgment. He found himself caught up in the deplorable conditions under which they fought, and in the reactions of their fierce fan base.

Jason grimaced. "Ugly."

"That's the point. It's not for me, but some of these guys, if they had decent coaching, a real league? A couple of them could make it. They're just stuck in the wrong place," Gabriel said.

Fans came and went: young men in jeans and T-shirts headed to the beer stands, to the porta-pots, or to the taped-off smoking areas.

Against the current, one group stood out. They arrived late in the fight card and made a beeline for the ringside seats. Three of their group-of-four were middle aged and reeking of corporate downtime.

Only the fourth seemed at home. He was younger and blessed with the carved physique of a professional athlete. His hair obscured by a knit beanie, he wore tight black jeans, and his muscular torso was cleanly outlined by the wafer-thin sweater that clung to his frame.

He turned to sit down, and Gabriel froze.

Ray elbowed him. "What's up?"

Gabriel nodded toward the men.

Ray squinted. His face tensed.

"Holy fuck."

THE BIGGEST LIFE LESSONS MAY be taught early, but they gain focus with age, or so Gabriel had been told, in the moments when a person looks back and recognizes what he had once been too blinded by youth to understand. Gabriel had bought into that line of thinking for years, assuming that his collection of experiences would somehow, some day, make perfect sense.

After seeing Arturo sitting ringside with three men who looked as though they belonged in corporate suites, he wasn't so sure. He wondered instead if the true lesson was that the moment the pieces of your life start to fall into place, something comes along to knock them all out of alignment.

"I thought he was in Japan," Ray said.

"Last I heard…"

Lucha libre had a fan base in Japan, most recently mined by the LC and spearheaded by one of its most popular rudos, El Cadejo.

"Miguel didn't mention anything?" Ray asked.

"No," Gabriel said.

He spoke with Miguel often—on the phone, in chat rooms, on Skype. Though they lived fifteen hundred miles apart, Miguel still managed Gabriel from afar. And he had said nothing about Arturo Guerra coming to Los Angeles.

"Let's get out of here," Gabriel said.

He made a hasty retreat; Jason followed silently in his footsteps. Ray was the only one who suggested they stay, if for no other reason than to figure out what was going on, because he was certain that he also recognized one of the executives.

"The American. The guy with the silver hair and sunglasses—and what the fuck is up with that, anyway? That's Matt Baron, president of the League of American Wrestlers. You know, the guy who gets in the ring and says, 'I am the LAW!'?" He mimicked Baron's Texas accent, badly.

"I knew I recognized him," Gabriel said. "You don't think—?"

He looked toward the kitchen, where Jason had been leaning against the counter, listening but not speaking for nearly half an hour. His contribution to the conversation had been limited to a "yes," a "no," and an occasional grunt since they'd left Pico Rivera.

Ray shrugged.

"It may be nothing more than some promo trip," Ray said. "You should check again with Miguel. Or maybe Oscar knows something."

But Miguel's contacts at the Triple L were suspiciously mute on the subject of El Cadejo.

He responded the day after receiving Gabriel's text. He'd gone straight to the top, to Oscar Chavez. Oscar had mumbled something about a possible promotion and changed the subject.

"If Oscar knows something—and Oscar *always* knows something—he's not talking," Miguel said.

So he'd gone down the line: agents, trainers, luchadores, and even league assistants.

"I got nothing," he said.

By the time Lucha Bang threw open the doors to the Pyramid the following weekend, Gabriel knew no more than he had in the hours after the cage match.

He set it aside as best he could and prepared for the show. He lined his eyes in gold and his lips in glittered rouge; he set his mask in place. He laced his boots to mid-thigh and kissed the cross hanging from his neck.

He approached the ring and leapt atop the turnbuckle, looping his cape between his fingers so he could raise it winglike toward the audience, toward the ringside seats—where Arturo Guerra sat alongside Matt Baron, Oscar Chavez, and another man he could only assume was affiliated with the LC.

They disappeared as soon as the match ended. They didn't come backstage. They didn't corner him in the dressing room. They slipped away without a word.

The message appeared in his email the next morning from Oscar, cc'd to Miguel.

SUBJECT: Meeting
Gabriel, I enjoyed Lucha Bang last night, and I'm sorry I couldn't stay to say hello, but I had a late meeting with our friends from the LC. We have agreed in principle to an event I want to discuss with you. I'd like to meet Monday at 10 a.m. at the Triple L office in Culver City. Miguel, you can join us on video.

Acid churned in his stomach. Gabriel had always thought that he had forged and maintained a good relationship with the Triple L executive since their first meeting, but Oscar had appeared like a specter in Los Angeles, along with a ghost Gabriel thought he had exorcised long ago.

FROM THE MOMENT THAT GABRIEL first convinced Oscar Chavez to alter his Triple L contract allowing his move to Los Angeles, it had been clear that the league had a plan for US operations, and at its core was American television.

The Triple L's presence in the US market had been small, but Oscar had forged relationships with American Spanish-language networks to broadcast the league's bouts from Mexico City. While the show's audience grew, Oscar had worked quietly with his American television partners to build his own network, a crossover business featuring content that would appeal to English-speaking Latinos who had grown up with Telemundo, Univision, and ESPN Desportes.

Triple L TV had debuted on basic cable, jointly operated by the league and its US network partners. The Americans would run it as an offshoot, a specialized sports network they had modeled as the ESPN for Mexican wrestling, with talk shows and movies padding the content between syndicated lucha shows.

But old movies and rebroadcast bouts from Arena México would not sustain it. Triple L TV needed a centerpiece, complete with sex, violence, and the style and quality of American television, to break into the young, English-speaking, and increasingly affluent market it sought.

Oscar explained it with rehearsed precision.

Gabriel sat in the glass-enclosed Triple L conference room with Oscar as Miguel looked on from his office at Gimnasio de la Ciudad, broadcast on a fifty-inch monitor at the front of the room. As he had in his office on Paseo de la Reforma, Oscar had made sure that his Los Angeles headquarters were built with sleek, modern fixtures and contemporary artists' takes on classic lucha libre imagery.

"We've had plans to take Triple L TV to the next level and now we think we have the formula to make it work," Oscar said. "Gabriel, you've been such an asset to us. You know that, right? You've brought in new fans and added something fresh to our lineup of estrellas. And you've helped us see that we can succeed in this market, and much faster than we had planned. We're about to take a big step and we want you to be a part of it."

Gabriel looked up at the monitor. Miguel listened, impassive. He wore his best poker face as Oscar spoke of Gabriel's short, bright history with his league. But when he finally spoke, Miguel cut to the quick.

"Get to it, Oscar. What are you up to, and how is the LC involved?"

Oscar chuckled and took a long drink of water before continuing—a practiced pause.

It had been an opportunity, both promotional and financial, that he couldn't turn down, he said. It would be an outstanding platform for the launch of *American Lucha,* Triple L TV's signature show.

The LC had successfully spent the past several years building an Asian fan base by exporting its young stars to compete in Japan. And the recent standout had been a rudo, one they knew well. El Cadejo had become so popular on the tour that he'd caught the eye of a visiting American wrestling executive, who wanted to buy out his LC contract and try him out on the US pro circuit.

"What does this have to do with Gabriel, or the Triple L?" Miguel asked. He made no effort to be the calculated negotiator of their first meeting with Oscar. His voice was firm, distrustful.

Oscar directed his response at Gabriel, watching him closely as he spoke.

"They don't want to introduce him to their fans cold. They need a launch platform. It needs to be big—something that will draw existing lucha fans to the American pro circuit."

Gabriel already suspected what was coming, or at least whom it involved. He could feel it in the buildup, in Oscar's reluctance to spit out the news.

"The LC has a good memory," Oscar said. "They've been watching your Lucha Bang shows."

It would amount to a three-way deal. The American league would buy out two years of Arturo's contract from the LC, which would still be free to use his likeness in its promotions. They would launch his US career on the *American Lucha* debut. The Triple L would have its signature match, a grudge bout between popular, attractive young luchadores with a history of bad blood.

"And Gabriel?" Miguel asked. The words escaped him as a sudden, defeated gust.

"It will be mascara contra mascara, a campeonato," Oscar said. "A championship of good versus evil. Our angel versus their devil, to the end."

The loser would give up his identity; the winner would move on to a bigger contract.

And Ángel would lose, by necessity, as well as by legally binding contract.

"What's in it for you?" Gabriel said. "This is going to be the launch of your American show, and you're going to let your competitor win?"

Oscar looked at Miguel, straight into the camera. There was no need to plead his case. What's done was done. He turned to Gabriel.

"You know why auto malls are so successful? Why car dealers line up next to their competitors? Because it's good for their business. It brings customers, new customers who might not have noticed them otherwise. This is the same thing. We leverage their popularity with their fans to bolster our launch."

"But why would you want to lose? It's *your* show."

"It's so they can set themselves up as the underdog, Gabriel," Miguel said. "And because they got paid."

"Exceptionally well," Oscar said.

Miguel squinted into the lens of his laptop camera as if his old friend from the Triple L were inside it.

"You still haven't said what's in it for Gabriel," he said.

"We'll set up a championship match a month or two in advance. Gabriel will earn the title, win a belt as the US champion luchador, the original *American Lucha* champion. No one can take that away from you, Gabriel."

"And what does that matter if he loses, if he can't be El Ángel anymore?"

"Someday, we'll resurrect El Ángel Exótico. In the meantime, you wrestle as someone else. Fans will figure it out. We can drop a tip to *Lucha Semanal.*"

The room went silent.

"So he starts over," Miguel said.

"Yes, like everyone else who loses a betting match."

Miguel shut his eyes. His chest rose in a deep inhale—a move Gabriel recognized as Miguel's way to calm his nerves, the same technique he had taught Gabriel.

"Why?"

"Residuals, Miguel. You know how this works. He'll come back bigger than ever, eventually."

There was a knock at the conference room door, and Oscar's assistant poked her head into the room. "They're here, Mr. Chavez."

He nodded, and she opened the door wide, beckoning in her guests: the executives of the LC, along with a quiet, solemn Arturo Guerra.

He looked different—older, larger, a bit rougher around the edges. His hair was shorn, close-cropped. A new line of tattoos extended higher than before, to the base of his neck.

They eyed each other cautiously, without greeting, while the promoters killed time with small talk. On the monitor, Miguel leaned on his elbows, supporting his chin with his clasped hands. The LC delegation took their seats, and Oscar started the meeting anew.

"We wanted to bring everyone together to make sure we're all on the same page," Oscar said. "We think this is a dynamic opportunity, to have three leagues working cooperatively like this. It opens doors."

"In one event, the LAW will launch the American career of one of the LC's most popular global luchadores, and the Triple L will kick off its new network featuring one of its rising stars," Oscar said.

"Yes," Miguel said, spitting out the words. "It's very *dynamic* to sacrifice one of your most popular luchadores. It's very *cooperative* to let him know he's been thrown under the bus minutes before your partners from the other leagues arrived."

Oscar turned to the visitors, trying to wrest control of the meeting.

"We only just shared our plans with Gabriel and Miguel—"

"So I *am* the last to find out," Gabriel said. He looked at Arturo, then up to the monitor, to Miguel, who looked as stunned and sick as Gabriel felt. "I see."

He pushed his office chair back from the conference table.

"Are we okay here?" Oscar said. A voice snapped back at him from the video screen.

"No, we're not. I'd like a chance to talk with Gabriel privately before you sit everyone down at the table to confirm something you've only just told us about. We'll be in touch."

The monitor went dark.

Gabriel could feel Arturo's eyes bore through him during the exchange, but he said nothing until Gabriel opened the door to leave.

"I only heard about this a few days ago," he said. "We get to wrestle together again."

Gabriel stared at him, silent and impassive. Arturo lowered his voice.

"Gabriel, this is it. We made it," he said. "Think of the opportunity."

"Think of Miguel's hospital bills," Gabriel said. He glanced back at the conference room, at Oscar's stunned face, turned, and left.

HE PACED THE ROOM FOR close to an hour in a repeated oval that led him through the living area, past the kitchen, to the window-lined wall—the one overlooking the mural of a setting sun.

About every third pass, he stopped in front of the glass and looked out at the fiery oranges, yellows, and reds dripping from the art, interrupted by rays of dark purple text.

Arms wrapped around his waist; a chest curled against his back. Jason nestled his chin on Gabriel's shoulder.

"Do you think it's setting? Or is it rising?" Gabriel asked, still focused on the mural.

"I think it's rising," Jason said with conviction. "Besides, it's on the eastern wall, so it can't be setting."

"And here I was about to say that you're just being optimistic."

"Always. But this? Pure science."

Jason turned Gabriel in his arms, drawing him close. He brought his hand around to Gabriel's chest and placed it over his heart. "I didn't want to interrupt you."

"But?"

"But I invited the girls over, and Ray. Some pizza, some company. You okay with that? I know you've got a lot on your mind, but…"

"It's good to be around family," Gabriel said, finishing the thought. He wrapped his arms around Jason's neck and swayed to the sounds of the street in a private slow dance. "And how much time do we have before they get here?"

"Seeing as that looks like Ray's car down the block, I'm going to say not enough."

Gabriel unraveled himself from the embrace with a disappointed grunt.

"You're not upset? You've just been off by yourself the past few days and…"

"…and you love me and want me to cheer up."

"Something like that," Jason said, smiling.

Heavy steps approached the door. Gabriel took Jason's hand and raised it to his lips.

"I love you, too."

He had quietly sulked for days, and he knew that an impromptu pizza party was Jason's gentle way of nudging him out of it. Perhaps he should have been annoyed to have company sprung on him without notice, but Gabriel couldn't will it. It was Jason's open heart that had drawn Gabriel to him in the first place. And the eyes, if he were being honest with himself. And the lips, definitely the lips.

He understood Jason's train of thought. When times are tough, it's best to be surrounded by family. And Ray? Ray was family, just as Lola and Bonnie, the odd couple of Lucha Bang, had become. Jason saw to it that Gabriel had his patchwork family at his side for support, advice or, if necessary, a game of beer pong.

Raising a six-pack aloft in each hand, Lola barged through the door. "You know what we need to do?"

"I'm almost afraid to ask," Gabriel said.

"Get sloppy drunk," she said, opening a bottle. "Bonnie's got the tequila."

"And a few other goodies," Bonnie said with a wink. She handed Jason the bag from Liquorama with a kiss on the cheek.

The foursome had a mission and it involved liquor and love. They wholly committed themselves to drawing Gabriel out of his funk through constant chatter—about sports, or art, or that hot underwear model on the new billboard down the street—about anything, so long as it got him talking. They could eventually shift to the subject at hand. He knew the game and slowly began to play along.

"Is there any way you get out of it? A loophole?" Lola asked.

Bonnie shook her head slowly. She had already asked a lawyer friend who handled her business deals to look over Gabriel's contract.

"Only if he wants to get fired—or sued," Ray said.

The Triple L had stood firm. They owned the rights to El Ángel Exótico and they were committed to their plans. El Ángel would become their US champion, and then be sacrificed for ratings, revenue, and the high stakes launch of *American Lucha*.

"What does Miguel say?" Ray asked.

"That I should be true to myself," Gabriel said.

As quiet as he had been around his friends, he had spoken regularly with Miguel, trying to find an out, a loophole, or some divine intervention.

Miguel played on Oscar's sense of tradition, on his business acumen, on their friendship—and failed.

"You'll still be able to wrestle. You won't be shamed," he had said, trying to soften the blow.

"You and I both know that's not true. Are you telling me to go along with it?"

"I'm not telling you to do anything. This is your decision, and it's not one I ever had to face. You've played clean. You pressed for change, but you always played by the rules in the ring, and the league's been good to you because of it—until now."

It had gotten to the point where the video calls would be interrupted by long moments of silence, mentor and protégé both deep in thought. They would break it up by changing the subject.

"Remember when you sat me down and lectured me?"

"Which time, Gabriel? There were so many."

Gabriel had rolled his eyes. It almost made him smile.

"About being proud to be an exótico, about how I represent my community, my family. When you introduced me to Rosalinda. When you told me there were straight exóticos."

"Yes."

"I was thinking about that the other day. It still gets under my skin. Why is it okay for there to be straight exóticos, but an out luchador can't be anything *but* an exótico?"

"What's your point, boy? Still uncomfortable?"

"I'm proud of who I am. I'm proud of Ángel. We pushed boundaries, but they can only bend so far. I could never *quite* break through. I thought coming here would change that. It didn't. I'm a prop."

It wasn't limited to his identity as an exótico. It was the entire structure of Lucha Bang and its televised successor, *American Lucha*.

"There's no respect for what this is, for the tradition. They aren't real bouts. No stories."

On the monitor, Miguel had covered his face with his hands, squeezing his temples and the bridge of his nose. His eyes were shut. He didn't look up.

"Gabriel? Have you ever considered what's next?"

His words had connected with Gabriel like a plancha. Of course he had. At workouts, alone in his thoughts on the treadmill. During sleepless nights, with Jason's arm draped over his shoulder. In the back pews of the Cathedral, which he had taken to visiting with increasing frequency.

Oscar had made a bold decision. He likened it to a television show killing off a favorite character. It always got people talking, and Oscar Chavez wanted people talking about *American Lucha*.

"He talked with Oscar again yesterday," Jason said. "He's not getting out of it."

"It doesn't change, does it?"

Bonnie got up from the couch and tucked her arm in his.

"What do you mean, honey?"

"It's never been my decision," Gabriel said.

"Then *you* make the change. You take their belt, and then you rewrite their script. They want change? You give 'em change. They want an *American Luchador?* Then we'll give them an American luchador."

Across the room, Jason began to smile.

"She's right," he said. "Your contract says that you have to do what the league says, and the league says it wants you de-masked."

"Yeah. And?"

"Gabe? They didn't say *how.*"

★ ★ ★

HE HAD STIPULATIONS.

He wanted at least three months as champion, even if it were champion in name only. He wanted enough time for the title to be established in the books. That shouldn't be a problem. The leagues still had logistics to be worked out.

He also wanted the belt and the exposure that came with it—and a bonus for being released from a popular character that he had developed for the Triple L.

And when the time came to take a dive, Gabriel wanted both a private dressing room, "a place to be alone with my thoughts," he would say, and to be released from the remaining months of his contract. He wanted, as Oscar himself had suggested, time off. He didn't want to fill the gap with a temporary character assigned to him by the Triple L.

Oscar Chavez didn't have to agree to anything. But Gabriel's terms were a small price to pay for having a popular luchador's cooperation, and for extending the possibility of working with him in the future. El Ángel Exótico's days with the Triple L might be numbered, but Gabriel Romero would likely be a luchador for years to come, preferably with the Triple L, eventually.

So he agreed, with his own asterisk. Gabriel had to sign a non-compete clause prohibiting him from signing any time soon with either the LC or the LAW. It would limit him to independent status, which would likely drive him back to the Triple L just as soon as he missed the limelight.

They set up the campeonato, a match against a Boyle Heights luchador, a former Marine who figured prominently in their future plans for *American Lucha*. They would play up the macho Marine versus glam exótico storyline to set up Gabriel's victory and eventual downfall. At the end of the bout, El Cadejo would emerge from backstage, claiming the title should be his and vowing revenge.

The stage was set for *American Lucha*.

★ ★ ★

CREATING CHANGE CAN BE MORE complicated than building from the ground up. What's too much? What's not enough? Is change in the details, or is it a thing that pushes one past a place of manageable discomfort to where the risk forces a leap, or a dive?

As the new owner of the Pyramid Theatre, Oscar Chavez had made sure that it underwent extensive renovation before its television debut. A ring, larger and sturdier than the original, had been placed near the center of the room, arena-style, so that bouts would be performed like theater in the round. The club had been turned into a makeshift television studio, with camera pens and platforms set strategically around the theater. It had exchanged some of its grubby mystique for primetime gloss. The league had enhanced the décor and added a bank of oversized monitors both for the benefit of the live audience and for a visual backdrop for television.

The league had completely remodeled the backstage to include a training room, locker bays, and both group and private dressing rooms, the largest of which had been assigned to Gabriel for debut night.

There was room for an entourage, but he requested only Bonnie to help him get ready for the match, just as she had been doing for the past three months.

Oscar wanted the characters "tweaked" for Triple L TV, "more relatable for American audiences," he had said.

Bonnie interpreted that as carte blanche for an overhaul: music, costume, makeup, props—nothing was off limits. And as the work came full circle, she added a final touch: a temporary tattoo on his shoulder, a rose in the style of Mexican folk art.

"For Rosa," she said.

"For Rosa," Gabriel repeated. "Thank you."

The night's card was already well underway, and the thump of a driving bass beat and the roar of the crowd pierced the room like muted thunder, accented by a soft tap, tap, tap. It repeated itself moments later, louder, the determined rap of knuckles against particle board. Jason opened the door and poked his head into the room.

"I'm headed to my seat. I just wanted to take a picture for Miguel… Whoa, wow! Damn, Bonnie."

She took an exaggerated bow for his benefit, then stood to leave.

"My work here is done. I need to finish getting dressed. I'll leave you two to it." She turned back to Gabriel. "And you—"

She hugged Gabriel and whispered in his ear. "Go get 'em. I'll see you out there."

Jason stood at the back of the room and held up his smartphone. "Miguel asked Ray to send him a picture. Okay?"

Gabriel nodded and struck a pose with his arms flexed, showing off Bonnie's handiwork.

"Be sure to get one with the wings. And the mask, don't forget—"

"I'm dodging the no-camera rule. I'll shoot some video," Jason said. He looked Gabriel up and down and shook his head. "You really do look incredible. You ready?"

Gabriel reached for his neck, feeling for the chain that held his cross. The pre-bout ritual was so engrained in habit that he rarely thought of it anymore. It had become the meditative moment of calm before he transformed into El Ángel.

"I just need to stretch a little more, and then put on the rest of the costume," he said.

"That's not what I meant," Jason responded.

"I know."

"I'm proud of you, you know."

"I know."

There was no doubt of it, or of the fact that he was loved.

"I'd kiss you, but I don't want to mess up Bonnie's work." He held his hand up toward Gabriel's face.

"Jason?"

"Hmm?"

"I love you."

THE RAP ON THE DOOR was almost inaudible against the incessant rumble from the studio. A Triple L TV assistant dressed in black, carrying a clipboard and wearing a headset, stepped into the dressing room.

"We're ready for you," she said, scarcely looking up from her notes.

Checking the laces, Gabriel adjusted his mask one last time. He reached for his cape—freshly designed, a billowy swath of iridescent white—and threw it over his costume, then pulled the oversized hood over his head.

He stepped into the hall just outside the studio door and took his place at the end of the line.

The muddled baritone of the *American Lucha* host drifted backstage, rising in volume and pitch with his introductions. A former telenovela actor who had bridged to American television through commercials and a series of sidekick roles, he had been handpicked for his crossover appeal. He had spent the past two months shadowing Lucha Bang on the road getting the patter down, and it connected. The crowd bellowed its approval of his introduction of El Cadejo and kept cheering as he announced the arrival of the técnico.

The production assistant threw open the studio door just as he rolled out the final, prolonged syllables: *"El Ángel Exóticooooooo!!"*

The room exploded in light: gold, pink, white spotlights focused on the door, the crowd, the ring. The crowd rose in waves, cheering, shouting, and dancing as El Ángel Exótico's longtime choice of reggaeton introduction music filled the hall.

Since his first professional bout as El Ángel Exótico, Gabriel had always treated the introduction as a solitary moment, a solemn march to the ring. El Ángel was not the good-time party luchador, surrounded by an entourage. That role had always belonged to La Rosa.

But *American Lucha*'s producers wanted something new, something dramatic, something that added to the drama of its grudge-match premier, and El Ángel was poised to deliver.

The doors opened to a dozen young men in gold booty shorts and wings, with their torsos and faces dusted in gold and pink metallic powder, each with a pink rose painted on his shoulder. They were models, dancers, and aspiring actors, Bonnie's friends who stepped up when she called in a few favors, who didn't mind the bonus of appearing on television.

Electra followed, along with The Cyclone, fresh off an undercard match, and the old Lucha Bang corps of luchadores and dancers, who marched into the room in solidarity with their comrade. The strippers had been particularly quick to sign on, even without pay. With the primetime *American Lucha* taking over Lucha Bang, burlesque would no longer be part of the act. No strip, no tease. The producers offered to instead cast them as "American Lucha Girls," a sort of ring girl-meets-cheerleader concept that was met with a resounding "fuck you" from the Lucha Bang regulars.

At the end of the line, letting the backstage door shut behind her, Fanny Vice emerged, sprayed head-to-toe in gold dust, wearing a gold lame bustier gown slit to her upper thigh, and gold, five-inch stiletto Louboutins.

The entourage circled the ring as a cue to dim the lights.

The music screeched to a halt, like a deejay scratching a record. From the darkness, the spotlights once again jumped to life.

With a crash, El Ángel's traditional entrance music was replaced with hip-hop, the regimented beat of Kanye West. The doors flew open, and El Ángel Exótico, obscured by hood and cape, stomped down the aisle in time with the music. He moved with single-minded intensity toward the stage without acknowledging the frantic crowd. There were no high fives, no greetings—just a determined and stoic march toward his opponent.

He stepped to the center stage in front of the ring, flipped back the hood that had covered his face, and held his arms out wide to the audience. He loosened the tie that held his cape in place and let it fall to the stage, revealing enormous white, feathered wings strapped to his shoulders.

He folded his arms, giving the wings the appearance of spreading out in flight, like the Jorge Márin sculpture he had once posed before with Jason. He paced and prowled the stage, letting the crowd noise reach a fevered pitch.

He looked out into the audience just long enough to see Jason, who nodded, mouthing silently: "Do it."

Gabriel bowed his head as if in prayer, and then slowly reached behind his neck, testing the laces. To the crowd, it looked as if he was posing, flexing, preening.

He stretched his torso, raising an elbow toward the rafters as he slipped his fingers beneath the mask, running them through the laces, loosening the fabric.

Just as suddenly as it had started, the music came to a thunderous halt.

Gabriel bowed his head and slowly turned his hand until it settled on the top of his mask.

With eyes closed, he inhaled—a long, settling breath.

He waited and, as the room went silent, he gripped the mask and slowly peeled it from his head. He curled his fingers into the fabric as it bunched around his face, tearing it away. His arm dropped to his side. He stood silent and grim-faced for long seconds before he loosened his grip on the lamé costume piece, letting it fall to the floor.

El Ángel Exótico looked up to the crowd, revealing his face for the first time. Bonnie had carefully dusted it in soft golds and pinks so the fabric mask was replaced by one of foundation, blush, and a strategic sweep of shimmer caressing his cheeks, brow, and hair.

He prowled back and forth on the stage in front of the ring. He played to the crowd and to the camera. On a final pass, he reached out to Fanny Vice, who stepped forward and unstrapped his wings, then carried them offstage.

He leapt over the ropes with a flip, landing squarely on his feet.

As the referee checked his boots, Gabriel chanced a glance at Arturo. He had been upstaged and, behind the thin fabric of his mask, his eyes had narrowed.

Gabriel recognized the look.

El Cadejo rushed from his corner the moment the referee signaled the start of the match, and El Ángel countered, ensuring that he would not be caught in his corner by the attacking rudo.

As they reached the center of the ring, they slowed to circle one another, assessing the opponent; each waiting for a momentary lapse of concentration, an opening.

They approached each other cautiously, then an open palm landed a hot slap to Ángel's chest. It was a common opening move, but performed with more concern for staging than for inflicting damage. He countered, pushing at El Cadejo's shoulders, forcing him to retreat toward the ropes.

El Ángel needed to stay close. To give El Cadejo room to throw his body into the ropes would create an opportunity for the rudo to rebound, to launch himself at the técnico, taking advantage of his well-honed acrobatic skills. But it was too late. El Cadejo let the ring absorb his frame, then propel him back toward the center with its power. He took El Ángel down, attempting a pin.

But this was not Gimnasio de la Ciudad. Gabriel had learned how to leverage the power of his legs to pop his body out of such moves.

El Ángel pushed El Cadejo off him and jumped to his feet, racing to the ring. He climbed the turnbuckle and launched himself at his opponent in a high-flying kick to the chest. He landed on top of the rudo, and the referee began the count to the crowd's deafening approval.

To the promoters, it should have looked as though the match were going according to script. It was to remain close, the first round to El Ángel Exótico, then the second and third to El Cadejo. But the combatants knew better.

The second round immediately took to the air. The luchadores ran at each other, grappled, attempted to throw each other to the mat. Instead, they both landed against the ropes and rebounded in flying kicks. El Ángel attempted his signature takedown, a flying tijeras that would lock onto El Cadejo's neck and whirl him to the mat. But the rudo anticipated this, ducking out of the way so that El Ángel landed in a heap.

El Cadejo attempted a plancha, landing chest-first on El Ángel, but was met with an illegal—and unnoticed by the referee—kick to the groin.

Momentarily stunned, he stared down El Ángel.

A técnico is supposed to follow the rules.

He retreated and El Ángel rose, but the rudo attacked again, driving the técnico into the ropes. He threw a punch that landed near El Ángel's eye socket, drawing blood. The técnico slumped into the ropes, and the referee called El Cadejo off. He would not be permitted to attack as long as his opponent was tied up in the lines.

El Ángel raised his head toward the crowd. El Cadejo taunted his opponent and played to the cameras and the crowd, encouraging their taunts.

"¡Traidor! ¡Fraude! ¡Maricon!"

He pulled himself up and rushed the rudo, driving him out of the ring. El Cadejo landed on his back at the edge of a camera pit. He righted himself just as El Ángel dove through the ropes, causing the técnico to miss and land headfirst on a barricade. It was the opening El Cadejo needed. He rolled on top of El Ángel, locking his shoulders down and pinning his legs.

El Ángel was slow to rise after losing the second round. He tried to get up, but his feet faltered and he slipped back to the floor, collapsing at the feet of the crowd that had scattered to avoid the flying luchadores. El Cadejo turned toward him, ready to attack again.

But the attack didn't come. Instead, he felt the gentle drift of soft fingertips on his temple.

In the fray, a woman knelt by El Ángel's head. Then another knelt by his shoulder, protecting him from a fight that had spun out of control. El Cadejo stepped back and looked to the referee, who waved him back to the ring.

The referee approached the ropes nearest El Ángel, and El Cadejo began his taunts anew. This time, they were met with boos. The fans were squarely in the corner of the fallen exótico.

With unsteady legs, El Ángel rose to his feet. The fans who had circled him offered their hands, their arms, their shoulders as support. He waved them off and moved slowly toward the ring. El Cadejo stood by, awaiting the call from the referee that would free him to continue the beating. He got his chance the moment El Ángel dragged himself back through the ropes.

El Cadejo ran at him, driving the back of his head into the turnbuckle. Shoving an elbow into El Ángel's windpipe, El Cadejo grabbed the cross that hung from his neck and yanked it free. He dropped it to the mat as the exótico slumped against the ropes, gasping for air and waiting for the moment the referee would pull his opponent off. But the rudo backed off of his own accord, giving himself room for a flying kick that missed the mark and sent him tumbling to the floor below.

With El Cadejo out of the ring, El Ángel pulled himself up to the top of the turnbuckle, fighting his weakened body, and dove over the ropes at the rudo, a dropkick from the heavens.

It landed with fury. He locked his ankles around El Cadejo's neck as he flung him to his side. The rudo landed in a heap, and El Ángel went back for more. He ran at the ring, gained momentum from his rebound, and hurled himself into a back handspring that landed between El Cadejo's shoulder blades.

El Cadejo attempted to kick out and hit El Ángel's inner thigh, slowing the aerial assault. But the técnico landed close enough to roll over him, leveraging his legs to secure El Cadejo's feet to the mat.

The referee began a count in slow motion.

One

The crowd erupted.

Two.

The announcer, long since out of superlatives, let it play out wordlessly for the television audience.

Cadejo spun out, and jumped to his feet and kicked at El Ángel's abdomen before the técnico could rise again.

It was time.

Gabriel shut his eyes and concentrated on the task at hand. He looked up, catching Arturo's eye, and slowly pulled himself up on his elbows. He left room for Arturo to attack, to knock them out from under him. It was met with a silent and subtle nod.

The kick leveled him. El Ángel fell in a heap, and El Cadejo jumped on his back, signaling the referee to call the match.

One, two, three!

The count was quick and final.

GABRIEL WAVED OFF BONNIE AND Lola, then Ray, and even Jason as he stumbled into the dressing room. He needed a moment, he said, and shut the door behind him.

Twenty minutes later, he had scarcely moved from his position, collapsed over his knees in a folding chair in front of the mirror. His body coated in sweat, blood, and glitter, Gabriel sat alone in the dressing room with his forearms stretched along his thighs and his head resting on his hands.

He heard a door open, then footsteps, and running water. Moments later, an inked hand held out a wet towel.

"Porque?" Arturo asked. "Why'd you do it?"

Gabriel shook his head, mute.

Arturo walked around to face him and placed his hand below Gabriel's chin, forcing him to look up. He dabbed methodically at Gabriel's bloody brow, gently cleaning his face.

"Why did you do it?" he repeated. He tossed El Ángel Exótico's mask on the vanity. "This doesn't belong to me."

"Keep it," Gabriel said. He straightened and took the washcloth from Arturo's hand, wiped the rest of his face, and tossed the cloth aside. "You won the match. The mask is yours."

"I don't understand."

Gabriel stood, slowly and painfully, and leaned against the lockers.

"You were right," he said. "I was as dishonest about who I was in that mask as you've been as El Cadejo. I'm done with that. No more hiding."

"It's just a role, Gabriel. It's just business."

"Not to me," Gabriel said. "When has anything in that ring been on our terms? You might go off script, but you still play by their rules, and you're trapped. I'm not letting that happen to me, not any more. If I was going to be de-masked, I was going to do it on my own terms. No more playing by someone else's rules. I'm done."

Arturo pulled his mask off his head. He grabbed a towel and wiped the sweat from his face and leaned back on the counter top.

"I didn't mean it to go like that," he said.

"You never do," Gabriel said.

Arturo's posture sank. He buried his face in the towel. He pulled the towel away and rested his hands on his thighs.

"I was better in Japan. I never lost control. I played by the script. I was good," he said. "Then I saw you again."

In the ring, Arturo had seemed larger than life. But slumped in the dressing room, he was small, powerless.

"When you pulled off that mask, it was like you were stealing something from me," he said.

"That's not true," Gabriel said. "I wasn't taking anything from you, just reclaiming it for myself."

Arturo nodded silently. When he finally looked up, his eyes were bloodshot and moist.

"You don't have to quit, Gabriel. After what you just did? How the crowd reacted? You could write your ticket. I bet the Americans would sign you, and you know Oscar will want you back. We could have a rematch."

Oscar Chavez had, of course, seen to it that Gabriel couldn't sign with the Americans, or with the LC, even if he wanted to. It had seemed like a sacrifice at first. With his final league bout behind him, it felt like a blessing, a release.

"No," Gabriel said. "You and I are never getting in a ring together again, understood?"

Arturo smiled. Gabriel had nearly forgotten he was capable of it, and how inviting Arturo's face looked when he allowed himself a rare moment of happiness.

"Understood. They'll want us to, though."

"Doesn't matter; it'll never happen. I won't let it," he said. "And what about you?"

Arturo shook his head. "I'm the *American Lucha* champion. From here I move on to American wrestling, and come back at some point to defend my title. I'm sure my defeat will be glorious."

"You don't have to do it this way. You don't have to be alone."

Arturo chuckled, a brief huff of a laugh that dripped with the bitterness of having a future pre-ordained by contract.

"I finally have a meal ticket with my own name on it," Arturo said. "And for the time being, I have a belt. You know that's what I always wanted. This comes with it. I'm not doing anything to jeopardize it. It's not like I'm going in with my eyes shut."

In the moment, Gabriel saw the Arturo that had eluded him for so long. Miguel was right. Arturo may have been a villain, but he was also alone in the world, able to share his confessions only in a brief moment with a former lover.

"You know, mythology says that there are two cadejos," Gabriel said. "The dark cadejo lures us to make bad choices. Some think he's the devil. But the light cadejo guides us, protects us from him. You don't have to be El Cadejo Oscuro."

Tentatively, Arturo stepped over to the lockers and took Gabriel's hand.

He reached into a small zippered pocket in the waist of his wrestler's tights. From it, he drew out the golden cross he had pulled free during the match. He turned Gabriel's hand over and placed the cross in his palm.

"Maybe when I retire," he said.

He picked up his mask and reached for the door handle.

"Tell the old man I'm sorry."

"Are you?"

Arturo pulled the mask over his face and opened the door.

"Every day," he said, and slipped from the room.

The door reopened behind him. Jason stepped into the doorway.

"Everything okay in here?" he asked.

Gabriel groaned.

Jason stepped into the room carrying a bottle of ice water in one hand and a bouquet of roses in the other.

"You all right?"

Gabriel nodded.

"You *employed*?"

Gabriel braved a smile, his lips clenched together, and shook his head. "Not really sure. Don't really care."

"You care," Jason said. He handed Gabriel the flowers, then the water. "You live for this."

"Maybe I shouldn't. All this time, I thought lucha was the thing that grounded me, a way to express myself."

"And?"

"Arturo had a point. He hid behind a character because he thought he had to in order to be a luchador. I did the same thing. I played by their rules because I thought I had to. They'll always want El Ángel Exótico, when I just want to be *Ángel*."

"Can you live with this?"

Gabriel reached up and took Jason's hand. He kissed the fingertips. "Yes."

"If you can't, I think you'd make a pretty good trainer."

Gabriel though about it and smiled.

"Maybe when I retire," he said.

"And you're not doing that yet?"

Gabriel drew a deep breath. He knew the room reeked of stale air and sweat, yet all he noticed was the warm aroma of Jason's cologne.

"I may be done with them, but it doesn't mean I'm *done.*" He pulled Jason close, and brushed his lips with a soft kiss. "What do you think of *El Ángel de la Ciudad?*"

"You'll need a new mask."

"No," Gabriel said. "No mask. No drag. No kissing. No thigh-high boots. No gimmicks."

Jason raised an eyebrow. "You sure you can't keep the boots?"

"Okay, maybe the boots—and I kind of like the glitter."

EPILOGUE

THE WAREHOUSE HAD SEEN BETTER days. The inspection had revealed rotted pipes, a cracked foundation, and a rat's nest in the overhead beams.

Still, it had potential.

The space was vast and adaptable and easily segmented into additional workspace: offices, restrooms, and locker rooms. The owners of the empty lot next door were more than happy to make the parcel available for parking. At ten bucks a car, they would make a tidy profit.

Some would call the neighborhood sketchy: the little industrial strip under the Gold Line track, in the shadow of Elysian Park. It didn't have the flash of Hollywood Boulevard. And while it technically sat within the downtown loop, it remained outside the costly hipster chic of the Bank District or Arts District or whatever district was next in the path of the fashionable steamroller of redevelopment.

But it was close. Its time would come, and until then, the neighborhood would welcome its new residents as family and open its protective arms to them.

By day, the trainers of Gimnasio de los Angeles would teach lucha libre, from athletic training to choreography to sessions on the origins and fine art of lucha storytelling taught via video conference from Gimnasio de la Ciudad.

And on select nights, the gym would become Club Angeles, the new home for a new brand of Los Angeles lucha libre that respected its origins, but embraced its possibilities. Lucha wouldn't be played with a laugh track at Club Angeles, but it would welcome bartenders, and burlesque dancers, and wrestlers of all stripes.

The gym had an enviable staff, from the onetime NFL prospect who led the gym's strength-conditioning program to the CFO, a former Cal business school standout who counted the gym as the future crown jewel of her real estate portfolio.

The boss had set out to build a business that straddled two worlds when he couldn't find an existing one that felt like home. By combining the resources of two gyms, in two countries, with a coordinated stable of some of the best coaches and luchadores in the business, he had found a path to blend old traditions with new aesthetics.

"Is it done? Move over Miguel, let me in!"

Rosalinda's smiling face popped onto the screen of Gabriel's tablet alongside Miguel, seated in the shade of their courtyard.

"Gabriel, have they finished?"

Gabriel laughed, threw his head back, and looked across the room, where two artists were placing the finishing touches on a mural she had sketched for the gym, a companion piece to the one at the revamped Gimnasio de la Ciudad.

"Just about. Want to see?"

"I'm not just here to see your handsome face, mijo."

He hit the flip function on the tablet and began to pan the brick wall, which was now filled with a colorful mural of luchadores, a few from the past, the legends. Others were modern luchadores less known to a broader audience, but mile markers on Gabriel's path: The Henchman, the tough rudo with the kind temperament; The Silver Cloud, the faithful and dedicated rudo-turned-técnico now training a new generation of luchadores in Mexico City; La Rosa, the smart and talented veteran wrestler who had become so much more than a trainer or manager, surrounded by an entourage of male dancers. There was a take-no-prisoners luchadora and a powerful black luchador, smiling like a kid on Christmas morning.

And in the far corner near an office door, a painting, nearly complete, of a young luchador in dark silhouette, strong and beautiful, draped in feathered angel wings and thigh-high wrestling boots, dusted in gold glitter, freeing himself of his mask.

"It's beautiful," Rosalinda said.

Miguel smiled and leaned toward her, snuggling against his wife.

"I don't know," Gabriel said, sounding self-conscious. "That last part is a bit—"

"Earned," Miguel interrupted. "It was earned, Gabriel. And now I get to see you every day, whether I like it or not."

Rosalinda slapped his cheek playfully.

"Miguel!"

Miguel took her hand in his and raised it to his lips.

"Fine," she said. She stood, letting Miguel's hand drift. "You two talk. And Gabriel? You'll visit again soon?"

"As soon as I can."

She kissed Miguel on the temple and, with a wave to his laptop camera, darted out of the picture.

"I wish I could talk you into coming up for our first event," Gabriel said.

"I'm a homebody," Miguel said. "Besides, too much fancy stuff."

"It's a warehouse. It's not that fancy."

"Just make sure someone is running a feed. I'll watch. I need to make sure Raymond behaves himself."

"I'm not sure how long he'll be wrestling for us," Gabriel said. "He got an offer."

"So I hear. He always wanted to sign with the American leagues. Good for him. Just make sure he has someone look over that contract."

Ray had sworn that he no longer wanted the old dream; that he thought of the new gym and its newborn league as home. But something in his eyes when he shared the news that the Americans wanted him to wrestle for them—at least part-time—suggested that the old dream wasn't quite dead.

"I'm going to have to find a new roommate," Gabriel said.

Miguel sat up straight, slowly and painfully stretching his spine. He cringed and kept his eyes shut while he took a breath.

"Somehow, I don't think that's a problem," he said. "Remember, I want a livecast on Saturday."

With that, the screen went dark.

Strong hands cupped his shoulders and gave them a squeeze. They moved down Gabriel's chest as warm breath brushed his cheek.

"How's my entrepreneur?"

Gabriel took Jason's hands and wrapped them across his heart. How was he? Should he be nervous? Worried? Unsettled? He had been told, countless times by friends and colleagues, that he should. He was taking a plunge, a risk.

But that was nothing new. When hadn't he?

It wasn't that at all. For the first time in memory, Gabriel somehow felt both settled and unfettered.

He pulled Jason's hand to his lips, and kissed his fingertips.

"I'm ready."

LUCHA LIBRE GLOSSARY

Batalla: A battle, a match.

Campeón/Campeonato: Champion/championship.

Carrera contra Carrera: Career versus career, a betting match where the loser must retire.

Cuadrilátero: Wrestling ring.

Empresa: Wrestling league.

Esquina: Corner.

Enmascarado: A masked luchador.

En Suicida: A move from inside the ring to outside the ring, such as a dive into the seats.

Exótico: A luchador, typically gay, who performs in drag.

Familia Luchistica: Wrestling family.

Jaula: Cage.

Lucha Extrema: Dangerous or "extreme" wrestling performed outside of lucha libre league guidelines, often fought in cages with obstacles such as razor wire, nails, or glass in the ring.

Lucha Libre: Direct translation is "free fight." The universal name for Mexican wrestling.

Luchas de Apuestas: A betting match, often for a mask or hair, or for a luchador's contract.

Máscara: Mask.

Mascara contra Cabellera: A mask versus hair betting match.

Maromas: Wrestling exercises.

Nombre de Batalla: Fight name, character name.

Padrino: A luchador's first opponent.

Parajas de Luchadores: Wrestling team.

Parejas Increibles: An incredible pairing, a star match.

Patada Voladora: Kick.

Plancha: A common lucha libre move where the attacker lands across the opponent's chest or abdomen, a splash move.

Quebrador: A so-called "back-breaker" move where the attacker drops the opponent so their back is bent backwards against a part of their body, usually a knee.

Rana: A pinning position.

Rudo: The villain or "heel" character in a lucha libre match; a rule-breaker or thug.

Super Estrella: Super star.

Técnico: The "face" or hero character in a lucha libre match; a technician who obeys the rules.

Tijeras: A head scissors attack where the wrestlers wrap their legs around the opponent's neck.

Tornillo: Any spinning or corkscrew move.

Trios Parejas: A tag team match involving teams of three luchadores.

ABOUT THE AUTHOR

Erin Finnegan is a former journalist and winemaker who lives in the foothills outside Los Angeles. A lifelong sports fan and occasional sports writer, she has had to dive out of the way of flying luchadores at matches in both the US and Mexico. Her first novel, *Sotto Voce*, received a starred review from *Publishers Weekly* and a *Foreword Review*'s INDIEFAB Silver Book of the Year Award.

Get to know Erin at Erin-Finnegan.com, on Twitter at @eringofinnegan, on Tumblr at eringofinnegan, and on Facebook at facebook.com/eringofinnegan.

One **story**
can change **everything.**

@interlude**press**

Twitter | Facebook | Instagram | Pinterest

For a reader's guide to **Luchador** *and book club prompts,*
please visit interludepress.com.

interlude ❖ press

you may also like...

Sotto Voce by Erin Finnegan

New York-based wine critic Thomas Baldwin can make or break careers with his column for *Taste Magazine*. But when his publisher orders him to spend a year with the rising stars of California's wine country, his world gets turned upside-down by an enigmatic young winemaker who puts art before business.

Sotto Voce is the story of love and wine, and how both require patience, passion, an acceptance of change—and an understanding that sometimes, you have to let nature take its course.

ISBN (print) 978-1-941530-45-0 | (eBook) 978-1-941530-46-7

Into the Blue by Pene Henson

Tai Talagi and Ollie Birkstrom have been inseparable since they met as kids surfing the North Shore. Tai's spent years setting aside his feelings for Ollie, but when Ollie's pro surfing dreams come to life, their steady world shifts. Is the relationship worth risking everything for a chance at something terrifying and beautiful and altogether new?

ISBN (print) 978-1-941530-84-9 | (eBook) 978-1-941530-85-6

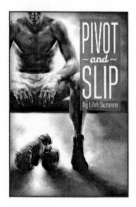

Pivot and Slip by Lilah Suzanne

Former Olympic hopeful Jack Douglas traded competitive swimming for professional yoga and never looked back. When handsome pro boxer Felix Montero mistakenly registers for his yoga for Seniors class, Jack takes an active interest both in Felix's struggles to manage stress and in his heart and discovers along the way that he may have healing of his own to do.

ISBN (print) 978-1-941530-03-0 | (eBook) 978-1-941530-12-2

NEW
LIBRARY

Westerly Public Library

3 4858 00468 2341

WITHDRAWN FROM
WESTERLY PUBLIC LIBRARY

CPSIA information can be obtained
at www.ICGtesting.com
Printed in the USA
LVOW11s1630091116

512299LV00001B/281/P